A LIFE
OF NO
COINCIDENCE

A LIFE
OF NO
COINCIDENCE

David Martin Lins

A LIFE OF NO COINCIDENCE
First Edition
Copyright © 2022 David Martin Lins

eBook ISBN 978-1-7365970-3-3
Paperback ISBN 978-1-7365970-4-0
Hardcover ISBN 978-1-7365970-5-7

Primary Line & Developmental Editor/Adrian Bumgarner
Additional Early Developmental Editing/Stephen Prat
Additional Late Developmental Editing/Lorin Petrazilka
Cover design/Lorin Petrazilka
Formatting/DTPerfect

DavidMartinLins.com

For the good ones.

The majority of the clergy
who sacrifice and pray.

The majority of law enforcement
who protect and serve.

The majority of humanity
who try and help.

PART ONE

MICHAEL

1.

M ICHAEL LOOKED DOWN THE CONVENIENCE STORE aisle at the back of a very angry man.

So this is why I'm here?

"Listen, sweetheart," the guy snarled. "I gave you a twenty, and I'm not going anywhere 'til you gimme my change."

Michael knew he had a few inches on the guy, but with a shaved head and a forest green tank that only partially covered an impressive collection of rippling tats, the guy was still intimidating as hell.

How about just one asthmatic, eighty-pound chess club champion next time? Michael asked the Voice as he grabbed a four-pack of Reese's and took in a deep breath.

"I don't usually need you for them," the Voice replied.

"Sir? I don't know what I can do. You only gave me a ten," the girl behind the counter said apologetically.

"That's a load of crap!" Mr. Three Percent Body Fat barked.

As Michael walked toward the counter, one last thought ran through his mind. *I don't want to die tonight, but if that's the plan, let me get through these peanut butter cups first.*

"Deal." The Voice acceded.

"Mister? They check the register at the end of every shift. I can't give you ten extra dollars." Explained the dark-haired girl, probably a co-ed from nearby Arizona State or Scottsdale Community College. "I would just give it to you out of my own pocket, but I don't have it."

"Callin' me a liar?!" The guy shook his head, fists clenched with simmering rage. "Ya know the last time someone accused me of being a liar—"

"Hold up. Can I take a stab at this one?" Michael interrupted as he approached from behind the man. "You treated yourself to a tattoo of a dove to remind yourself that peace is preferable to violence." Michael looked him up and down. "Only . . . I don't see it. You know what? Never mind. Really don't need to know where."

"What the . . ." The man turned slowly with obvious irritation. "You gotta be kiddin' me. A thief on one side and a comedian on the other."

Michael had been right. At six foot two, he was taller than the guy. But height never intimidates the intoxicated or the trained, and this guy looked to be both.

Unsure if he could look the guy in the eyes and keep his knees from buckling, Michael looked beyond him to the co-ed. "Wasn't trying to be all judgy. If you've got a tattoo, more power to you. I mean, unless it's your ex's name or in a foreign language, and you can't confirm what it says."

Thumping veins traversed the man's temples. "I don't know *who* you are or *what* you're trying to start." His stare bullied Michael into finally meeting his eyes. "But this has got zero to do with you. Sweet thing behind the counter tried to rip me off."

"Not trying to start anything at all." Michael somehow sounded steady. "Just here to make it right."

"Yeah? And how ya gonna do that?" the man demanded, still on edge.

Michael took a ten out of his wallet and slowly extended it

toward the man, who eventually snatched it out of his hand as if doing him a favor.

Michael stepped around him to face the girl. "Miss, may I purchase this delicacy?" He slid the pack of peanut butter cups across the counter and handed her a five. She was frozen. "What? Eight percent of the calories come from protein." Then, he continued in a conspiratorial whisper. "Only know that because of an argument with an ex-girlfriend." She just stared up at him. "We went on three dates. I think that qualifies her as an ex, right?"

Still a bit shaken, the girl began to ring him up.

Michael had hoped this would be enough to make Muscles McGee walk away, but he could feel the man standing firmly not three feet behind him. He turned quickly to face the guy.

"Hey! You're still here!" Michael realized that might've been a step too far and had to resist the urge to audibly gulp like that pothead in the old Scooby-Doo cartoons.

"Listen, kid. I can pay for my own beer. That wasn't the point!"

Are his muscles seriously twitching? What the hell? Michael suddenly felt a growing need for a handful of antacids. *Should I give him my peanut butter cups as a peace offering?*

"You'll live." The Voice promised.

I was really hoping for something with a bit higher downside.

Thankfully, the man broke the momentary stare down by looking past Michael and back at the girl.

"Screw this! I ain't ever coming back to this dump!"

The Voice whispered, "GMJ0614. His license."

Michael was fully cognizant that the guy was probably more afraid of a parole violation than a fight with a sarcastic millennial. But as the man grabbed his beer and quickly made for the door, Michael waited until the last second. "Oh . . . and buddy? GMJ0614!"

"Tell him not to hit her again. It's over."

Michael cringed as the man paused at the open door and looked back.

"What the hell?" The man snapped, not yet understanding the significance.

"Your license plate number. I noticed it when I got out of my truck. I need you to know if you hit her again, I'm going to know. The police will be back. If it happens tonight, if it happens tomorrow, I'm going to know. If you *ever* hit her again, I'm going to know."

The now-boiling cauldron of a man slowly walked back toward Michael.

You said I wasn't going to die. He resisted the urge to swipe his peanut butter cups from the cashier, unwrap them, and take a quick, final bite before the sweet relief of death finally caught up to him.

"I have no freaking idea what you're talking about." The man glanced at the girl. "Did I lay a hand on you? Well? Did I?!"

"You misunderstood me." Michael's voice remained outwardly calm.

"Enlighten me then!" The guy lurched into Michael's face as he shouted.

Michael didn't flinch.

"I wasn't talking about this beautiful young lady. I was talking about when you get home."

The man stared at Michael as if trying to solve a puzzle, working it out in his head. Michael waited him out.

The man leaned up and in, looking beyond Michael's shoulder as he whispered past Michael's ear, "I served, brother. I saw some messed up stuff and learned how to *do* some messed up stuff. Know what I'm sayin'?" He took a half step back to look straight at Michael. "It's a good idea to know what kind of animal you're dealing with before ya go pokin' it with a stick."

"First of all, thank you for your service, Rudy, but don't go worrying about me," Michael responded quietly, causing the man's eyes to flare at the use of his name. "I might look like the love interest in a low-budget Hallmark Channel release, but you should know this: I've got *nothing* left to lose."

"How did—" Rudy stopped short, looking confused. He then turned and left quickly, almost shattering the glass door in the process.

As his engine roared to life in the parking lot, the girl spoke in a bewildered tone. "Mister?" She paused, deciding whether to continue. "How *did* you know his name?"

Michael grinned, grateful he wasn't currently being beaten to a pulp. "No offense, miss, but it's late, and I really need some sleep. And the chocolate."

"Oh. Yeah. Sure thing." She fumbled through the register. "Here's your change. Thank you, you know, for what you did." She tried to produce a grateful smile but still looked like she might throw up.

"See? Like I said, beautiful." He knew she needed to hear it, so he said it.

"Sure. Whatever." She slid the peanut butter cups back across the counter, too wounded by someone—or something—to believe him.

"You are most welcome, Kim," he said warmly as he took the snack and went to leave.

After a long beat, Kim called after him, "Hey!"

Halfway out the door, Michael explained. "It's on your name badge." And with a flash of a smile, he was gone.

As Michael finished his late dinner, he got up from a rickety, faded green card table, tossed an empty Styrofoam cup into the white plastic trash bin under the sink, and opened the kitchen window so the odor of cheap noodles would dissipate a bit more efficiently. He washed his only fork and set it on his only plate with a clink that echoed throughout the hollow condominium.

Looking around his bare kitchen, Michael took a deep breath, let it out with a sigh, and headed to the bathroom. He brushed his teeth and peeled out of his clothes but skipped the shower. His bones needed rest more than his skin needed soap. The grind was relentlessly wearing him down, like the Colorado carving the Grand Canyon just over two hundred miles to the north.

As he lowered himself onto his mattress, Michael could've sworn every molecule in his body felt a little extra gravitational pull. He looked up through his tired, caramel eyes to watch his ceiling fan get pushed into a slow rotation by the cool air emanating from his wall vent. The rhythmic movement calmed him, and his eyes grew heavy. Finally, his left leg twitched in one last protest as he began to go under.

Then, as Michael was about to finally sink into a deep sleep, the Voice spoke. Despite what his body felt, it seemed it wasn't quite time to relax just yet. He needed to be somewhere. Michael blinked and willed his eyes back open. Sleep was going to have to wait yet again.

So help me God . . .

Michael dragged himself from the lonely mattress, which had become the last remaining piece of furniture in his bedroom. He grabbed a black t-shirt and a pair of jeans from the neat stacks of clothes he'd set against one of the barren walls and dressed quickly. Moving urgently through the condo, Michael snatched up his wallet and truck keys on his way out the door and down the steps.

He cranked up the engine of his old truck, a blue '74 F-250 that had seen better days but still got the job done, and pulled out of the complex with a roar.

Driving into the night, he squinted his eyes in an effort to fully regain his sight.

"Left." The Voice directed.

He turned left, now heading south through the desert metropolis.

"202 West."

As his truck approached a freeway, Michael swerved onto it heading west past Tempe Town Lake toward downtown Phoenix. *A bit more of a heads-up next time would be lovely.*

He merged onto another freeway and drove through the Papago Freeway Tunnel, a divided half-mile underpass snaking beneath a park in the center of the city. Its dirty tiled walls curved gradually, lit in a yellow haze reminiscent of a street racing game. He flew out the far side of the tunnel and merged onto yet another highway heading God-knows-where. He exited a few miles later and made his way south a few more miles into southwest Phoenix's industrial district.

Michael had lived in Maricopa County for about six years now but had never ventured into this part of town. No reason to. The road he found himself driving was lined on both sides by the high chain-link fences topped with the barbed wire of auto salvage yards.

"All by myself. Don't wanna be . . . all by myself . . ." Michael sang to himself, wondering why he was suddenly the only car on the road. If he had anything of value to leave behind, this road would have been great motivation to write his will.

Eventually, he saw another vehicle a short distance directly before him on what appeared to be the set of *Mad Max*. The intermittent street lights flashed momentary spotlights on an old, dusty jeep that looked like it belonged in the surrounding salvage yards. The jeep drove about another half mile before abruptly turning into a low-lit parking lot tucked between more high barbed wire fences.

As Michael approached, he turned into the lot as well.

Michael saw the tiny dirt parking lot belonged to a hidden shack of a pawnshop, and there was no way for him to maintain subtlety. An old, frail man with a denim cap and coke-bottle glasses had already gotten out of the jeep.

When the lights of the truck swept around the corner and struck him, the man froze. Then, as if realizing after a moment that his lack of motion didn't actually make him invisible, the man fumbled his way back into the jeep.

When Michael's truck pulled up next to him, the old man slammed his jeep into reverse, kicking up a plume of soot and dust, shifted into drive, and was gone before the cloud resettled.

Should I follow Roy Orbison's jeep? No? Then, why the hell was I even here?

"That was all you needed to do."

Michael slapped the palm of his hand on the steering wheel so hard he would've gotten a face full of airbag in a newer model. *This is absolutely ridiculous.*

2.

THE UNWELCOME MORNING SUN WAS BLASTING through Michael's window several hours before his body had recovered. *Make it go away. Please. For the love of all things good and holy and righteous. Bring on nuclear winter. Or death. Nuclear winter or death.*

"Not this morning, Michael," the Voice replied, refusing to end his suffering.

Although he had been the one who made the commitment years ago, there was no way Michael could have known how far it would go. Now he couldn't hold down a job because even managers at fast food joints get impatient when the fry guy abandons his post and walks into the dining area to find an old lady before saying, "I know you just bought a number five combo meal with a prune juice, and I also know it's been over five years since you and your brother spoke, but you need to call him today. I think he might have undiagnosed pancreatic cancer. Enjoy your combo meal."

On top of that, his financial stockpile had evaporated. It had been a few years since his loss was the gain of Hillary Nettles of Apache Junction. Well, not Hillary herself—but her cause—a place called Hillary's Closet. The charity was a resource for foster parents to get used clothes for their kiddos at no cost, and she had an abundance of them. Every parent in the metro area had the ability to part with some garments, but very few were willing to part with cash to help Hillary pay the rent. Just before she would have been forced to close the doors for good, she received a miracle donation from an anonymous source.

Now, with his money all but gone, Michael was out of personal belongings to sell online, and he wouldn't be able to hang on to his condo much longer. And yet, financial problems were not his greatest sacrifice. Not by a long shot.

Completely alone, he had given up on any kind of intimacy some time ago. No parents to visit on holidays. No brothers or sisters to be proud of or disappointed in. No girlfriend to argue with or make up with. No best friend to bail out of trouble or share a laugh with.

No one could understand his world and—in truth—no one even wanted to know something like it was possible. A life like his, a life directed by some all-knowing Voice, would disturb their comfortable lives and open them up to a reality they could never come back from. *Like when Neo took the red pill. Or was it the blue pill? Whatever pill it was, that's what it would be like.*

Michael needed breakfast to face the day.

The kitchen itself had become a reminder of Michael's downward financial spiral. There was a rickety refrigerator that emitted a buzz at random intervals, an unpredictable toaster with a mind of its own, and that single place setting on the counter. Apparently, it would be all he'd ever need.

He went about preparing his typical breakfast: two pieces of wheat toast and a glass of milk. Grabbing the toast—*extra crispy today!*—and milk, he headed into the living room. It was worse than the kitchen, consisting of a folding chair, a card table, and an outdated desktop computer that looked like it might have Oregon Trail preinstalled.

As was his ritual, Michael powered up his computer, slowly; got online, slowly; and browsed a few local websites for news. He had begun the ritual years ago in an attempt to shed light on his previous day's activities. Yet, this habit never seemed to have the desired effect.

As he perused the local headlines, he saw nothing that seemed to apply. Monsoon season had arrived quietly overnight with light showers throughout the valley, there was a shooting in Glendale, and a single mom had seemingly vanished. He found nothing about a beat-up jeep or convenience store and held out hope that the lack of relevant information was a result of headlines he had somehow prevented.

But Michael's curiosity wanted answers. *Why did I follow that old jeep? How did I know a license plate number I never actually saw? How did I know Rudy's name or that he was abusive? God? Psychic gifts? A brain tumor? Bitten by a radioactive spider?* Yet, as big as those questions were, those types of occurrences were not that out of the ordinary since he made the most one-sided deal in the history of Western civilization.

The memory of that day was now little more than a haze. More like a legend than an actual memory.

3.

THE FEELING OF EMPTINESS WAS HARD for Ezekiel to justify. After all, he was married to his dream girl. They lived on rich, vibrant green land. They had meaningful friendships with neighboring families and fellow church members. All these things added up to a life of tremendous blessing. Yet, that sum total never added up to enough to fill the aching void left by infertility.

Ever since Ezekiel was a boy, his dad had been his hero—the essence of authentic masculinity who somehow maintained the perfect balance of warmth and strength. It was what Ezekiel longed to become more than anything else in this world. And now, as a man, the role of a father was the one thing he could never attain. But worse than his own disappointment was the impact on his wife.

On some level, Phyllis assumed marriage would be followed by children. Initially quite nervous at the prospect of motherhood, the slow realization that it might not happen seemed to fuel a desire within her.

In time, the desire grew into an inferno, and it wasn't something as shallow as wanting what she couldn't have. It was the discovery of a great, dormant desire that had always been there. She didn't know how, but it was supposed to happen. She was meant to be a mom.

For the following several years, with the support of Ezekiel, Phyllis would spearhead the effort to investigate every possible avenue of growing their family. As soon as Ezekiel would leave well before the slightest hint of dawn to work the farm, Phyllis would resume her mission.

Each day, she would remove a box of files, forms, and notes from the hallway closet and spread it across the dining room table. And only after Ezekiel asked her why she packed it away before he came in every night did the dining room achieve a state of constant chaos. She never confessed it had been her effort to spare him the heartache she felt every time she looked at the stacks of papers that had become a material manifestation of the Herculean effort.

She reached out to domestic and foreign adoption agencies, pregnancy centers, foster care agencies, churches, hospitals, and any other conceivable option that could be pursued. Finally, she convinced Ezekiel to take foster parent classes and open their home.

Together, they took a series of heartbreaking classes on Saturday mornings where they were taught to spot and deal with the aftereffects of all sorts of unthinkable abuse. Instances of behavior that would only make sense when understood in the light of trauma. Smearing excrement all over the walls of a bedroom. Reenacting a sexual act. Running out of the room in a panic when a cigarette is lit.

After enduring the class, it wasn't long before a precocious five-year-old named Jack showed up on their doorstep with a black trash bag containing two extra outfits and a collection of three Matchbox cars. The dining room table was no longer an operations base but a nightly gathering space for the potential family of three. Hope began to flicker as Phyllis quickly took to the boy. Before the week was out, little Jack had plenty of clothes, more Matchbox cars than he knew what to do with, and was enrolled at the private Catholic school in a nearby town. A week later, he began calling Phyllis "mom." Little Jack was the second boy to steal her heart.

Within a month, Child Protective Services was at the door with some serious questions for Ezekiel. Little Jack had casually mentioned to the kindergarten teacher that his daddy used the belt on him when he was bad. While the teacher was fairly certain Jack wasn't referring to Ezekiel, she was not allowed to make assumptions and was required to report it.

The questioning was thorough and uncomfortable for Ezekiel, but on a much deeper level, the realization of what little Jack had already endured broke his heart.

As the questions ceased and the authorities left, the new knowledge of Jack's past triggered a protective instinct in Ezekiel. Suddenly, Little Jack was his boy as well.

But three weeks later, CPS was back, and this time, it wasn't about abuse. An aunt had been located in Rockford, Illinois. In cases such as these, blood trumps all.

In the aftermath of Little Jack, the dining room table never returned to its former state of messiness. It now morphed into a monument to silence. Ezekiel and Phyllis would eat their meals together without a word. They still held deep love for one another, but intuitively understood the other's deep hurt. There were just no words for this kind of pain. No words that could bring consolation. No words worth saying.

Over the next few years, time reassembled the shattered pieces of their hearts, except the one piece that would always be missing—Jack. That missing piece would always be there, invisible and undetected by anyone but Ezekiel and Phyllis. Despite the hurt, they gradually began talking again, timidly, a single step at a time.

The call came out of the blue as Phyllis and Ezekiel arrived home from church one Sunday.

"Phyllis! Are you still certified to adopt?"

It was Donna. She had met Phyllis at the church's shawl ministry and seemed to enjoy the gossip more than the knitting, but she was more than happy to be the public face of the ministry, delivering shawls to the Synergy South County Hospital where she worked.

"Donna, we've been through this before. You know that we decided . . ."

"Jesus, Mary, and Joseph, Phyllis! I know. I know. I know! Just answer me this very second! Are you and Farmer John still certified to adopt?"

Phyllis' heart dangerously fluttered at the prospect of opening a painful door long shut and ignored. "Yes, Donna. Of course we are, but—"

"There's been a miracle!" Donna could hardly breathe. "There is a baby boy. He is about a week old. His name is Michael. And, Phyllis, here is the best part! All the paperwork is signed. No one can change their mind."

"Donna." Phyllis was filled with the instinct to hang up on her friend and hide from another journey toward inevitable heartbreak. And the good Lord knew she couldn't endure another round of this cosmic cruel joke. "Please . . . don't."

"Phyllis? Don't spit in God's eye! We know what you've been through. God knows what you've been through. And as I see it, he dropped this baby from heaven right into your lap. I've told everyone I can about your story and how you are the most good-hearted people I've known in my forty years on this earth!"

Phyllis ignored Donna's blatant miscalculation of her own age. "Donna. It is very sweet of you to think of us, but I'm sure there are procedures and applications . . ."

"Stop it! You stop it right now! There is a lady who wants to meet with the two of you as soon as possible. I already gave her your number, and she is going to call you tomorrow. I just wanted to prepare you. You want this baby, Phyllis. Ezekiel wants this baby. And this baby needs you!"

The day they finalized the adoption of Michael Ezekiel Bale later that year proved to be the happiest day of their marriage, despite the unspoken feeling it might still get reversed like a rug being pulled out from beneath their feet.

As time went on, the Bales realized it was real. This time, it was permanent. This time, there was no cruel punchline. They were a family of three.

Determined to give their child an amazing head start on life, they came up with a plan over the very dining room table that had witnessed so much heartache. They sold the family farm on the outskirts of Racine, including all of the equipment, all of the livestock, and every last acre of property—a pretty penny from the developer who planned on turning it into a subdivision. Then, they said goodbye to lifelong friends, purchased the smallest two-bedroom home they could find in the working-class suburbs of Milwaukee, and invested the rest in a secret account.

Ezekiel picked up a job at a meatpacking plant, providing just enough for them to get by. Meanwhile, Phyllis's earnings from babysitting half the neighborhood were added to the secret account. On the day of his college graduation, Michael was going to get a check he never saw coming.

At least, that was the plan.

4.

MICHAEL COULDN'T HELP BUT BE A bit disappointed. It was the morning of Christmas Eve, and it wasn't even snowing outside. The weather was unseasonably warm in Wisconsin with temperatures hovering well above freezing.

He was expecting a call from his dad any time now, letting him know they were about to head across southern Wisconsin to Madison and pick him up from the University of Wisconsin where he was halfway through his sophomore year.

They had expected him to ask for a car when he was approaching his sixteenth birthday and then again when he was about to leave for college, but he always told them he would let them know when he needed one.

He loved spending Christmas with his folks, and it hurt his heart a bit that he had told his parents not to pick him up until Christmas Eve. But the student bookstore really needed him to cover right up until the last minute. Just then, the phone rang.

"Hey, pops!"

"Sorry to disappoint you, honey, but it's your mother."

Michael never understood how the same voice could express

love and shovel guilt simultaneously, but his mom could've taught a master class.

"Well, I do love him twice as much." Michael playfully needled. "Are you two crazy kids coming to get me or what?"

"No, we thought we would just leave you there and enjoy time alone this Christmas." Michael had learned his sarcasm from his mom, who went on. "Of course we are coming to get you! We've been counting down the days ever since Thanksgiving, Michael. Your dad is in the garage warming up the car as we speak."

That's when it hit him, like something invisible had reached into his chest, twisted, and wouldn't let go until he understood.

"They shouldn't leave now." The Voice spoke for the first time, as clearly as any audible voice would sound. "In an hour. In two hours. On Christmas Day. It really doesn't matter. Just. Not. Now."

"Honey? Are you there?" The momentary silence made Michael's mom think she had lost connection.

"Yeah, mom. I'm here . . . were you two planning on leaving right now?"

"Well, yes, Michael. Or should we wait 'til New Year's Eve?" She paused for a second. "Do you need a little time with your secret girlfriend before we get there?"

"No. That isn't it." He paused, searching for words. "I was just thinking . . . the two of you should stop for a nice breakfast together before you head this way. A little time together, just the two of you on Christmas Eve."

"Now, Michael," she said with a perfect motherly tone. "You know I love your father. I always will. But since you left for college, all your father and I *get* is time together. Until we found you, all we *had* was time together. We get plenty of time together. What we *want* is more time with our son."

"Okay, but . . ." It was all he could muster. *It's just a feeling. It's a beautiful day, and I'm probably just being paranoid.*

The Voice was clear. "Any time but now."

Got to think of a reason just in case . . .

His mother paused only a beat longer before she was done waiting. "See you soon, honey. We love you."

He gave up and said, "Love you too."

The line went dead.

5.

NOT LONG AFTER THAT FATEFUL DAY, Michael took up running again. He was pretty good in high school, but after a few years off, he couldn't finish more than a few miles. But each month, his endurance grew, and as Michael set off in an effort to let go of yesterday's insanity, he knew he could push the ten-mile mark without collapsing into a puddle at the end.

In high school, running was just something he could do, a natural fit for his long and lean frame. Now it had become an escape where his brain could switch off, and life was nothing more than the physical task at hand. The simple beat of feet padding the ground, each arm shifting to the rhythm of breathing as the continuous pat-pat-pat drove away every thought, if only for a time.

When he wasn't distracted by running, one question was always there: *Why do I continue to hold up my end of the bargain?* So—for now—running was a refuge. In fact, it was what had initially drawn him to his condo complex, a property bordered by an all-purpose trail that cut through the heart of Scottsdale.

After five miles or so, Michael turned around and headed back home.

Upon arriving back at the edge of his condo complex, he bent over, clutching his shorts at the knees in an attempt to bring his breathing back down, when he heard a woman yelling. From what Michael could make out, it sounded like she was pleading with someone. He listened more closely.

She was crying out for another chance. Something reached into him and twisted, one of his uncomfortable, familiar signals.

"Get involved."

Fine. But if it requires anything remotely physical, it better be an asthmatic because I'm wiped. Michael slowly straightened and began walking toward the voice where he saw a short woman with long black hair standing in an open doorway with her back to his approach. She seemed to compensate for a lack of stature with an abundance of fire.

"I told you! I don't know what you're talking about! I didn't talk to anybody! I wouldn't do that to you, mi amor! I wouldn't even know what to say!" Her begging was soaked in desperation. "They wouldn't understand! You know I don't blame you!"

Then, a familiar voice bellowed from within the building. "Just stop! Stop! He knew! He knew everything! So spare me your lies and just let me leave before—"

"No! Please, baby!" She begged again. "Please don't do this, Rudy!"

Definitely not the asthmatic I ordered.

Then, the woman stumbled backwards out of the doorway. In her place stood the man from the convenience store. Carrying a large box under his arm, he quickly walked past the woman, glanced up directly toward Michael, and froze. His jaw visibly clenched, and he looked back at the woman.

He hissed furiously, "How are you gonna deny it now? He must've gotten here a bit early!" Then, he looked back up at Michael and snarled, "Whatever, bro. Enjoy my leftovers."

As he started off, the woman called after him, "Rudy! Wait! You forgot one thing!" He hesitated and looked back. She ran inside as she yelled over her shoulder, "Let me grab it!" Rudy looked over at Michael with contempt and waited.

The woman ran back out with a broom. Confused, Rudy muttered, "What the—"

She reared back and swung, slamming the broom onto Rudy's shoulder. "I am no man's leftovers! I am . . ." She struck him with the broom a second time. ". . . a beautiful queen!"

Rudy dropped his box of belongings in order to shield himself with his arm. It was too late as she connected a third time, and he fell backward.

People began peeking out their windows to watch whatever was going on without getting involved.

Now, sitting on the sidewalk, Rudy attempted to sit up, arm still trying to fend off the swinging broom. "Loca! Stop this!"

"Say it! Beautiful queen!" She swung one more time, connecting to the right side of Rudy's head. He fell over but quickly rolled into a crouch. His face contorted in an angry glare.

Michael ripped the broom from the woman's hands and stepped forward between Rudy, blood now collecting on his right temple, and his girl. "Don't even think about it." He raised the broom like a baseball bat.

Rudy squinted in consideration for a moment before grunting. "Another time. The both of you." He turned, picked up his box of mostly broken junk, and stomped off as even more silent witnesses observed from the safety of their units.

The woman walked past Michael taking several steps after Rudy in a last, futile effort to plead her case. "No! You can't leave! I don't even know this guy!" She turned to Michael, deadly serious. "Give me my broom."

Michael shook his head. "Not a chance."

"Who *are* you? What did you tell him?! What did you say?!" Accusations as much as questions.

Michael made sure to hold on to the broom while he gently responded, "Listen, I just told him to never hurt you again."

A look of horrified recognition flashed across her face before it could be buried.

"Wait. Why would you even say that? Why would you *do* that?" Her voice became even more shrill. "You don't know what you've done! He kicked me out of his apartment last night. And this morning, he comes over here and takes the last of his . . . you know what?! It doesn't even matter! This is all because of you! This is all your fault!"

Hold on one freaking second! One, he was physically abusing you! You should be grateful he's gone! Second, you just took a freakin' broom and clocked him with it! That just might have encouraged him to leave! Not that he didn't deserve it. He did. For hitting you. He HIT you. Which is why I'll just say this . . . "Listen. I'm sorry for what you've been through."

"You're not sorry! It's your fault!"

"I need to be clear, lady. I'm not apologizing for Rudy leaving you."

"Oh! You think you know us? You think you are helping? You are just making it worse! And why do you even care?" She paused for a brief moment before her face morphed into a vengeful smile. "Maybe I *do* know who you are! You've been watching me!"

"Wait. What?" Michael didn't know where she was going, but he didn't like the implication one bit.

"You hear that, everyone?" She spun theatrically as she spoke louder. "I thought I saw someone watching me when I was on my balcony the other night! I thought maybe it was all in my head! Maybe I had one too many! But no! I saw a shadow in the darkness!"

"Can you not do this?" Michael pleaded to no avail.

She went on, gaining confidence. "But I thought I was just being paranoid! Well, I guess I should've listened to my instincts! I should've paid attention when the hair stood up on the back of my neck!" She looked around to her growing audience. "Did you listen outside my door too? Is that why you think you know something? You heard just enough to make a crazy accusation and ruin a happy couple's life? You're sick! You need help!"

God. If you've ever loved me, smite this woman with instant—and permanent—laryngitis.

He stood his ground as more neighbors began to venture out of their homes and watch the spectacle. Finally, mercifully, she began to run out of steam. "You know what? You need to tell me who you are right now!"

"Miss? I don't think that will—"

"No! You tell me who you are! Right! Now!"

"Michael Bale." He confessed, not quite sure why. "Please never let Rudy back into—"

"I don't need your empty advice, Michael! Go ruin someone else's life! I don't ever want to see you again!" She turned to the people looking on at the spectacle. "Shut your blinds and close your drapes, girls! We've got ourselves a perv in the complex!" The woman gave Michael a discreet, vindictive smile, turned away from him, and marched through her door, slamming it behind her.

Michael gently set down the broom and swiftly walked past accusing eyes back through the complex toward his unit.

On the plus side, I'm pretty sure any time I show up to the community pool, I'll have the whole place to myself.

He turned and looked back to see a guy quickly look up at a tree like he was birdwatching.

I just want to get back to my unit and lock the freaking door.
"Check your mail first."

What? For a Bed Bath and Beyond coupon?

But he made his way past his building and across the parking lot.

New deal. I'll keep answering every call, but I get to punch the next ungrateful man in the neck. As for the next ungrateful woman . . . I get to punch the man nearest her in the neck.

Standing before one of the complex's mail stations, Michael

pulled out his usual stack of mail entirely composed of credit card offers and grocery store advertisements. He tossed it all in the trash can next to the homeowners' association bulletin board, but instead of turning and heading back to his condo, he took a moment to glance at the notices.

Several unrelated pages were pinned to the board. There was an announcement for the next association meeting. Next to it, a bright yellow sheet simply said, "Slow Down. Turn Down." in a font sized to fill half the page with a pencil hanging next to it on a string. It was a campaign asking residents to slow down and turn down their radios when arriving home. Whoever came up with the idea somehow expected signatures to convince the offenders. There was one signature. And where the pencil dangled, there was a safety notice that the pool area would be repaired by the end of next month. The smaller notes on the board included a canceled Pilates class, a lady looking for a lost ring, and some free kittens.

The last thing I need right now is a cat. Unless it's big enough to sit on while watching the television I no longer own.

As Michael went to walk back across the lot, a car that he had seen in a movie somewhere came careening around the corner.

Nick Cage in Gone in 60 Seconds? *Or was it Keanu Reeves in* John Wick?

As his mind struggled to make the connection, he realized he was about to get run over and lunged out of its path behind an overly manicured bush.

Okay, fine. I've officially changed my position. I am now completely on board with "Slow Down. Turn Down."

He carefully rolled over and sat up next to the bush, brushing the dirt from his shirt.

A senior citizen with a leathery, pruned face slowly waddled up with her walker, stopped, looked down at Michael, and said, "When you are done here, the hedges next to building three need trimming as well." She sped off at a clip of about one mile per hour.

I'd be happy to if there's a paycheck involved . . . or . . . maybe there is. He turned and looked back at the plant to his side. He pulled some branches apart and saw a faint glimmer, a hint of light in the darkness of the landscaped vegetation.

Michael walked back across the lot with a ring that looked vintage and quite expensive—if the rock it held was genuine—in one hand and his cell phone in the other. He went back to the bulletin board, got the number of the lady who lost the ring, and waited less than two seconds before he heard the phone get picked up and fumbled for a few seconds. It was followed by a man's raspy morning voice. "Mom. I told you, nobody's called."

"I might have the wrong number because I'm pretty sure I'm not your mom."

The voice instantly woke up. "You are definitely not my mom! Sorry, bro. It's just that . . . never mind." The voice stammered. "I would be Rob, son of Brindy. How may I be of service?"

"Well, I saw a note on a bulletin board . . ."

"Oh, buddy!" Rob interrupted. "Do *not* tell me you found the one ring!"

"Well actually—"

"Not the ring to rule them all?"

This is not going to be a quick transaction, is it?

"Well, I don't think it's *that* ring."

"If it's my mom's ring, trust me, it is."

"Well, I hope it's your mom's then." Michael just wanted to keep the conversation moving.

"You are *so* my hero right now!"

"We don't even know if it's the right ring . . ."

"Heck yeah it is! I can sense these things. I've got what you might call an advanced intuition."

Rob, you have no idea what a truly advanced intuition looks like.

Rob went on. "I'm in the complex! You need to get over here right now! Is that kosher?"

"Yeah. I'm . . . it's kosher."

"*Nice.* Can you type the directions into your phone? Because this is a little complicated."

Michael looked down at his first-generation flip phone. "No, I don't think that'll work, my friend."

"Well, just rip my flyer off the bulletin board, and write on that."

"Are you sure? We haven't even confirmed it's the right ring."

"Dude."

Convincing argument.

Michael ripped the flyer off the board and grabbed the dangling pencil. "Okay. Got it. Lay those directions on me, brother."

What felt like twenty minutes later, Michael set off with a full page of directions, half of which were scribbled out and none of which seemed to make any sense whatsoever. But Michael did find the ring, and he was fairly certain he was supposed to return it. He paused for a moment, looked around, crumpled up the directions, and stuffed them in his pocket. Then, he just walked and ended up approaching a random door less than fifty yards and one right turn from the mailboxes, toward the back of the property.

***

"The ringbearer, I presume?" Rob said with a grin as he opened the door.

"In the flesh," responded Michael.

"I never got your name. I'm Robert Safranski."

Rob was a handsome young man who looked to be about the same age as Michael, with caramel brown skin, dreads, and thick black-rimmed glasses. The name Safranski came as a bit of a surprise.

Sensing Michael's confusion, he went on. "I'm Polish."

"Cool. I'm Michael." He extended his hand, which Rob

shook firmly, smiling warmly through his thick beard. "And I have no idea what I am."

Rob cocked his head. "What do you mean by that?"

"Ah. Yeah. Overshare. My bad. Adopted. So I don't know my biological heritage."

"No freakin' way! Me too, bro! I don't know my *biological heritage*, either." He mocked the formality of biological heritage with his best James Earl Jones impersonation before continuing. "But I've got a bit of an advantage on you." He held up one of his arms. "Thanks to my impressive tan, I can pretty much surmise I have some African or Carribean ancestry."

Michael snickered. "Yeah, I think you might be onto something. Now, about the ring—"

"Adopted by two people of mostly Polish descent. So I consider myself a stunning 'Polfrican American.'" Rob smiled widely as Michael silently guessed he worked at an organic food store. Then, Rob's face went serious. "Well, Mikey. You might be adopted like me, but the real question is, are you some kinda vampire?"

"Excuse me?"

"Well, it's quite simple really. Vampires cannot enter your home unless specifically invited. At least, that is what has been written throughout history. And you haven't entered. Therefore, you have left me in the unenviable position where I cannot invite you into my dwelling."

Michael cocked his head to the side trying to decipher what Rob was telling him.

"Now, if you were to enter my home without my invitation, I would know you aren't a vampire, and we could potentially be buds." Rob stepped back from the doorway.

Okay. I'll play the game, but if he's not grateful for the ring . . . punch to the neck. "Is that an invitation, Rob?"

Rob shook his head slowly. "Definitely not."

"In that case." Michael looked directly at Rob and flared his eyes for a long moment before breaking into a wide smile and walking past Rob and across the threshold. Michael was taller than most people, but he noticed Rob pretty much equaled him.

Michael entered the condominium to find furnishings that could best be described as a bit bipolar. On one hand, there was what appeared to be a very expensive leather living room set. The coffee table, end tables, and dining room table were all fashioned from solid dark wood. Probably artisan crafted. And there was a 60-inch flat screen mounted on the wall. On the other hand, the wall also had several vintage Van Halen posters, taped, not framed. There were several piles of clothes strewn about the room. And then there was a beanbag that looked like it had been victimized by a chihuahua on crack. It was situated prominently in front of the expensive couch, obviously Rob's favorite piece of furniture in the room.

"Thanks for getting here so fast, Mikey. My mother is going to be stoked."

"I know you have a strong gift of . . ."

"Perception!" Then, Rob flashed an exaggerated smile. "See what I did there? It's a gift, really."

"Obviously, but I was thinking we better make sure it's your mom's ring." Michael began to dig it out of his pocket.

"If it'll make you feel better." Rob waited for the ring in question to be produced. He then looked at it and back at Michael with a look of boredom before saying, "Yes. It is the ring. Shocker."

"Well, good. I appreciate you humoring me. I'll just leave the ring with you."

"No, no, no. It doesn't work that way with my mom. I was under specific instructions to call her as soon as someone found the ring. So after you called me and said you'd found it, I followed orders. Anyway, she's on her way right now . . . and trust me, the way that woman drives, it won't be long."

"Oh, um, alright." Michael looked at the furniture and the

flat screen and remembered back a few years ago to when he had money.

"Can I get you a beverage?" Rob was already stepping carefully over a stack of clothes on his way to the refrigerator.

"No thanks. I'm okay."

Rob turned. "Allow me to break this down for you. If mom shows up and you don't have something to drink in your hand, she's going to tear into me for being a bad host. So for my sake, here are the options. I've got acai juice, chocolate oat milk, and a pitcher of purified water. What's it gonna be?"

Acai juice? Oh, I absolutely nailed the organic food store guess.

"Well, I'm certainly not here to cause a domestic dispute, so I guess I'll just have a glass of water."

Besides, I've already been involved in one too many domestic disputes today.

"The essence of life. Good call!" Rob said as he poured a tall glass and then reached back into the refrigerator. "But me? I'm still hitting up the chocolate goodness!" Rob paused as if lost in thought for a minute. "Had an ex who called me that."

Pretty sure my overshare was just trumped.

As Rob walked with the glass of water in one hand and a half-gallon of chocolate oat milk in the other, he motioned Michael over to the cluttered kitchen table.

. . . and where is Rob's glass?

"Hold these a sec." Handing both drinks to Michael, he swept a whole pile of open maps right onto the floor. Smiling, he took back his half-gallon of the chocolate drink and started to guzzle it straight out of the carton.

Does the hippie drink straight from the water pitcher too? Smart money says yes. So now I have to distract him from the fact I have no intention of drinking my water.

"You sure seem to have a thing for maps . . ." Michael fished. Rob bit, quickly slamming the oat milk down and wiping his mouth with his wrist in excitement.

"Sure do, Mikey! I get them all from the camping supplies store where I work."

Not an organic place but pretty close. Maybe Rob has two jobs? Okay. Not likely.

Rob continued. "Some are maps of places I've been. Others, I have yet to get to." He reached down and plucked a map up off the floor. "See? This one here is of Rocky Mountain National Park. Personal favorite. There are elk, mule deer, moose, wolves, black bears, marmots—"

"Wait a minute. What the heck is a marmot?" Michael pretended not to know. Anything to keep Rob's attention away from the full glass of water.

"It's like a squirrel that hibernates at high altitudes. So basically, its whole existence is eating, getting fat, and sleeping. Pretty much my spirit animal."

"You're making this up, aren't you?"

"What? You don't believe me? How far do we go back?"

"About five or ten minutes now." Michael clarified quickly.

"Whatever dude! Marmots exist and are friggin' awesome! If I had to live in air that thin, I'd only want to eat and sleep too. Heck, that's already what mom thinks I do."

Ding!

"Speak of the mother!" Rob slammed down the rest of the chocolate goodness, jumped up, and bobbed to the door.

Ding!

Rob swung the door open to reveal a woman in oversized sunglasses, a pink cap, a silver tracksuit with a white collar, and pink Nike swooshes. The ensemble made the woman look like she just finished a tennis lesson, but Michael had the distinct feeling she hadn't played in a very long time.

Obviously a lady who is trying to take twenty years off.

"How's the best momma in the world?!" Rob exaggerated.

Without acknowledging the question, she lowered her glasses and surveyed the scene.

"Robert? What happened? It looks like you were burgled. The piles of clothes. The maps everywhere and the beanbag! Goodnight, Irene! I thought we agreed you'd burn that!"

"Momma? Sweet, sweet maternal force of nature? *You* agreed I'd burn it. I didn't. Think of the air pollution. Think of the birds of the air." Rob knew he was playfully getting under his mom's skin and could barely contain a grin.

"No. I clearly remember *us* agreeing. And, Robert? Stop calling me momma!" She ordered through her artificially-filled lips.

"I humbly apologize, matriarch of our loving and close-knit family." Rob decided to go all out by leaning in for a hug. She wouldn't have it, blocked him with one hand, and walked in from the doorway.

Rob looked at Michael and said, "I guess the books were wrong."

"What books?" Michael was confused.

"Vampires," Rob whispered, eyes wide in mock terror.

With her sunglasses completely removed now, she shifted her focus to Michael. "Oh. Hello there. I'm Brindy. Brindy Safranski. You are?" She kicked a pile to the side in disgust on her way to the table, then faked a smile and extended a hand.

"Michael. His name is Michael, mom . . ." Rob informed her from the doorway still open behind her.

"Matthew. Wonderful name. Now, you have the ring?" She pulled up a chair, wiped at it violently, and sat across from Michael.

"Yes, ma'am. It's right here." Michael dug the ring out of his pocket and handed it across the table.

"Please, Matthew! I'm not much older than you. Call me Brindy," she replied, never looking up as she delicately took the ring. "Oh, there it is! My great-grandmother's ring!"

"You said it was your grandmother's." Rob seemed to question, sauntering toward the table.

"Yes. After my great-grandmother gave it to her. It's called inheritance. Something you may never get to experience." Brindy folded her arms, raised her eyebrows as much as past surgery would still allow, and let her empty threat sink in for a moment before turning her attention back to Michael. "I apologize for my son. Here, I want to write you a check for finding my ring."

"I thought it was your great-grandmother's ring," said Rob with a big trouble-making smile plastered across his face.

"Please shut your face, you little tree hugger." The words were said quickly and quietly as if from a prim and proper sniper. Brindy quickly straightened in her chair and regained her composure. "Again, I apologize for my son. I'm pretty sure extended time at high altitudes has adversely affected his brain."

"If I wasn't adopted, I'd guess genetics." The smile grew as Rob was on a roll.

"Matthew? What is your last name?" asked Brindy as Rob smacked his forehead with the palm of his hand in disbelief.

"Bale. Michael Bale."

She pulled out her cell phone. "Do you have Venmo, PayPal, Zelle, Apple Pay, Google Pay?"

"I'm sorry . . ."

"Fine." She dug into her handbag and removed a checkbook. "Name again?"

"Michael Bale."

"Ah. That's a good name. Nice . . . and . . . short." She finished writing, tore off the check, stood as she handed it to Michael, and headed for the door. "Burn that beanbag!" She ordered over her shoulder as she put on her sunglasses, headed out the door past her son, and started down the steps.

Michael looked down at the check. It was written for one thousand dollars.

"And that . . . is why she thinks she can act like that, Mikey," Rob said with a smile.

6.

MICHAEL WAS A REGULAR AT THE Sunday evening church service. He made it his usual practice to slip in at the last minute and slip back out right after the final blessing. Human interaction was not the reason he came, and he was doing his best to avoid the eager youth group leader who kept trying to recruit him to help. He was apparently qualified due to his pulse, his Mass attendance, and the fact he was still under fifty years old.

Still, he knew he was supposed to be here. Maybe it was Catholic guilt. Maybe it was an effort to honor the memory of his parents. He would find himself staring off at a beautiful stained glass window and being transported back to his childhood. As a boy, he would drift off looking at a window depicting St. Francis of Assisi. Eventually, his dad would notice, pat him on the shoulder, and point his attention back to the altar.

If Michael were able to be honest with himself, he might also realize he went to Mass because it was the only place where his life made sense. Unbelievable things were completely possible here. They said wine could be turned to blood. People could be turned into pillars of salt. Angels spoke. And people heard them.

A short, pudgy man in a dark blue suit, which he appeared to be very proud of, brushed past Michael and snapped him back to the present. The man walked up to the front, bowed reverently, and proceeded up the steps to the ambo. Searching for the correct page, the pudgy man bumped the microphone with his book several times and cleared his throat. Then, emerging from this little character, came a rich, deep voice.

> *"There he went into a cave and spent the night. And the word of the Lord came to him and said, 'Go out and stand on the mountain in the presence of the Lord, for the Lord is about to pass by.' Then a great and powerful wind tore the mountains apart and shattered the rocks before the Lord, but the Lord was not in the wind. After the wind there was an earthquake, but the Lord was not in the earthquake. After the earthquake came a fire, but the Lord was not in the fire. And after the fire came a gentle whisper. When Elijah heard it, he pulled his cloak over his face and went out and stood at the mouth of the cave."*

The man continued reading, but Michael stopped listening. A message received in a whisper . . . that sounded familiar.

Michael knew better than anyone there was a steep price that went with ignoring the Voice, but the costs associated with heeding them seemed to be slowly building with no end in sight. He decided to come back tomorrow and try talking to the guy in charge of this place.

Returning from church, Michael passed his reserved parking spot and drove to the back of the property instead.

My reputation in this remote part of the complex might still be intact.

He pulled his truck into visitor parking and hopped out. While he had walked the property toward the green belt virtually every day, he had never explored the paths beyond the pool area at the back of the complex. The walk proved to be less than thrilling.

The sidewalk wormed back and forth through several more buildings that looked exactly like his. The complex, while clean, struck him more like a Hollywood backlot than a place where people made their homes and lived their lives. Every house was unique back in Wisconsin.

He paused to sit at the bottom of some steps and thought about the antiseptic landscape before him. Too perfect. Too orderly. This didn't feel like home.

Just then, he heard someone humming, loud and out of tune, from around a building toward his end of the complex. Despite being quite horrible, Michael recognized the tune as the death march and the perpetrator as his new buddy, Mr. Robert Safranski, who sauntered around the corner holding his beanbag solemnly.

"Hey, buddy. Whatcha up to?" Michael couldn't contain a curious smile while asking.

"Well, dude, there comes a time in every beanbag's life when the dumpster beckons." He appeared to be serious.

"No." Michael protested in mock horror. "You aren't suggesting . . ."

"It is time, my friend." Rob was still as serious as could be. "I'm in the middle of the funeral procession for Mr. Beanbag right now. You want to join me?"

Michael couldn't quite tell how real this was for Rob.

This might actually be a solemn ceremony.

"You know? That might not be appropriate. I hardly had time to get to know Mr. Beanbag."

"Okay. You're right. This is a path I need to walk alone." And with that, Rob resumed the worst humming Michael had ever heard as he walked down the path and around a corner.

Michael watched him go.

If he is that loyal to a beanbag . . .

"Can I help you?" A woman's voice interrupted his thoughts, startling him.

Standing before Michael was a scene both beautiful and comical. A stunning young woman was struggling to hold on to five bags of groceries.

I really should have wandered back to this part of the complex a long time ago.

"Umm . . . bub? These groceries are a bit heavy, and I don't want to be rude. But you are sitting on my bottom step." Her blue eyes seemed to twinkle at him. He realized that even worse than not getting up to help, he was just sitting there directly in her path.

"Oh! Oh, crap! I'm so sorry!" Michael scrambled to his feet. "Can I help you?"

"No, but thank you. I think I got it."

As if on queue, one bag slipped out of her grasp and smashed onto the walk. More embarrassed than frustrated, she looked back at Michael, flashed a nervous smile—a perfect smile—and did a small curtsy as if to say, "I'm a bit of a klutz. Love me as I am."

Get a grip on yourself, man!

Michael jumped up from the bottom step to beat her to the bag. As he lifted it, he heard the unmistakable sound of broken glass shifting. He straightened up to stand before her and tried again. "Are you sure you don't want me to carry this up for you?"

"No, no," she said as she tried to shift the four bags she was still holding on to. "I got it." She managed to extend three fingers from her left hand. Michael noticed a bare ring finger. She motioned with a glance at her fingers and repeated herself. "I got it."

As Michael gave her the fifth bag, feeling like the least chivalrous man in the world, he said, "I'm sorry you broke your groceries."

I'm sorry you broke your groceries? Is that the best you've got, moron?

Her face broke into that killer smile again. "I'm sorry I broke my groceries too. But I *do* need you to move out of my way."

"Oh! I'm really sorry Miss . . ."

"Rebecca."

"Miss Rebecca . . ." Michael tried for more.

"Yeah. I think Rebecca is more than enough for a random guy just sitting on my bottom step who won't let me pass," she said.

"I'm not a random guy." Michael protested. "I'm Michael Bale." He reached out to shake her hand while she was still struggling to hang on to all five bags of groceries. Michael quickly changed his extended hand into a goofy wave. It was official. He had just become an idiot.

Rebecca laughed, probably at him. "Well nice to meet you, Mr. Michael Bale. I'm still Miss Rebecca. Please excuse me for not waving in reply. Now, I really have to get these bags up my steps."

"Yeah . . . of course." Michael moved aside, and Rebecca began ascending the steps. Just then, a voice boomed from around the corner.

"Friends! We are gathered here today to mourn the loss of Mr. Beanbag! He was a good—no—he was a great beanbag!"

Rebecca turned to look at Michael, slightly confused. "Did you hear what I . . ."

"Yes. Yes, I did."

Should I say it? No, Michael. Don't say it.

"He's a friend of mine."

Why did you say it?

Rebecca looked confused as she strained to hear her first funeral for a piece of furniture.

"Oh, Mr. Beanbag! You brought comfort on a daily basis while doing a thankless service! You saved my home from becoming a pretentious den of snobbery! In return, I treated you like an ass. You will *never* be forgotten! So long, good friend!"

Then, came the sound of a dumpster lid slamming down.

"This guy is a friend of yours?" Rebecca whispered, feigning concern.

"A new friend."

"Oh, he's a *new* friend now?"

"Hardly know him, really." Michael held Rebecca's eyes for a moment before there was another sudden slam around the corner, and Rob could be heard murmuring.

"I'd best get going. Sounds like the funeral is over." And with that, she turned to ascend her steps, fumbled her way through her door, and was gone.

A distraught Rob came back around the corner carrying his beanbag. He looked up and saw Michael still standing there.

"I'm weak, man! What can I tell you? I just can't do it! I can't!" Rob looked disappointed in himself.

"Rob? There comes a time in every beanbag's life, right?" He put his arm around Rob's shoulder. "It clearly is *not* Mr. Beanbag's time, brother. Keep your chin up. I think you made the right call."

"Really?" Rob looked relieved that his new buddy wasn't condemning him.

"Absolutely! Now, let's get that thing back in your living room where it belongs!"

As the two walked down the sidewalk to restore Mr. Beanbag's rightful place, Michael glanced over his shoulder at a second-story window where a white curtain was falling back into place.

Maybe this isn't such a bad place to live after all.

7.

THE DOORBELL SEEMED INCREDIBLY LOUD AS it woke Michael from his first deep sleep in months, maybe years. He stumbled out of bed and threw on some shorts and a t-shirt as he made his way toward the front door.

Is it too much to hope Miss Rebecca secretly followed me home yesterday and is bringing me a waffle, bacon, and coffee?

The obnoxious blast hit him again without warning.

Ding!

"On my way!" Michael hollered irritably.

He opened his door and was stung by a high wattage blast of Arizona sunshine. As his eyes adjusted, two people were standing directly before him. A small, yet strong man of about forty was just a few feet from his open door. He was wearing a dark polo shirt and slacks and had a dark complexion with well-coiffed, jet-black hair, a mustache, and a sparse beard. A little to the side and one step down stood a slightly younger woman who was wearing a dark blouse with slacks. She was sporting a short, dark black ponytail and intense eyes—eyes that were burning a hole through him. Both were wearing Glock 40s on their belts right next to

42

their badges. They also had extra magazines and a pair of hand-cuffs visible.

"I can't afford your Thin Mints, but thanks anyway."

Mom always said I became more of a smart ass when I was trying to hide anxiety. Maybe she had a point.

"More of a Samoas fan myself. Sir? Are you Mr. Michael Bale?" asked the man.

"Yes, uh, officer. How can I help you?" Michael was still try-ing to shake off his slumber while trying to ascertain what was going on.

"Mr. Bale? I am Detective Alvarez and this here is Detective Gradillas. We were hoping we could have a word with you."

"Uh, sure. Come on in." Michael opened the door wide and motioned the officers in. *Rising anxiety. Don't be a smart ass. Don't be a smart ass.*

Alvarez pursed his lips and gave a curt nod as he stepped past Michael. Gradillas glanced up at Michael quickly and strode into his condo, surveying the sparse room as she took up her position near a window. Michael shut the door and began walking toward the kitchen.

"Can I get either of you something to drink?" He continued into the kitchen.

"Sir?" Gradillas attempted to get Michael's attention.

"I've got . . ." He was almost around the corner and to the fridge.

"*Sir!*" Gradillas ordered. "Please stop. We'd like to talk to you here. Now."

Startled, Michael realized the gravity of the visit. "Sorry about that. Just trying to be a good host. I'd offer you a seat, but as you can see—"

"Not a problem, Mr. Bale. You seem to live very simply," said Alvarez. Even. Calm. He took out a small notepad. "She must've had a good divorce lawyer, huh?"

"Stop projecting, Alvarez." Gradillas snapped.

"Oh! No. Never married. I guess all a single guy needs is a bed, a refrigerator, a table, a chair, and his computer," Michael responded nervously.

"So sparse apartment, no roommates," Alvarez said aloud purposefully as he jotted onto his notepad.

"Condo, actually," Michael involuntarily interjected.

"Pardon?" Alvarez looked up.

"It's a condo. Means he owns it," Gradillas replied.

"Or the bank," Michael said with a smile that vanished when both detectives gave him matching unentertained looks.

I am such a moron.

"Fine. Was really concerned about that." Alvarez glanced at Michael. "Back to you. No wife. No ex. You got a girlfriend, Mr. Bale?"

"No sir." How many questions had they already asked Michael? It was time for one of his own. "Hey, can I ask you folks what this is all about?"

Alvarez lowered his notepad to his side, looked at Michael, and said, "Sir, we have a complaint against you. Do you know a Sonia Ordoñez?"

"I've never heard the name before, officer."

"It is vital you answer honestly," Gradillas interjected.

"I've never heard that name before."

"Okay," Gradillas responded with a hint of disbelief. She turned and walked several paces to another window, looking carefully outside while continuing to listen intently.

Alvarez wanted to lock in a final answer from Michael whether it was the truth or not. "So you are sure you have never heard of Ms. Sonia Ordoñez?"

"Positive." Michael knew the answer to the next question before he asked it. "What is this all about, officer?"

Gradillas turned from her second window to reply, "Actually, you can refer to us as detectives." She went on. "Ms. Ordoñez has given us a reason to believe you may be giving her inappropriate and undesired attention. You followed her boyfriend to a con-venience store and discussed intimate details with him. These details caused a dispute between Ms. Ordoñez and her boyfriend. A dispute they caught you eavesdropping on."

Then, Detective Alvarez rejoined the conversation. "Does any of this ring a bell, Mr. Bale?"

Michael's heart sank and it showed. Alvarez and Gradillas looked at one another and back at Michael.

"Listen. I'm just observant. I was driving home the other night when I got the munchies. I stopped at a convenience store. When I walked inside, I saw a man being confrontational with a young woman behind the counter. I've seen the type a million times. So I took a stab in the dark. I told him that if he ever hit his girlfriend again, I would call the police. I must've been right because he got pretty spooked. Then, I ran into them at my apart-ment complex. This apartment complex. Those were the only details I knew. Shouldn't *he* be the guy you are interviewing?"

Gradillas' face showed her instant displeasure. "Sir? If it is all the same to you, this might not be the best time to give us advice. Why don't you stick to answering *our* questions?"

"But I didn't do anything."

"We have already established that isn't entirely true," Gradillas said from the window.

"And it's our job to discover how untrue it is," Alvarez added. "So let us do our job. Unless you're an undercover detective?"

"Currently unemployed," Michael responded.

"Hardly any belongings." Gradillas turned to Alvarez. "And he's unemployed. Can't imagine why he's single."

"Hey! I'm standing right here." Michael was starting to get frustrated. He stopped an abuser, and he was the one being scrutinized.

"Mr. Bale," Alvarez said, getting things back on track. "We will look into your version of the story, but I hope you under-stand it is rather common for someone being accused to make counterclaims. Why didn't you approach the police if you thought there was abuse?"

"Officers. I mean no disrespect, but did you really expect me to come walking into the police station and say I saw a man who seemed like an abuser? I called him on it, and he got spooked. I don't know where he lives or even his last name. But could you check it out?"

"That sounds reasonable enough." Gradillas jumped in. "But you just brought up another point. Ms. Ordoñez told us you knew her boyfriend's first name. If you just met him in a gas station for the first time, how did you know his name?"

Combined, these two didn't miss a beat.

"Truthfully?"

"Always a good policy, my man." Alvarez suggested.

"I'm not sure. The best answer I can give you is that I got it from somewhere while I was in the convenience store."

Michael *was* being as honest as he could, if not entirely forthcoming.

"Alright, Mr. Bale," Alvarez said, ready to wrap up the interrogation. "I'm going to ask you to avoid all areas of this complex except for your parking area and your condo. I'm sure you understand why. If you see Ms. Ordoñez before we speak again, turn and walk in the opposite direction. Do not attempt to speak with her. Do not attempt to contact her. Am I clear?"

"Yes, sir. Sounds ideal." Michael wasn't so much angry as frustrated.

"I promise we will look into your version of the events with the same professionalism I showed this morning during our discussion," Gradillas said.

Alvarez shot a glance at Gradillas. "Thank you for your time. We'll be in touch. Gradillas?"

Gradillas was still at the window, studying the view again. After a moment, she turned and walked out the door without looking at Michael.

8.

As soon as Michael knelt in the musty darkness, a rich Irish brogue came from the other side of the screen. "In the name of the Father and the Son and the Holy Spirit."

"Forgive me, Father. It has been about a year since my last confession." Although Michael didn't take advantage of it often, he had always been grateful this old priest made confession available at various times throughout the week.

The voice behind the screen replied, "Welcome back. What do you need to confess, son?"

"I'm just . . . I'm struggling with God."

The priest could be heard shifting in his chair. "Well, that's a bit general. At the risk of badgering the witness, how so?"

"I don't understand why my life seems so unfair. I'm just constantly doing things for other people, but nobody does anything for me. So I dunno. Maybe you'd call that selfish? And I pretty much question God all the time."

"At least you are on speaking terms," the priest said with what sounded like a warm smile.

"Yeah, but it feels like a one-way relationship."

"Ahh." The priest seemed to consider for a moment. "So it feels like God sets high expectations, and the rewards aren't worth the trouble?"

"You nailed it."

"Of course I did. I think every good priest has struggled with that at least once or twice." The priest chuckled. "Okay. Why don't you tell me more about what you do for others?"

"Father? There is a line outside the confessional, and what you're asking for could take a while."

"And you are currently at the front of that line."

"You sure?"

"Listen, son. I'm not trying to be nosey. I just need a little context so I can be of assistance."

"Okay. Well. It was Christmas Eve, a few years ago. My parents were going to drive halfway across Wisconsin to pick me up for the holiday. I knew they shouldn't come."

"Intuition."

"Not in the common use of the word but defined as the power of direct knowledge without evident rational thought . . ."

"Okay, Rain Man."

"No. It's just that I've had this conversation before," Michael added.

"Got it."

"Anyway, it can take on many different forms."

"At the risk of sounding too priestly, have you considered it might be the voice of God?"

"If it is, I didn't respond accordingly that day."

"How so?" Michael heard the priest shift again.

"I wasn't able to stop them. Truth is, I didn't try very hard, and that was the day they both died in a car accident."

"Oh, son . . . that sounds like a tragic coincidence."

"Father? I don't believe in coincidences anymore."

"Not sure I know what you mean, but I'd love to hear more." The old priest could be heard leaning back into his creaky chair.

"Completely your choice, but if you'd like to talk more, I'll be heading to the Galway Pub in about ninety minutes."

"What about confession?"

"I still haven't heard you mention any sins. Besides, son, there is a line."

Michael waited anxiously atop the barstool nearest the entrance. He felt strongly self-aware and desperately wanted the old priest to arrive soon. This was not his scene, and he was certain every other patron in the place knew it. Then, the door opened, and the man he was waiting for arrived.

The priest had thick, flowing white hair that he kept trimmed neatly. It matched his perfectly manicured white beard. He wore dark sunglasses, which he quickly removed to reveal sharp, deep eyes. Eyes that somehow made it possible for the old man to maintain a youthful countenance in his older years. He wore black fleece over his Roman collared shirt and black slacks with functional black shoes.

He immediately spotted Michael eyeing him, and with nothing more than a jerk of the head, summoned him to follow deeper into the establishment.

"Hey, Father! You dining alone today?" A pretty young waitress approached.

"Oh, come now, Stephanie." The priest smiled smoothly. "You know I don't come here to dine alone. Those rumors would besmirch my flawless reputation of sanctity. My friend here will be joining me."

He motioned to Michael.

Stephanie looked at Michael with the confidence necessary to navigate a bar such as this as an attractive employee. "Okay, then. Let's go, boys." She turned and began walking toward the back, and Father followed as Michael moved quickly to catch up.

Stephanie moved them swiftly to a corner spot. As Father slid into one side, she turned to Michael who was still a few steps behind. "Welcome to Father's table." She then turned back to Father as Michael silently slid to the opposite side. "The usual?"

"Besmirching, Stephanie. Besmirching."

Stephanie just smiled and waited. A single hand on a hip.

"Two of the usuals. I don't drink alone."

"Of course not, Father!" she responded overdramatically. "You would never, *ever,* have a drink all alone in this very spot!" Her face went neutral. Then, she turned and was off.

Monsignor William Fitzgerald was a blend of never-ending oxymorons. He was a man with the natural grace and authority of a king who would correct you if you called him anything more formal than "Fr. Fitz." Although an elderly gentleman who had the effortless charm of a ladies man, he had always been entirely faithful to his vow of celibacy, in practice if not always in his heart. Fr. Fitz was a kind man of God whose strong hands betrayed the boxing matches of his youth in Ireland.

Stephanie was back in a flash with a pint for each of them and vanished just as quickly.

One of Fr. Fitz's thick hands reached up and grasped his pint. "Losing my parents were two of the hardest days of my life. I can't imagine losing them both all at once." He took a sip and looked across the table with deep compassion.

"Yeah. It sucked pretty bad." Michael took a sip even though he had no love for the taste of Guinness. He was in a pub sitting across from the manliest priest he had ever met. When in Rome, or Dublin . . .

"Where were you when you heard the news?"

⸻

Ezekiel was driving about ten miles per hour over the speed limit. Earlier, when Phyllis glanced over at the speedometer disapprovingly, he had told Phyllis that was the slowest he was willing to go. They had waited long enough to be reunited with Michael this Christmas. And although she was usually a stickler when it came to the speed limit, this was the one time Ezekiel would get no argument. They both rode in silence, holding each other's hand in anticipation of seeing their son.

Ezekiel felt like the most blessed man alive. The woman he had loved as long as he could remember was beside him. The son he never thought he could have was waiting for them. In his heart, everything beyond those two blessings was just gravy.

"Honey! Watch out!" Phyllis screamed as an extraordinarily muscular deer exploded from the side of the freeway and streaked across the lanes not one hundred feet in front of them. Ezekiel quickly slowed the family wagon as he watched for the beast's running buddies.

When he was finally satisfied the deer was a rogue and dared to breathe again, he glanced over at Phyllis, who still hadn't recovered. Her eyes were wide, and her breathing was shallow. She was letting her mind linger a bit too long on what might have been.

"If we hit that thing, we would have had venison for a month," Ezekiel whispered.

"A year," Phyllis quickly responded, still barely breathing.

"Actually, if we hit something that big, we might not be eating any solid foods for quite some time." Ezekiel winced. As soon as he heard the words coming out of his mouth, he knew they were exactly the opposite of what his wife needed to hear just then. "You know what? I think we should be extra careful and just cruise toward Madison at the speed limit." He eased off the gas once more.

"Good. Because if you get us killed, I'll murder you."

"Phyllis? Honey? I don't think it works that way in heaven . . . which is clearly where you will end up."

Vehicles of all shapes and sizes were now passing them on the left, a fact that was not lost on Ezekiel. By driving so slowly, he was taking one for the team—as well as his wife's heart.

"You think I won't be able to murder you in heaven? You doubt the ferocious nature of a mother kept from her son on Christmas?"

Ezekiel glanced over just in time to catch a tiny smile on the lips of his wife.

"No. I'd never doubt such a thing." He smiled widely, glancing at her again. "I just don't think heaven works that way."

As the words escaped his lips, a car to their left slammed on its brakes. At the screeching sound, Ezekiel looked back to the road ahead and saw a semi that had just rumbled across the small grass median and directly into their path.

"Ezekiel!"

As he slammed on the brakes with a futile swerve, he seemed to understand the words he spoke would be his last. "I love you Phy—"

—

Michael had been going crazy for several hours. He had called his parents four times and lost count of how many times he had gone outside to look for them in the parking area.

When he heard the knock on his dorm room door and opened it to see two uniformed policemen, his heart sank. He had known something was going to happen. He just couldn't have known what. Who possibly could?

"Hello. Are you Mr. Michael Bale?"

No.

He fought the moment.

No, no, no, no.

"Are you Mr. Michael Bale?"

"Yes, sir."

"Son of Ezekiel and Phyllis Bale?"

Oh God.

"Yes."

"We received a call from state patrol. There's been an accident."

"Please, no."

It was all he could muster.

"I'm sorry to inform you . . . that both your parents . . . they . . . well . . . they are deceased . . . they died in the accident."

Although the officer continued to speak, Michael's brain changed channels, and he wasn't listening anymore. Grief and loss overtook him. They were gone. Both of them, gone.

In his heart's search for a foothold, his thoughts were drawn to the conversation with his mom. He kept replaying the instant when he seemed to instinctively understand something horrible was going to happen if his parents didn't change their plans.

Where did it come from? How did I know? Something stronger than coincidence.

Second-guessing is what had gotten him here. This realization untapped in Michael a disgust at his own inaction.

Questions led me to hesitation, hesitation resulted in disaster. I'm done hesitating. From this moment forward, action without question.

Michael's knees buckled.

The officer closest jumped to steady him. "Son? Son?"

The word suddenly stung.

"Yes, officer. I'm sorry. Could you both come in and repeat whatever you just said? I'm struggling a bit, and I don't think I heard anything beyond my parents . . . beyond that they died."

Michael's wobbly legs barely carried him to his couch. His heart didn't want to continue beating as the few known details were filled in. At some point, grief counseling was offered and advised by the well-intentioned officers. Further condolences were expressed before the officers reluctantly left Michael alone. Completely alone.

Fr. Fitz had finished his beer and was watching Michael intently. "Well, I'll be damned."

"That's pretty much how I feel, Father."

"Explain where that feeling comes from, Michael."

"I'm sorry. I'm not trying to feel sorry for myself. It's just—"

"Michael. Stop. Don't worry about my opinion of you. Be real for a minute. Why do you feel damned?"

"Well." Michael continued slowly as if taking stock. "I'm adopted, which means my birth mom didn't want me. My parents both died in a tragic accident. I don't have any real friends, much less a girlfriend. My truck is on its last legs. I live in a barren apartment. I can't keep a job, and I'm about one paycheck from being homeless."

"And all this because you've responded every single time ever since the day your parents died?"

"Pretty much."

"Pretty much every time or every time?"

"Every single time." Michael chuckled at the insanity of his own life.

"Astonishing. So no friends at all?"

"Not really. My life hasn't exactly made that easy. Although . . ."

"What?"

"There *is* Rob."

"And who is Rob?"

"This hippie guy in my condo complex I recently met."

"And he gets along with you?"

"Yeah. I think so."

"And you can stand him?"

"I wouldn't put it that way." Michael laughed. "He's kind of a unique character, but there's something there. It's like he is who he is. I don't know how to explain it."

"Do you have contact information for him?"

Stephanie returned and grasped Fr. Fitz's empty glass without moving it. He looked up and shook his head. No second glass today. She took it and hastily wiped the table.

"Yeah. I've got his phone number."

"And no girlfriend?" Fr. Fitz asked as Stephanie moved to reset a table a few feet away.

"Not even close." Michael smiled sadly.

"Where were you the last time you saw a beautiful woman in person? Other than Stephanie, our extraordinary waitress, of course."

"Thanks, Padre. You're the best." Stephanie fired back without turning around.

"Again. My condo complex." Michael looked down at the table.

"How old would you say she was?"

"About my age." Michael shrugged his shoulders. "Maybe a few years younger."

"Good. Did she have any unfortunate jewelry?"

"Huh?"

"Was she married, Michael?" Fr. Fitz shook his head.

"Uh, no. No. She wasn't married."

"Name?"

"Rebecca. Didn't get her last name."

"Do you have *her* contact information?"

"No."

"Beautiful. Unmarried. Lives within five hundred yards, and you didn't get her number? But you got the hippie's number." Fr. Fitz's face fell into the palm of his hand.

"Pretty much sums it up." Michael grinned.

Fr. Fitz smirked. "Maybe you should've taken the vow of celibacy instead of me."

"You're probably right."

"No. No. It sounds like life has been pretty rough the past few years. But Michael, hidden underneath that grief, what I hear is that you were conceived by a strong and selfless woman who took the heroic path. You were then raised by two wonderful people who chose you to be their son. By your grief, I assume you got two of the good ones. Since their passing, you have made your life about serving others. You have a vehicle. You have access to fresh water. You've never gone hungry. Blessings can be obscured by grief but never eliminated by it."

"Yeah." Michael swallowed hard. "I'm sure everything you're saying is true." He looked down at his empty glass, unable to look at Fr. Fitz.

The priest went on. "But the fact that other people somehow have it worse never negates the pain we feel and the struggles we endure."

Michael didn't respond because there was nothing to say.

Fr. Fitz continued. "Having said that, I guess the pressing question is, are you good with a hammer?"

"Excuse me?" Michael looked up with a single eyebrow raised.

"I know you have problems, Michael, but I have problems of my own." Fr. Fitz looked at Michael with a hint of a grin. "I just had one of my maintenance crew move away last week."

"Are you offering me a job, Father?"

"Yes, I am. And I think you should take it because I am already aware of your eccentricities."

"Well then, I accept."

"You don't even know how much I'll pay you."

"It will be more than I'm making now."

"We'll work on your negotiating skills later. For now, show up tomorrow morning at seven."

"I can do that."

"And I want you to call your new pal and loiter wherever it was you saw that woman. And if you see her and don't get her number, I'll fire you." Fr. Fitz paid in cash, patted Michael warmly on the shoulder, and exited the pub.

9.

MICHAEL THOUGHT HE WAS GOING TO receive absolution. What he got instead was homework. Make a new friend, stalk a neighbor, and show up to work at seven. He decided to get to it. Rob was the easiest box to check off the list.

Rob answered the phone but was talking to someone else. "No, dude. I swear. You can make an omelet in a Ziplock bag! No. I don't know if it's toxic, but I would guess clean air and the calming effects of being one with nature offset any adverse effects." Rob then quickly switched his attention to the phone. "Rob here. Expert outdoorsman and foosball player. How may I brighten your day?"

"Hey, Rob. Michael here. Wondered if you wanted to go grab lunch?"

"Flattered, but who is this?"

"Michael." Nothing. "Michael Bale." Still nothing. "I'm the Ring-bearer."

"Aw, bro. Wish I could! Hold on. Hey. Little man. Yeah, you. Step . . . away . . . from the bear repellant. Seriously, little dude. Nothing good will come of you messing with that can." Michael heard a loud metallic clang. "Hey! I need a parent up here! Any parent! Don't care if this is your child! Oh. Hi there. Is that your offspring? I was wondering if you could keep him away from the industrial-strength pepper spray. Sweet. Thanks." Rob paused a minute to make sure everything was "kosher" again. "Hey, bro. Yeah. I wish I could, but I'm workin' all day."

"You could've just let the kid spray some of that stuff in the store."

"Good ideas given too late are no good at all."

Then a voice could be heard yelling, "Dude! I've got a good idea! Get back to work!"

"You know I can multitask, boss! Talking to my buddy and saving you from a lawsuit at the same time!" Rob hollered. "Hey, Mikey. I've got a great idea too. Why don't you pick me up something and stop by? If you drop off a burrito for me, I'll give you a gift in return."

"Hey! What about me?!" his boss hollered in the background.

"Are you payin'?"

"Fine! But you are paying for his gift, and the burritos better not be over twenty-five bucks! I own a camping store, not a bank!"

Rob tried to give Michael directions, but he said he knew where it was. As soon as he hung up, he fired up his outdated computer and looked up directions to local burrito places and Humboldt Camping Supply.

<hr>

Humboldt Camping Supply was a very small place on the tail end of an eighties-era strip mall where the variety of backpacks, tents, and sleeping bags was significantly smaller than the big chain stores, but everything was high quality, and the advice from anyone who worked there was top notch.

As Michael carried lunch through the front door, Rob and

his boss were distracted by a very important debate, which gave Michael a chance to admire some of the most amazing facial hair he had ever witnessed. The boss looked to be in his sixties and had what could best be described as a paisley beard. It was a goatee only attached to the remaining hair on his head on the left side of his face. It was a look that wouldn't stir up a lot of interest in the world of online dating, but Michael doubted that was really a concern for a guy like this.

"Dude. I'm telling you. Springsteen destroys Dylan," Rob proclaimed.

"Rob, I'm begging you." His boss pleaded. "Do not say that again, or I will be forced to fire you."

"Please. Dylan was a great lyricist. One of the best of all time, but have you heard the man sing? Makes a guy seasick."

"First of all, he is the *best* lyricist of all time. Secondly, you are saying Dylan's lyrics were better than his voice?"

"Absolutely, bro."

"Not your 'bro.' We are not related. And back to my point, the same is true of Springsteen! I won't argue his lyrics are strong, but the man sings like a guy who can't find his inhaler."

"Lower your voice. You are talking about the Boss."

"No. He isn't the Boss. I am the boss, and now you have officially forced me to fire you."

"Hey, guys," Michael finally interjected. "I've got the burritos. Does Rob still have a job?"

"Oh. Yeah. Bossman fires me about three times a week, but I just keep showing up and he keeps paying me."

"Must be an accounting error," his boss mumbled as he approached.

"Hello, sir. I'm Michael." Michael extended his hand.

"And I'm the boss." Rob's boss shook Michael's hand, passing him a twenty at the same time. "Now gimme my food."

"Sure thing." Michael passed him a burrito, and the boss immediately wandered his way into a back office.

"You gotta give me my burrito to get your gift." Rob reached out his hand, palm up.

"I don't need anything, buddy. Your boss paid." Michael handed over the food.

"Deals a deal! Now the fun part. You get a vacuum-sealed water bottle, a multi-tool, or a first aid kit. Hero's choice."

"First aid kit," the Voice only Michael could hear interjected.

Michael thought the multi-tool would come in handy, but he was left with no option. "I'll take the first aid kit."

"The healer reveals himself."

"Thank you, buddy. It wasn't necessary."

"Hey, dude. Rob always takes care of his friends."

"Did you just go third person?" asked his boss from the back. "Don't make me fire you twice in ten minutes."

"Sorry captain, my captain." Rob turned back to Michael. "Hey, Mikey. You got any plans tonight?"

"Not yet." Michael knew this was subject to change but decided to keep that to himself.

"Now you do. Video games and dinner. Mi casa. On the ocho."

"Sounds great. I'll be at your door eight o'clock sharp."

"Hey, kiddo." The boss had wandered back out front. "Are you gonna work and split Rob's paycheck? Because if you aren't, I need him to get back to work."

"Sorry, sir," Michael apologized.

A loud snap echoed from the back of the store.

"Got him!" Rob exclaimed and jogged toward the source of the sound.

"Took ya long enough!" the boss called after him.

Michael followed Rob to the back where he found his friend tossing a freshly occupied rat trap into the trash.

"You would not believe how long it took me to get that guy, and I'm glad I did! Bossman was getting pissed paying for MREs that were just going toward that rat's nutritional needs."

"So a little cheese on a trap did the trick?" Michael guessed.

"Naw. That's just it. This was a smart one. His instincts told him it was a trap. A little cheese wasn't enough. I had to figure out what it would take to tempt him so strongly he would ignore his instincts."

"And?"

"Peanut butter sprinkled with a couple of bacon bits and a touch of honey."

"I hope we eat that well tonight."

"I was just going to order a pizza."

"Fair enough. Should I bring anything?"

"Just the mental fortitude to suffer humiliating video game losses." Rob beamed.

"We'll see about that. I better go before I get you in more trouble."

"Cool beans. Thanks for stoppin' by."

As Michael headed for the door, he checked off the first of his three homework assignments and decided there was no time like the present to knock out another. He headed back to his condo complex.

—

As Michael pulled his truck back into the complex, he decided to park in his spot and just walk back to Rebecca's building. He remembered the detective's orders, but she was worth the risk.

He got out of his truck with every intention of heading that way when he saw a little toddler shuffling in another direction with no supervision. He jogged toward the little guy but lost him behind a building. As he turned the corner, he saw the boy push through the faulty gate to the pool area. Michael broke into a sprint.

"Hey, hey! Kid!" Michael didn't know what else to yell.

The pool area was empty except for the little guy waddling along the perimeter of the pool toward the deep end. He was looking at a red inflatable ball floating just off the edge. Michael burst through the gate. It flung around and slammed against the metal fencing.

The crash made the little boy jump, slip, and fall into the pool with a splash. Michael remained in a dead sprint, dove into the water fully clothed, and quickly located the toddler. He spun the child away from himself, reached underneath his arms, and swam on his back to the edge.

Between the little boy's coughs, he heard footsteps approaching quickly. He steadied himself on the edge as arms reached down for the boy. He looked up to see a woman who appeared to be the boy's mother lifting him out of the water.

"Oh, Ricky. Ricky! What were you doing? You can't run away from me like that!"

She hugged him close as she walked him away from the water. Still in the pool, Michael pulled out his cell phone, now a paperweight, and set it on the side of the pool.

Halfway to the gate, the mother turned back to Michael who was now dragging himself out of the pool. "Thank you, mister! Thank you!" She turned again and walked out the gate. "I should sue this dump," she mumbled under her breath. "Ricky! You know better!"

As she walked off, she passed Rebecca who was just standing there staring at Michael, sitting on the edge of the pool. Fully clothed. Completely drenched. His shoes, socks, and the bottom half of his jeans were still submerged in the pool.

"Hey, Rebecca. Wanna join me for a swim?" Still sitting, Michael pulled off his shoes one at a time and poured water out of them back into the pool.

Rebecca walked up toward Michael on the outside of the pool fence. "Yeah, um, I'm gonna pass. Didn't bring my suit with me."

"Neither did I, but if you're chicken . . ." Michael stood up to face her. His soaked shirt clung to his still-heaving chest.

"I think you're great and all, but . . ." She began as Michael reached up and pulled off his t-shirt, turned, and wrung it out over the pool. "But, uh, I don't typically swim in other people's laundry water."

Michael turned around with a twinkle in his eye. "Hold on. You think I'm great?"

"It depends. Did you actually just save a little boy who fell into the pool?"

"What? No. I don't know what you think you saw." Michael closed the distance between the two of them. "But my washer is broken, and this was the best idea I could come up with." He pulled the wet shirt back on.

"Ah. That makes so much more sense." She leaned on the fence.

"Do you still think I'm great?"

"Well. I'm a bit disappointed that you aren't David Hasselhoff, but I guess you're alright."

"Do you ever have dinner with guys who are just alright?"

Rebecca stood up straight. "Of course not. I recently made a resolution. I only have dinner with extraordinary men."

"In that case, you have just over twenty-four hours to decide how you feel about me. At six o'clock tomorrow night, I'll be sitting at a table at Macayo's Depot Cantina Restaurant in Tempe. I understand I might be dining alone, but I sincerely hope not."

"Hmm." She stepped back from the fence. "How *do* I feel about you?" She turned and walked off to her condo.

10.

I JUST SAVED A KID. FIRST OF ALL, *that was awesome, and the mom was actually mildly grateful. Nice for a change. As a major bonus? I saved the kid while a girl I was about to ask on a date was watching. Seriously? Heroic acts are so much better than a cute puppy.*

He closed his door, immediately stripped out of his wet clothes, and looked at the clock on the oven. He still had several hours until he was expected at Rob's place. He wanted to go for a run, but he would have to walk right past Sonia's unit, and he didn't want to see those two detectives again any time soon.

"Just go to Kiwanis."

I just want to jog. No more heroics today.

"Go for your jog."

At 125 acres, Kiwanis Park wasn't big enough for distance running in and of itself, but it bordered a canal that had a dirt path you could run along for an entire day.

As Michael rolled into the park, he was still floating on cloud nine, and the weather was perfect for a quick run thanks to cooler than normal temperatures connected to the yearly monsoon season. Clouds were gathering, and a breeze was picking up, but he still had a window before the weather turned if he didn't delay. He stretched a little before starting off around a small lake, past some bustling picnic areas and a cluster of sand volleyball courts.

After Michael finally ran up the incline to the edge of the canal, he planned on one more good quad stretch before really letting it rip. He stood straight, steadied himself with a small utility pole with a random leash looped around its base, kicked back his right heel, and grabbed his foot. As he pulled the foot up behind himself, he bent forward to get the full stretch. He looked down along the concrete that sloped to the flowing water's edge while realizing life was looking up for the first time in a long time. There, about a foot above the water, he spotted what looked to be two fake fingernails. He shuffled a few feet over and squatted down to get a closer look. Something didn't feel right, so Michael got down on his stomach to get even closer.

This isn't good.

"No. It isn't."

Michael rushed back to the nearest picnic area and borrowed someone's phone to call the police.

The process seemed to take forever. First, he had to wait twenty minutes for the officers to arrive. Then, Michael watched as they slowly approached from the distant parking area. Next, there were the obligatory questions and discussions on whether or not the fingernails were really worth calling in. Their call back to cop central consisted of details on the scene, the broken nails, and Michael's full name. It was followed by a request for Michael to stay put. The next wait was about forty-five minutes. That was when the fun really began as none other than Detective Alvarez came jogging up to the scene.

"Hey, Michael! It seems like only yesterday!" He smiled broadly. "You, my man, are having one helluva week!" He slapped

Michael on the shoulder as he walked by to confer quietly with the officers. He glanced back at Michael a few times while getting up to speed. The conference seemed to end abruptly as Alvarez slapped one of the officer's shoulders, apparently an Alvarez go-to move for crime scenes.

He began walking along the side of the canal. The officer he had been talking to peeled away from the group and was texting someone. The other officer, a bear of a man, was walking back toward Michael. Alvarez slowed his pace as he made his way along the edge of the canal. He made it to where the water flowed through the large grate and underground. Then, he laid on his stomach lowering his face just inches above the water.

"Sorry for the delay," the bear apologized. "The detective just wants to check things out personally before letting you go. We want you to know we really appreciate your vigilance and even if this turns out to be a false—"

"Hey! McElroy!" Alvarez yelled from down the canal a short distance. "Get the fire department! Now! Then, get me the emergency number for SRP! Schneider! I need you to secure the scene!"

Alvarez began walking with purpose back up the canal while texting someone.

As he put his phone away, he shouted, "Michael! I need you to step back from the canal. Stand in the grass please."

The next fifteen minutes went by in a flash. The smaller Schneider was putting up a police line at a significant distance from the canal's edge. McElroy was on his radio constantly. All the while, Alvarez was asking Michael every question imaginable.

"I'm sure our visit caught you off guard. What did you do after our visit yesterday?"

"Just because I like to be thorough, are you good with me checking out your story?"

"Out of curiosity, how often do you visit this park?"

"With the understanding that you are currently single without many connections in the area, could you tell me all the times over the last three days that no one could account for your whereabouts?"

"To the best of your memory, when was the last time you visited this park?"

"Why were you here today?"

"I'm known to be a pretty observant fellow, but two fingernail fragments in that location? That is impressive. How did you notice something so small?"

"Did you see anyone acting suspiciously within view when you arrived on the scene?"

As the clouds darkened and the wind began to pick up, the cavalry arrived. The arrivals included the fire department, many more uniformed police officers, some officials, a news reporter, a cameraman, and Detective Gradillas. She said something to McElroy, who headed straight for the news crew. She walked up with three glass water bottles, tossed one to Alvarez, and extended one to Michael.

"Alvarez said you'd been here quite a while and were putting up with his incessant questions. Probably parched."

"Really. It's no problem." Michael chugged from the bottle. In the chaos, he hadn't realized how thirsty he had become. "Who is . . . was the person?"

"Can't say for sure yet," Alvarez replied. "Hey, Gradillas. Can I have a word? McElroy! If you would?"

Alvarez walked Gradillas up the incline to the canal's edge, pausing only to whisper something to Officer McElroy the Bear, who made his way back down to Michael.

"See what I was sayin' before? You were vigilant, and because of that, we found this lady. Well done, Mr. Bale."

"Right place, right time." Michael finished off his water bottle. "I just wish I could've prevented whatever happened to her."

"You're tellin' me! I'm the cop here, man. I'd love to catch the guy who did this to her. I mean, that's assuming it wasn't an accident. Here. I'll toss your bottle for you. Wouldn't want to fine you for littering." Officer McElroy the Bear reached out, took it out of Michael's hand, and walked back through the police line.

The body was recovered from the water minutes before sundown. Matters were complicated by the impending thunderstorm that had been brewing for hours.

The weather was set to turn ugly soon. Inside the police line, there was a flurry of activity as the assembled army was scrambling to record everything they could before it was all washed away. Alvarez directed a photographer as Gradillas made her way back to Michael.

"Sir! Sir! What is your name?" A reporter approached Michael from out of nowhere.

"Um. Sure . . ."

Gradillas stepped between Michael and the news crew.

"This man has been through quite an ordeal today and will not be answering questions from the press. Isn't that right?" She turned to Michael.

"Fine with me."

"Aw, come on detective!" The reporter protested, clearly frustrated to be the first on the scene without a witness interview to show for it.

"In order to protect his privacy and maintain his safety, we feel it's best for him to be questioned by the police rather than the media for the time being." She took Michael by the shoulder and began walking away from the scene.

Once they were at a safe distance Gradillas stopped and whispered, "Hey, Michael. You are free to go. We just need a number in case we need to follow up."

"I don't have a phone anymore."

"Well, that certainly isn't going to help the girlfriend situation, now is it?" She seemed much friendlier than just thirty-six hours ago.

"Probably not. But I *did* get a job."

"Really? Since yesterday?"

"I've been busy. Just ask your partner. He's got it all down in his notebook."

"Not a shocker. In a scenario like this one, we have to cover our bases in order to cover our asses."

"Understood."

"Anyway. If you are okay with it, no talking to reporters for a while. It's for your safety until we figure out what went down here. Now, get out of here if you want to beat the storm."

As Michael was being escorted from the scene, his water bottle was being sealed and given to Detective Alvarez.

11.

MICHAEL WALKED THROUGH THE DUSTY MONSOON wind to knock on Rob's door, not because he wanted to hang out but out of obligation.

Rob opened the door with a look of amusement. He was wearing a faded Pac-Man print t-shirt and cargo shorts. No shoes. "Look what the cat dragged in."

"Buddy. I am . . . so . . . sorry," Michael responded.

"Whatever, dude. I ate without you. Plus, do you seriously think I crash before two?" Rob backed up and motioned Michael in. "As long as you're okay with cold pizza."

"At least you've decided I'm not a vampire."

"I ordered garlic on the pizza."

"So you are seriously gonna make me eat my pizza cold?"

"You're lucky I'm in a forgiving mood." Rob smiled as he pulled a few slices out of the oven where he'd kept them warm and tossed them on a plate.

"If it helps, I've got a stellar excuse."

Rob leaned back against the kitchen counter. "Spin your yarn, my friend. I got the time."

Michael proceeded to walk Rob through the entire Kiwanis Park adventure. During the tale, Rob mindlessly ate the slices he'd pulled out for Michael and began digging into a fresh half gallon of mint chocolate chip ice cream with a spatula.

"Dude. So I have one question. Do you have a superpower, or are you Sherlock Holmes?"

"Why would you ask that?"

"Because either you have superhuman powers of observation or you only have extraordinary powers of observation. I just wanna know which."

"The fingernails?"

"And mom's ring. People walked by that bush for over a week. I'm pretty sure a landscaping company trimmed it. No one saw the ring. And then the partial fingernails. People walked by that spot all day, and no one saw them." He paused for a beat before continuing. "They were hanging on to a steep concrete decline. I don't understand how you spotted them."

"How do I put this? Stuff just kinda happens to me."

"What, like Forrest Gump?"

Michael took a deep breath, fully understanding he was standing on the edge of a cliff. He knew if he answered Rob's questions, he was jumping and there would be no coming back. Michael also knew that if he wasn't entirely honest, his potential friendship with Rob would be doomed. He was at the end of the road, and he chose to jump.

Michael told Rob everything. The day his parents died. The vow he made. How his life had spiraled since. Rob listened while finishing up the ice cream and licking the spatula clean.

As Michael wrapped up, Rob pointed the spatula at him and smiled. "You want to be my friend."

"Lack of options."

"No. Seriously. You want to be my friend!"

"Now you're just making this awkward."

"As I see it, being your best friend is dangerous."

"Who said anything about best friends?"

"And if I am gonna be your wingman, if I am gonna be your Robin, if I am gonna be your Ed McMahon . . ."

"How old *are* you?"

"I am going to need some training."

Rob started putting on a pair of burgundy Chuck Taylor All Stars.

"What are you talking about?"

"I need to see you in action. Let's go, sensei. Snap to it."

Rob then pulled on a gray sweatshirt.

"It doesn't work that way. I can't force it."

"Well, bro. Tonight, you will just make yourself available. We'll be like Starsky and Hutch, letting dispatch know we're on duty."

"Again . . . seriously . . . how old are you?"

"Grew up watching reruns with my pop." Rob opened his front door to a downpour and pulled up his hood. "Where is your ride, kemosabe?"

"Fine. Let's go."

—

As his old truck roared into the soaked night, Rob was looking at everything like a sugar-riddled cat with ADD after five cups of coffee. "So where are we headed?"

"No idea."

Rob fidgeted. "But it will just happen, right?"

"No idea."

"What about that guy? He could be dangerous." Rob pointed through the rain at a man of about three hundred pounds walking down the road eating a churro.

"Only if you're that churro. Calm down."

"What can I do?"

Realizing Rob was just going to get more frustrated with the lack of action, Michael decided to have a little fun. "Relax, turbo. I'm going to grab something to eat."

"How can you be hungry? I'm stuffed."

"I bet you are."

Michael pulled into Josebertos, a twenty-four hour Mexican food shack with a drive-thru.

Through the dull patter of the rain, a voice said, "Hello and welcome to Josebertos. What can we make for you?"

"Yeah, um, I'd like a chicken quesadilla with sour cream."

"Anything else?"

Michael turned to Rob, who let out the kind of belch some men only unleash in the company of other men—or wives of five-plus years. "Needed to make room for chips and guac."

"Add an order of chips and guacamole."

"I've got a chicken quesadilla with a side of sour cream, chips, and guacamole. Please pull up. We'll have your total at the window."

Michael pulled up to the window, and it slid open.

"That'll be eight fifty-three."

"I got it, bro." Rob fished out a ten and handed it across.

The window slid back shut.

Michael twitched his head and made his eyes go just a little Manchurian Candidate. Rob took notice.

"What's up, bro?!"

"Um . . . nothing. Nothing you need to worry about."

"Ohhh. It's happening! Talk to me!"

The window slid back open.

"Here is your change. And here is your food. Have a good night."

It was time.

"Thank you. Oh, and call your aunt Beatrice. Tell her to get out of the house. Now!"

Michael pulled away from the window quickly.

"Dude! I knew it! I knew it! You are a freakin' superhero!"

Michael rolled with it by doing his best falsely humble, deep voice. "I'm no hero, Rob. I'm just a man trying to make a difference."

"Bro. You saved Aunt Beatrice."

Rob opened the bag, pulled out the small plastic container of guacamole, and peeled off the top. Michael quickly checked his rearview mirror before slamming on the brakes. He slid to a stop on the wet pavement.

"Don't eat that!"

He grabbed the guacamole, rolled down his window, and flung it across the road. Then, he proceeded down the road as the rain finally let up.

"Whoa. What was wrong with the guac?"

Michael tried not to smile. "We'll never know."

Rob looked back into the bag. "Do you think the chips are alright?"

"Pretty sure. Say. Do you know any Lionel Ritchie songs?"

"Is that the dude who did 'Ghostbusters'?" Rob started munching his way through the chips.

"No."

"The dude who did 'Party All the Time'?"

"No."

"The dude who did 'Dancin' on the Ceiling'?"

"Bingo! I knew it!"

"I don't understand, but I guess I don't need to." Rob made short work of his chips and eyed the quesadilla.

"You gonna eat this?" he asked, his big round eyes pleading.

"Hand me that bag. Now."

"Fine." Rob handed over the bag and looked around. "Hey! Where are we headed?"

"Tempe Marketplace. There is one more thing we need to do."

Michael turned into the outdoor mall at the crossroads of the 101 and the 202. It included shopping, restaurants, and a large movie theater. The stores had closed hours ago, but it had plenty of foot traffic thanks to the food, the flicks, and the rain finally ceasing. Michael found a spot close to most of the restaurants.

"I'm going to need you to sing." Michael warned as he turned off the truck.

"Como say what?" Rob looked over at him.

"This is serious. I'm going to need you to sing."

"I don't understand."

"Let's go."

Michael got out of the truck with his bag of Mexican food, and Rob followed him toward the center of the outdoor mall.

"What the heck are you talking about?" Rob called after Michael.

Michael kept a quick pace. "There is someone here who has gone through a lot. I don't know what. I don't need to know what."

He stopped abruptly to face Rob. Deadly serious.

"All I know is that 'Dancing on the Ceiling' means something to them. They need to hear it."

"And you want me to sing it?"

"That is exactly what I need you to do."

Michael turned and resumed his quick pace toward the crowd of revelers, making their way back to their cars or across the walkway from one establishment to another.

"But all I know is the chorus!" Rob called after him.

"That will be enough," Michael said over his shoulder.

"Why don't *you* sing it?"

"Because I can't carry a tune."

"Aw, man!"

Michael stopped next to a small stage used for outdoor concerts on the weekends. "This will do."

"Wait. What? You want me to stand up there?"

Michael did his best serious voice again. "It is the only way to make sure the person hears you."

Rob just stared at Michael for a second. "Right now?"

"Right now."

Rob took a deep breath, gathered his courage, and stepped up onto the stage. Michael took a few steps to a nearby bench, took out his quesadilla, and prepared to enjoy the show.

Rob looked at him and took one more breath. "Whoa!"

Several people looked over from their conversations.

"What a feelin'!"

Several more stopped talking.

"When you're dancin' on the ceiling!"

"Shut up!" someone yelled.

"Oh! What a fee-li-in'. When you're dancin' on the ceiling. Come on!"

Michael had to give Rob credit. He didn't go halfway.

Then, a group of five inebriated guys suddenly all sang, "Whoa! What a feelin'!"

A group of college girls laughed, but one joined the small chorus. "When you're dancin' on the ceiling!"

Another turned to her. "Cindy? You know this song?"

"Lionel Ritchie was my grandpa's favorite ever since the Commodores," she responded too quietly for either Rob or Michael to hear.

Rob kept going, encouraged by the growing choir, and to Michael's amazement and amusement, Rob led the crowd in the refrain three more times. Each time, more people joined in until a security guard broke it up by making Rob get off the stage.

The guard, who was just doing his job, was booed vigorously.

On his way back to Michael, Rob high-fived several people and got one particularly random kiss on the cheek from a girl. He wore the lipstick on his bearded cheek with pride as he sat on the bench next to Michael.

"Dude! That was gnarly!"

Michael was suddenly hit with a wave of guilt. His original thought was to come clean with Rob so the two could share a good laugh. But it seemed they were past that now, and Rob's feelings would be hurt. He needed to put a stop to the fun.

"Rob, I need to tell you something."

"Sure, dude, but I need to say something first."

"Rob—"

"It'll just take a sec, Mikey." He looked over at his friend with a big smile. "I want to thank you for giving me a taste. Now I understand what it must be like when it *really* happens."

"Pardon?"

"I mean, I'm sure it's different when it really happens. But, if we are buds, it'll eventually happen, right?"

"So . . . you knew none of that was real?"

"Of course, man. I told you. I have great powers of observation."

"And you aren't mad?"

"I ain't mad, bro, but you owe me a guacamole."

"Can you take a raincheck? I just remembered I've got somewhere to be in about seven hours."

"Well, I guess we best get going before something really happens."

As they walked away, Cindy pulled a picture out of her purse and smiled a real smile for the first time in over a month.

12.

MICHAEL PULLED UP TO THE CHURCH ten minutes early and had no idea what to do or where to go. He knew where the parish office was, but he was pretty sure it wouldn't open for several more hours, so he found a bench directly between the office and the church. Fr. Fitz was bound to find him here and give him further directions. Eight minutes later, he was proven correct.

Fr. Fitz emerged from the front of the church in full vestments. He looked over at Michael, tipped his head with a smile, and turned to face the doors. Moments later, a smattering of about seventy-five parishioners made their way out behind him, most of them over sixty years old and a majority of them taking an extra few minutes to wait in line to exchange pleasantries with Fr. Fitz. Five minutes in, he was down to the last person. She was about eighty years old and was showing no signs of letting him go.

"... and that is why I'm convinced we'd get more youth coming to Mass if we reinstated a Folk Mass."

"Mrs. Abrams? I know you saw it work wonders in the seventies, and I'd love to hear you out, but this young man has volunteered to help around the church, and today is his first day."

"Volunteering?" Michael attempted to clarify.

"Oh!" Mrs. Abrams smiled widely. "You are such a good boy. Don't you think a Folk Mass would bring young people back to the Church?"

"Well . . . I . . ."

"Mrs. Abrams? This is a conversation that begins with us. And that will need to happen later."

"Well, I wasn't trying to make any waves. I was simply interested in the young man's opinion."

"Of course. I just don't want to waste his time when he has so generously volunteered his time and talent."

"Volunteered?" Michael questioned again.

"Volunteered!" Father happily boomed.

"Volunteered!" Mrs. Abrams happily confirmed. "God bless you." She patted Michael on the shoulder and waddled off toward her aircraft carrier of a Buick.

Michael stood up, cocked his head, and asked, "So I'm volunteering?"

"Of course not. But if I told Mrs. Abrams you were getting paid, she'd present me with a list of references and want to resume her career as a bookkeeper after a twenty-year sabbatical. Plus, it is a virtual lock she will be bringing you a small mountain of baked goods tomorrow. You're welcome. Now, follow me."

The priest led Michael to his locked office and sat behind a beautifully ornate desk covered in piles of paper, envelopes, messages from his secretary, and a few baked goods that must have been dropped off at the front desk and placed in his office by a receptionist since he was last at his post.

"Sit down, son." He motioned to a chair on the other side of his desk, then picked up a tin of muffins.

"Want these?"

"Uh, I think they were made for you."

"Suit yourself." He placed the muffins, along with the other baked goods, in a box next to his desk. "I send a quick email to my secretary whenever there is something in the box, and she takes it to a local shelter. But she insists that since the poison was made for me, I have the option of eating it first. I allow it because it gives me the opportunity to write a thank you note." He smiled kindly. "But enough about baked goods. Have you done any of the homework I gave you?"

"Homework?"

"Reached out to your potential friend? Located the girl you let get away? To summarize, do I have to fire you after you've been on the clock for thirty minutes?"

"Actually Father . . . I hung out with the potential friend yesterday afternoon and again last night."

"So you were avoiding the girl?"

"Nay, nay, Padre. I saw her too, and I might have a date with her tonight. Do I get a raise for that?"

"First of all, no raises for a year. Second, I don't even want to know how it is that you aren't sure whether or not you have a date tonight. Finally, if you are doing what you claim to be doing in your free time, you are a hero, and that *still* doesn't give *you* the right to call me Padre. Father, Fr. Fitz, or Almighty Supreme Ruler of My Paycheck are all acceptable, however."

Michael winced at the word "hero," and Fr. Fitz noticed.

"What? Can't take a joke, son?"

"I'm not a hero, Father."

"Explain that."

"Bluntly? I let my parents die."

"Tragic to be sure. But I give you Batman, Superman, Robert Downey, Jr."

"Ironman?"

"Sure. And the one who shoots arrows . . ."

"Hawkeye or Arrow?"

"How would I know? Probably both. And Spiderman."

"That was his Uncle Ben."

"Is that who they named the rice after?"

"I don't think so, Father."

"Besides, if Spiderman is being raised by his uncle, there is a good chance his parents bit the bullet."

"His parents *bit the bullet*? Really?"

"I'm sorry." Fr. Fitz immediately recognized his error. "That may have been insensitive, but I'm old, and old people are allowed to say insensitive things. It's the law."

"I don't think that is a thing."

"You obviously didn't know any of my grandparents."

"Interesting family insight."

"I have stories I could tell you, but you are on the clock. Now that I've shot a hole a mile wide in your 'living-parent-heroism-qualifier theory,' do you have anything else to back your case?"

"Sure. For one, I don't go out looking to help people. I just react. I find myself in circumstances, and I respond."

Fr. Fitz smiled and slowly shook his head. "And you think that means what you do isn't heroic? The men who stormed the beaches of Normandy. The first responders who died on September 11th. Teachers across our land who forego higher-paying jobs to teach our children. Those aren't heroes?"

"They all signed up for it."

"They follow through because it is what they were made to do." Fr. Fitz dismissed Michael's argument.

"Well, agree to disagree." Michael looked away.

"No. That's not good enough," Fr. Fitz said with authority. "Let's talk this through. Some of the boys at Normandy were drafted."

"So some of them didn't even have a choice."

"Some people dodged the draft, but most of those who were drafted still served. They might have felt as if they didn't have a choice, a bit like you, I imagine. And yet, here you are . . . still doing it. And the first responders didn't know what would be asked of them on 9/11, but they signed up and agreed to run toward danger in order to save others. If I'm understanding this correctly, that is exactly what you do." The priest waited for Michael's eyes to meet his own before going on. "And the teachers had career options . . . options that may have blessed them in ways teaching never will, but someone needs to do it. And every day, they wake up knowing they could have a better car, live in a better neighborhood, and have no psychotic parents to deal with. But they do the job. With the exception of the parent aspect, that sounds an awful lot like you. So either you are a fantastic liar or a hero."

Michael sat there in silence. He might've understood what the old priest was saying, but he didn't have to accept it.

Fr. Fitz abruptly picked up his telephone and dialed a number. "Hey! You here yet? Good. I got that new guy for you. He needs to leave today at four. No later." Michael smiled at the priest's help. "And start him in the bathrooms." Michael's smile vanished.

"Who was that?"

"That was John. You report to him. Older guy. Former military. Although I don't think he has fully realized the 'former' part as of yet. This is just his new assignment. Good man, if a bit tightly wound. He'll be waiting just outside the offices for you. We'll take care of paperwork once my secretary gets in."

"Sounds great. Thank you for the job." Michael stood up and went to shake Fr. Fitz's hand. The priest grasped his hand with the strength of a former boxer.

"No need to thank me. You will be earning your pay. I want those bathrooms cleaned heroically."

13.

MICHAEL DECIDED TO ARRIVE AT THE restaurant about fifteen minutes early just to be safe, but the complete and total lack of parking this close to Arizona State, one of the nation's largest universities, forced him to park nearly six blocks away.

He got out of his truck and checked his reflection in the window. Most of the young women in the area would readily agree his height combined with his classic good looks more than made up for his slightly aged polo shirt and worn blue jeans. But Michael didn't care what the consensus might be. He just hoped he looked good enough for Rebecca.

He walked a little too quickly and probably looked like an idiot or like a grandmother power walking at a local mall. He didn't want to be late, but if he ran, he'd risk becoming a sweaty mess. Less than ideal on a first date.

He was within half a block, and he just needed to keep moving when a voice called to him. "Excuse me, sir? Could you help me?"

Nope. No, I don't have the time. A beautiful young woman might be waiting for me.

"Excuse me? Sir?" The voice became familiar.

Michael turned to see Rebecca wearing a gray blouse with a large rose print and jeans.

Wow.

It was the only word his lizard brain could conjure.

"Sir. I need your help." Rebecca's eyes twinkled playfully.

"Well, miss, I hope I can be of assistance."

"You see. There's this guy. I hardly know him, but he asked if I would meet him for dinner tonight. Do you think I should go through with it?"

"Depends."

"On what?"

"Is he handsome?"

Rebecca smiled broadly. "He's passable." Michael scrunched up his face in mock disapproval. Rebecca went on. "I mean he is tall, in great shape, and tried to help me with my groceries . . . if you are into that sort of thing."

"If he tried to help you with your groceries, he might be a great guy."

"It *is* a possibility."

Michael paused as if to consider something carefully. "May I speak freely?"

"Please."

"I know we just met, but you strike me as quite a captivating woman."

"Really? Maybe I should forget all about the other guy and have dinner with you."

"I'd like that very much. Besides, that other guy was probably a jerk."

As they silently approached the restaurant, Michael was careful to walk beside Rebecca until they neared the door. He jumped ahead and held the door open.

"Why, thank you." Rebecca did her version of a small curtsy.

"Most welcome, madame," Michael responded in a poor French accent.

Quit it, dummy.

When they were led to their table, Michael pulled out Rebecca's chair.

"You're really trying to score points, aren't you?" Rebecca said as she sat.

"Don't read too much into it. If I didn't do it, my mother would've risen from the dead and smacked me upside the head," he replied as he slid into his own seat.

"Well, be careful, Michael. A hundred years ago, you would have been considered a gentleman. Now, some people consider opening doors and pulling out chairs offensive."

"How's that?"

"You could be insinuating I'm somehow weaker. What do you have to say for yourself?" She took a long sip of water, partially obscuring her face as she waited for his answer.

"While I could probably take you if we arm-wrestled, I would never assert that the gender who can endure childbirth is weaker than the gender that often faints at the sight of it."

A waiter stopped by, sold them both on the nightly special, and shuffled off.

She didn't order a drink. But I guess I didn't order a drink either. Are we just having ice water? Crap! Now I look cheap. Gotta bring up drinks in the context of—

Rebecca continued. "So why did you do it?"

"Do what?" He was pulled back from his momentary insecurity.

"Hold the door and pull out my chair."

"Hmm."

I don't know how to say this. I need words. Give me the words.

"I guess I just wanted to serve you."

"Well, that's interesting. Care to elaborate?" She grinned while raising a brow.

She's smiling. That's good. Hope she's still smiling after this answer.

The waiter returned, dropping off chips and salsa.

"I enjoy serving others, taking care of others. Doesn't mean I'm making any assumptions. I just think you deserve to know what to expect if there is a second date or anything beyond that."

"That's a big if."

"Certainly is." Michael took a sip of his ice water. The ice clinked a bit too much.

She is gonna know you're nervous. Ask questions 'til you can calm down.

"Now that we've hopefully established I'm not a misogynist, it's my turn to learn about you."

Rebecca lifted a salsa-covered chip. "I'm an open book, my friend," she said and punctuated it with a confident crunch.

Start with the basics.

"Were you born in Arizona?"

"Yup. Born in Mesa. Proud graduate of Mountain View. Go Toros."

"Nice! An athlete?"

Rebecca burst out in a laugh. "Oh, God no! Total band geek."

"Oh. Wow." Michael's eyebrows shot up.

"What was *that*? Are you judging me?"

"Well, I mean. You just aren't at all who I thought you were." He teased.

"Excuse me?!"

Incredibly attractive when she gets a little fired up.

"I'm kidding."

Rebecca relaxed. "Good, because I played a mean flute."

"Can you still play?"

"I don't."

"But *could* you?" Michael pressed.

"What? If I was drunk, probably a little."

"Should I order margaritas?"

"Not on our first date."

First date.

"Fine. Next time."

"Don't be presumptuous, Michael." Another crunch. "I recently escaped a relationship."

"Oh?"

This was not good news.

"He was a good-looking guy. Super intelligent . . ."

"Wow. Must've been horrible."

"That was the thing about Patrick. It started off normal enough. When he began talking about himself as God's gift to humanity, I assumed he was joking. But gradually, I began to realize he was just pretending like he was joking. People can only hide who they are for so long."

"Let me say it again and this time without the sarcasm. Must've been horrible."

"My fault for not recognizing his narcissism from the start. Only thought people like that existed in television shows."

"Well, we've already spent enough time on him. Ready to move on?"

Rebecca nodded.

"Were your siblings in the band too?"

"Only child," she responded with a wink.

"That explains it."

"Explains what?!" Rebecca was ready to pounce again.

"Why you've been hogging the chips."

"Alright . . ."

The waiter came back with the entrees.

Michael looked up at the waiter. "The lady might need a box because she quite possibly ruined her appetite on the chips."

"Ignore him," Rebecca interjected. When the confused waiter left, she turned back to Michael. "I hardly had any!"

"Why are you getting so defensive?"

"Because you just tried to assassinate my character!"

"It shouldn't really matter what that waiter thinks of you."

"But he *is* kinda cute." Crunch.

"*So* not cool." They both laughed. "Not cool at all."

"Like I said, band geek."

They looked across the table at one another a second too long before Rebecca looked down at her plate. "Looks delicious, huh?"

The conversation veered into pleasantries about how noisy the place was, how good the food was, and observations about other people within view until Michael decided to bring the focus back to Rebecca.

"Actually, I think it's really cool that you were in the band."

"Are you mocking me?"

"No. I'm being serious." He paused and waited for eye contact before he went on. "You can play an instrument. I can't."

Rebecca appeared a bit disarmed. "Thank you, Michael."

They ate silently for a few moments, before he said, "That was a lie. I can play one instrument like a boss."

She dabbed her mouth with a napkin quickly. "Really? What instrument?"

"The kazoo. I'm a bit of a prodigy." Rebecca rolled her eyes. Michael went on. "No. Seriously. You should hear me."

"Alright." Rebecca folded her arms.

"Alright, what?"

"Alright, big talker. Bring the kazoo on our next date."

Next date? Score! Okay, Michael, just calm down.

"Only if you bring your flute."

"I don't own one anymore."

"So if your days of flutistry are in the past, what do you do now to stay busy?"

"I'm a full-time student at Arizona State. Go Devils."

"And Toros."

"Of course."

"What are you studying?"

"Special needs education."

His eyes smiled. "That . . . is amazing. How did you choose it?"

Rebecca blushed just a bit as she answered, "In high school, a friend convinced me to volunteer with the Special Olympics for our required service hours. When we earned enough hours, she moved on—"

"And you didn't."

"And I couldn't. I fell in love with them."

Look at her. She's beaming.

Rebecca went on. "It didn't take me long to realize what I wanted to do for a living."

"Beautiful." It was all Michael could muster.

"It doesn't make me a saint, you know."

"Obviously. A saint would share the chips."

She shot him a look.

Without warning, Michael jumped out of his seat and bolted past Rebecca. She spun around to see him steadying an elderly woman who had been dining alone. She has apparently lost her balance while transitioning from her booth to her walker.

"Oh! Thank you!" The woman smiled adoringly at Michael.

"Here you go." Michael made sure her hands were steady on the walker before he let her go. "You got it?"

"Yes. I'm fine. But no need to rush. I haven't been held by a man since Bernardo went to be with Jesus." She smiled flirtatiously through the wrinkles.

Rebecca snorted and quickly covered her face.

Michael looked at her, grinning, and back to his latest admirer. "I'm afraid the stars aren't aligned for us. I'm on a date with this beautiful young lady," he said as he motioned to Rebecca.

The old woman shifted her walker to face Rebecca's chair. While looking straight at her, she said, "Oh yes. She is beautiful, and she likes you. Don't mess it up by paying any more attention to an old hag like me." She shifted the walker again and shuffled off just as the waiter brought the check.

Michael grabbed it as he moved back to his seat.

"We can split it," Rebecca offered.

"I asked you to dinner." He lifted it to see the damage.

Good God! Sixty-five bucks with no drinks before the tip? I'll need to keep finding rings.

"Thank you, Michael."

He looked up at her.

Yeah. I can keep finding rings.

"You're welcome, Rebecca."

"I just have one problem . . . and no. I don't want more chips."

"What's wrong?"

"You know I was born here, I'm an only child, and I'm studying special needs education. You even know where I volunteered in high school!"

You played the flute, have a huge heart, don't want people to think you're a saint, have a soft spot for chips and salsa, and are embarrassed when you snort.

"So what is the problem?"

"What do I know about you?"

"I don't know. What *do* you know about me?" he asked playfully.

"Hmm." She pretended to think for a second. "Your voice stays steady, but your hands get a bit shaky when you're nervous. You need to be better about speaking up when you want something. Oh! And my main competition might be eighty-five-year-old grandmothers."

"Can't take a little competition?" His smile sparkled.

"I'll just have to keep you away from the early bird specials."

"Fair. Let me take care of this real quick." He held up the bill before leaving the table.

—

As they walked back outside, the wind had picked up and ominous clouds were beginning to populate the sky.

"I love monsoon season in Arizona." Rebecca smiled at the sky. "I love the sunshine, but sometimes a few clouds are a nice change."

Just then, her cell phone began to beep, along with everyone else's devices within earshot. The few who weren't already looking at their phones pulled them out.

"Looks like there'll be more than a few clouds tonight, though," Rebecca said. "Severe storm warning with a flash flood warning for parts of Maricopa County."

"Then let me walk you back to your car."

"Nonsense. We've got time. We should walk down toward the lake. Unless a little rain will make you melt."

Tempe Town Lake, a 225-acre reservoir that ran east to west through northern Tempe with Arizona State and the college district to the south and the 202 freeway to the north, was the largest body of water in the sprawling Phoenix metro area.

"While I appreciate your concern for my obviously delicate constitution, I'm pretty sure I'll be alright. I grew up where bad weather can hit any time of the year," Michael retorted.

"And where might that be?" Rebecca jumped at the opening.

"Wisconsin. Let's go."

"I'm not going to Wisconsin with you. That would imply all sorts of improper things."

"I was talking about the lake."

As they began walking through the wind, Rebecca continued to satisfy her curiosity. "So you lived in Wisconsin with your family?"

"My mom and dad. Yes."

"Brothers? Sisters?"

"We gave them away."

Rebecca shot a look at Michael.

"I was an only child."

"Ah. So you were spoiled."

"Hold on. *You* were an only child."

"Aw, you remembered!" Rebecca teased.

As they crossed the street and entered Tempe Beach Park, the weather continued to worsen. The wind kicked up a few more notches, and it began to sprinkle.

Rebecca hesitated. "Maybe I *should* head back to my car."

"If you are tired of my company, you can just say so."

"No. I just—"

"It was a joke. If it gets any worse, I'll drive you back. My truck is in that parking lot." He pointed to a small lot just over a small hill. "I think it's about to—"

The rain intensified as she pointed to the east where the wind was just beginning to whip from. There were several individual columns where the rain was so intense they had created solid walls of precipitation from sky to earth.

As Michael looked to the east, the words hit him. "Head to your truck. You have somewhere to go."

I'll drop her off at her truck first.

"Not enough time."

This cannot not be happening.

Michael felt the oppressive weight of hopelessness. He was given another glimpse into an alternative future. A future that held the promise of companionship and maybe even love.

What if I just said no?

The skies turned angry in a matter of seconds, and intensifying sheets of water began to slap the earth.

"Michael! We've gotta get out of here!" She had to shout just to be heard over the roar.

I can't take her with me. I'd have to explain, and she'd try to have me committed. Not that abandoning her is any better. How am I going to say this? How could she possibly understand?

"Michael!"

"Rebecca! I'm so sorry! I've got to go!"

"Yes! We've got to go . . . now!"

"No! I can't explain now, but I've got to go!"

"What are you talking about?!"

"You won't understand! There's somewhere I have to be!"

"You aren't leaving me here!"

"I can't explain!"

"Then I'm coming with you!" Rebecca shouted through the rain.

Michael considered this for a brief moment. This was new. In the past, people had been angry or confused, but no one ever suggested coming with him. She had no idea what she was signing up for. Neither did he.

"Michael!"

"Okay! Alright! Let's go!"

"You were gonna just leave me in the middle of the worst storm of the year? What the hell *was that*, Michael?!"

The truck was barreling through the downpour at twice a reasonably safe speed.

"It's complicated."

"How complicated can it be, really?"

Michael involuntarily scoffed. "Ask me any question you can think of, and I promise I'll answer it."

"Fine. I repeat. What the hell was that, Michael?"

"I need you to be more specific," Michael said as he slid onto a freeway on-ramp.

"We were having, frankly, the best first date I've had in a very long time, and you had offered to take me back to my car, when all of a sudden, you went just a bit nuts and decided to abandon me in the middle of a monsoon. I'd like to know why."

"I had to go somewhere."

The majority of the vehicles were pulled off to the side of the freeway as the rain was now falling faster than any windshield wiper could handle, but Michael pressed on.

"Okay. Where?" Rebecca pushed for clarity.

"I'm not sure yet."

"I don't know what that means, Michael."

There was a break in the conversation as Michael heard the

Voice again and took another ramp connecting to a northbound freeway.

"Michael!"

"What's your question, Rebecca?"

Rebecca thought for a moment as Michael was now blasting his way through the storm without regard for staying in any particular lane. No need. There were very few people still attempting to drive through nature's onslaught. He was just weaving past stubborn drivers who wouldn't give up but were hardly moving.

"Did I just go on a date with another psycho?"

"I'm not a psycho."

"Then how is it that you have to go somewhere, but you don't know where that is?"

"I don't know."

"You said you'd answer me!"

"Rebecca, I'm answering you as honestly as I can."

After a moment of thought, she asked, "Seriously. Are you mentally stable?"

Michael silently shook his head.

It always ends this way, although usually not this dramatically or quickly.

"Depends on who you ask."

"I'm asking you!"

"I believe I am, but there were times when . . . not so much."

"How long ago was that?"

"A few years ago, when both my parents died in a car accident."

This revelation softened Rebecca's face for a moment. "Well . . . I'm sorry you had to experience that, Michael."

Not sure I had to experience it if . . .

"Me too." Michael swallowed. "Ask another question."

"You didn't really answer me a second ago. How is it that you know you are supposed to go somewhere, but you don't know where?"

"I get a sudden . . . push."

"A push?"

"Yeah. I sorta hear a voice. Then, I know I'm supposed to do something. Something specific."

"Did you say you hear voices, Michael?" The concern in her own was noticeable.

"Sort of." Michael, without taking his eyes off the road ahead or where he *hoped* it was, anyway, finally lost a bit of his patience. His voice strained. "Haven't you ever felt like you were supposed to call a relative? Or tell someone you loved them? Or you knew you weren't supposed to go on a date with someone, but you went anyway?"

"Well, yes. But that's a bit different."

"It is pretty much like that but magnified several times over."

As the rain began to relent, Michael knew what he was saying sounded nuts to Rebecca. People felt little whispers of intuition from time to time but taking it to this degree? Rebecca was probably feeling like she shouldn't have gotten into the truck with Michael. She could have run to the nearest building and waited out the storm, but now she was stuck in a truck going God knows where. Literally, only God knew where. For now, Michael decided to focus on the road and do his best to avoid killing them both.

"Take Pima north."

He finally exited the freeway and continued straight north, ascending a long road up toward the expensive and exclusive communities in the elevated desert northeast of the Phoenix metro area.

Although the rain had all but stopped, Michael and his truck now had to contend with a series of deep washes that rushed across the road at unknown depths. Cars were pulled to the side waiting for the levels to subside. Michael never hesitated. He just accelerated. As a result, Rebecca, who wasn't the most spiritual person on the planet, was suddenly becoming very communicative with the Almighty.

Finally, about six miles north of the freeway exit, the truck approached several cars parked in a line as if at a traffic light, but they were waiting on a police car that was partially blocking the road at an angle with its lights flashing. Michael coasted alongside the lineup toward the front. He stopped the truck when he saw the officer get out of his car and walk up to the driver-side window.

"It's flooded and impassable. The only way into the Cave Creek/Carefree area from the south is Cave Creek Road."

Up ahead, Michael saw a dip in the road where the water was rushing across it with such fury there were actual waves of muddy water building and crashing. There was no telling how deep it might be at its worst.

"Where is Cave Creek Road, officer?"

"With all the washes flooded, you'd have to turn around and drive back down to the freeway, head west eight miles, and get on it from there."

The Voice spoke. "Attempt the wash. You'll make it."

Michael looked at the turbulent water.

"Please drive to the back of the line, and shut off the truck. I'll let you know when it is safe to proceed. If the worst of the storm has passed, it will recede within the hour."

Michael took a deep breath, still looking at the rushing torrent just ahead. On the far side, there was another police car, another officer, and another shorter line of cars and trucks.

"Thank you, officer."

The officer turned and headed back toward his cruiser.

"Well, I guess you weren't supposed to drive up this road. What happens when you're wrong?"

"That's just it. When it comes to this stuff, I've never been wrong."

Just as the officer opened the door to his cruiser, he heard the truck's engine rev loudly.

"Michael, no," Rebecca said in vain.

Michael gunned the truck.

"Hey!" the officer shouted as the truck blew by. "Stop!"

The old truck blasted into the water with a thud. Michael and

Rebecca lurched forward as the truck's momentum was almost stopped by the impact.

Almost.

The wheels clawed for traction as the truck crept forward. Rebecca screamed, and Michael looked to his right to see muddy waters flowing through the bottom seals of the passenger-side door and the waves lapping up to the door's window. Michael strained harder to keep the truck moving ahead, but it was now moving as much to the left as it was moving forward. It was becoming a race to get free of the water before the truck would be pushed off the left side of the road and into a muddy wash. Michael spotted the officer on the far side sprinting toward the truck, yelling into his radio.

With only inches of pavement remaining, the truck miraculously found footing and accelerated out the other side, past the other officer who was now shaking his head while shouting his opinion of Michael.

They drove the next few miles in silence until Michael could stand it no more.

"You alright?"

"You're nuts! Completely nuts!"

"Rebecca. I'm sorry . . ."

"I don't even care about your whackadoo impulse control issues! You just nearly killed us back there!"

"We were going to make it."

"You knew that for a fact?"

"I did."

"Michael, let me out of the truck."

The Voice interrupted. "Take the next left. She'll be fine."

"We're almost there."

Michael slowed and turned left onto another road that bobbed up and down before it weaved around a boulder larger than his truck.

"Please, Michael. I need you to let me out now." Michael

heard the fear in her voice, and the realization that she had just crossed from anger to fear sickened him.

As he approached another spot where the road curved to circle around a tractor-trailer-sized boulder, he pulled to the side of the road and jumped out of the car.

Rebecca watched as he ran off the road to the far side of the boulder without explanation. "My new worst first date ever." Then, she noticed the keys were still in the ignition.

Michael was sprinting across the muddy terrain dotted with cactus while trying to avoid accidental acupuncture when he almost ran into a car that had slid off the road and into the far side of the boulder.

The front of the car was crumpled up like tinfoil. Behind the wheel, an older man was leaning face-first onto the steering wheel. His glasses were sideways, and there was blood on the right side of his head. He didn't appear to be conscious.

Michael went to open the driver-side door, but it was jammed shut. He circled to the passenger side. No luck. It was just as impossible to open. At a loss, Michael turned and ran back around the boulder toward where he had left the truck.

Rebecca had moved behind the wheel and didn't understand why she couldn't bring herself to leave this lunatic behind and drive the truck back down to Tempe. Then, she saw Michael sprinting back onto the road.

He frantically ran to her door and swung it open. "Do you still have your phone?!"

"Yeah. Why?"

"Call 911." He was struggling to speak calmly. "Tell them to trace the call. We are somewhere west of Pima in North Scottsdale or Cave Creek. I don't know exactly. There was a car accident. An elderly man is pinned in his car. I think he's unconscious. We need help right away."

With that, Michael grabbed the first aid kit from behind the seat, turned, and ran off again.

PART TWO

GABRIEL

14.

GABRIEL WAS WAITING FOR THE INEVITABLE.

He favored relaxing to the sounds of Rachmaninoff emanating from his home theater system while enjoying Balvenie Week of Peat whiskey in the late Arizona evening. He wasn't hoity-toity by any stretch of the imagination. He just had grown to appreciate quality.

Accordingly, he was wearing a Burberry funnel-neck cashmere sweater in preparation for an active night while everything he could possibly need was already in his toolbox and ready in the trunk of the only car he'd ever owned, the one his father had given him about ten years ago.

When the call came, he was in the classic Shelby Mustang and on the road in under two minutes.

He headed south through the heart of Scottsdale. Just after entering Tempe, he turned right for less than a mile before turning left onto Mill Avenue. He weaved through minor construction as he drove under a freeway overpass before Mill divided into two one-way bridges that span Tempe Town Lake. Quite a sight after sunset, the bridges were lit by beautifully strung white lights that sagged between poles about every twenty yards along both sides of each bridge and reflected in the shimmering water below.

Gabriel impatiently made his way past the many bars and clubs that make up Arizona State's college district before continuing south through Tempe.

About five miles further south, Mill Avenue took him directly to Kiwanis Park.

He turned off his radio, slowed to a crawl, and listened to the night through his open windows. Within moments, he heard it . . . a small dog yipping in the distance.

He pulled his car off to the side of a residential road and retrieved the toolbox. Gabriel quickly put on what he thought he might need and grabbed his Maglite before heading back toward the park. He knew he was running out of time and would have to hurry.

As he quickly walked toward the sound of the dog, he passed a dark grouping of sand volleyball courts. Then, Gabriel crossed a silent park road and came upon a small parking lot that contained only one remaining car, a dark Beamer. He knew the park was closed for the night, and everyone else had left for home. He clicked on his flashlight and continued into the darkness.

The dog was still doing its best to get someone—anyone—to pay attention, but it wasn't having any luck. If anything, an over-zealous homeowners' association president was probably thinking about calling the cops to shut the dog up.

Gabriel crested a small hill to see the back end of the park, bordered by a canal.

As he climbed the berm, he saw a cocker spaniel on a loose leash standing at the canal's edge next to some sort of utility pole sticking out of the ground. In addition to the incessant barking, he could now hear the water rushing by. Monsoon season in Arizona caused the canals to flow more briskly than normal. His flashlight found a jogger clinging to a crevice on the side of the fast-flowing canal, completely underwater except from the neck up and the single arm she was using to hang on for dear life.

She seemed to be in her early thirties, sandy blonde hair, beautiful but frantic eyes, and quite a pretty face if she weren't straining so hard to hold on.

Gabriel's eyes quickly followed the flow with his flashlight to where the canal flowed through a huge steel grate as it passed below a road. If the woman lost her grip, she would either die from the impact or be trapped against the grate and quickly drown. There would be no saving her, so he had to move quickly.

Looking up at him and with the last bit of strength she had left, she begged for his help. He could barely hear her over the dog that was losing its mind and nipping at him. In an instant, a million options played through Gabriel's mind. His eyes came to rest on the utility pole just up the sloping, gritty concrete side of the canal above her.

He set down his flashlight, turned to the faithful little dog, picked it up with one of his leather gloves, walked to the utility pole, and looped the leash around it.

There, little doggy. Safe and sound while I get to work.

As he returned over the top edge of the canal's forty-five-degree slope of rough concrete, the woman looked up at him with a sudden combination of confusion and fright because he was just standing there smiling. Aided by a sudden burst of adrenaline, she managed to pull hard enough to reach up with her other hand in an effort to find something, anything, to grip. As her free hand scrambled for a hold, one of her painted nails scratched along the grit of the embankment and snapped well above the waterline. Her momentary surge of fearful strength ran dry, and the arm fell back beneath the flow.

"Hey! Relax, lady! Your adorable little mongrel is safe and sound." His eyes glistened as he smiled from ear to ear. Then, he crouched down low, steadied himself, and kicked at her remaining hand. With the last bit of fight left within her, she launched her submerged arm in an attempt to grab on to him and struck his ankle. All it accomplished was a second snapped nail.

The impact caused her grip to falter, and within moments, she disappeared under the current.

"Why? Why, Gabriel? You are meant to help."

He quickly got up and dusted himself off, then turned to make his way back across the park toward the abandoned BMW. Quietly, he began singing, "Rollin'. Rollin'. Rollin' on the river . . ." and smiled at his own demented sense of humor.

As he approached the car, he dropped to his knees and took a look under the driver-side door. Sure enough, there it was. A small plastic key container held to the bottom of the car with a magnet. A great little device if you find yourself locked out of your car. A horrible little device if the wrong person knows where to look for it. He knew where they were because he was supposed to save her, and this would've been the fastest way to get her to the local hospital. Or something like that.

Hey, I saved the dog. That's the more valuable life to most movie audiences anyway, right? So should I just take the car? Naw. Don't want to deal with Augustine at the chop shop on this one. Plus, it was a cute pup but noisy as hell. Shouldn't leave my car anywhere near here in case anyone investigates.

The car held sentimental value, after all. No. This would have to be kept simple.

He stood back up, dusted himself off a second time, and unlocked the door. Quickly grabbing the purse, he scanned the interior for other valuables. After he snagged anything worth taking, he shut the car door, locked it, and put the key back where he found it.

To most, the risks associated with murder, or in this case, assisted swimming, for the contents of a purse might not seem to be worth the risk, but this wasn't how Gabriel had come to see it. The lady would've died anyway if he hadn't shown up, so this was really more of a small, involuntary inheritance he was collecting.

And there was no risk. The only witness was a dog. A dog he chose to spare.

Gabriel always spared dogs. Dogs knew how to show gratitude.

In addition to the lack of witnesses, he had taken precautions. He'd worn gloves. The monsoon that was going to hit later would obscure any footprints he had left at either the canal or the car. It took less than an hour of his time, and he would make a few hundred. He didn't particularly mind these small jobs because he could always arrange something bigger when he needed to.

Clancy was a perfect example.

15.

THERE WAS A SLIGHT CLICK. It signaled the bedroom shades beginning to separate, letting in the morning light as "Ride of the Valkyries" by Wagner began to play on a bedside speaker. Bad guys in movies always seemed to like it, so he adopted it as a theme of sorts.

A moment later in the bathroom, the shower turned itself on. The automation wasn't cheap but was worth every penny. Gabriel got out of his pillow-top king and strode into the steam for a shave and a shower.

Upon emerging from the bathroom, it was time for the rest of the morning ritual: grabbing a cup of Kona and surfing the net in search of news stories that might shed light on his previous night's activities, a self-gratifying exercise every time.

This morning had quite the variety of stories to entertain the bloodlust of the masses but nothing out of the ordinary. Another entertainment industry honcho caught in a sexual harassment scandal. Another politician accused of something horrible by the opposition. Another hot summer day in Phoenix. An elderly man found wandering three miles from his home in the extreme temperatures. And there it was: a single mom who never came home after leaving her child with a babysitter.

Bingo! Single mom, eh? Not that it makes any difference. The first ones were parents too. And that kid was better off without 'em. Probably this one too. You're welcome for the early inheritance, kid.

While Gabriel enjoyed his mystery adventures, he didn't much care for the chores that followed. Like driving fifteen miles to toss worthless evidence in a dumpster behind a church, then turning around and driving twenty miles in another direction to the seediest place he had ever seen. It was the kind of place the police didn't care about. As a result, it was also the kind of place that would buy certain questionable items—meaning anything that was obviously stolen—without questions or fingerprints and take full ownership until they were able to be resold for profit.

***

He rolled into the church parking lot, took a quick look in every direction, and proceeded to the lone dumpster at the back of the lot. It seemed to Gabriel that there was no parking lot more abandoned in an entire city than a church parking lot on Sunday afternoon. The congregation had all gone home, and the clergy were exhausted. He left the car idling as he grabbed a small garbage bag and tossed it into the dumpster.

Here's your ten percent, Big Guy.

He quickly hopped back into the car and was off to make some quick cash.

***

"Heeeey, Jim!" Gabriel said as he entered the shop. "Clancy ain't in today, is he?" Gabriel always used his good ol' boy persona when dealing with the guys at the shop. It was a voice he could easily recall and use on command . . . it was the voice of his father working on the truck outside with his pals.

Jim, a hefty man wearing a rather unfashionable Hawaiian shirt and sporting a Magnum P.I. mustache, did not even bother to look up from the magazine he was flipping through behind the counter. "Yeah. He's in the gun room."

The pawnshop consisted of three rooms. The main room spanning the front of the building was filled with old and mostly obsolete electronics, appliances, knives, and jewelry. The back half of the old building was split in two. The back left was called the storage room. In reality, it was filled with random boxes, but it also housed a small refrigerator, a microwave, a toilet, and toilet paper—usually. The back right was the weaponry. Thanks to Arizona's unique combination of old west heritage and most residents having moved from hunting-friendly midwestern states, business was always good.

"Clancy! Ya old coot! I know yer back here! I spotted yer piece o' crap in the parking lot!" Gabriel purposefully boomed as he made his way back.

Slowly, a frail old gentleman wearing a white button-up shirt with thin blue horizontal stripes stood up from behind a glass counter. With the aid of his thick glasses set in black plastic horn-rims, he had been dusting the merchandise on the lowest shelf. In his seventy-eight years of existence, Clancy still couldn't figure out how dust could get into an enclosed glass counter.

"Hey, Billy."

In all his dealings with the pawnshop, Gabriel always referred to himself as Billy. He couldn't afford to use his actual name, and Billy seemed a fitting tribute. In every situation Gabriel was led to, he took the most he could, and oftentimes, this is where he took it. Calling himself Billy only seemed natural.

Although several generations older than Gabriel, Clancy continued to look down at the glass case.

"Clancy," Gabriel said in a suddenly hushed tone, grabbing the glass case between them with both hands and leaning in. "What happened, man? I know yer a good man. *God* knows yer a good man. And we both know you want things to change before it's too late."

Gabriel held his stare silently until Clancy found the strength to look up through his glasses back at him. He began to visibly break. "I don't know if I can."

"Then explain to me why I've been . . . " Gabriel broke in, a little louder than he realized, until Clancy held up his hand gently.

"Billy? Ya gotta know how much I appreciate what you think I deserve. How much I value all the thought you put into this." It was Clancy's turn to lean forward using hushed tones. "In truth, I was gonna go through with it last night. I packed a bag and came back to get everything I could, but someone was here. They were just idlin' in the parking lot." Clancy looked at the entrance to the room. "Now, I can't be sure, but maybe Jim hired someone to keep an eye on the place nightly until he gets the cameras fixed. In any case, I took it as a sign or maybe a last chance to back out. I mean Billy, you know this whole thing never sat right with me. No offense."

"Clancy? Listen to me." Gabriel cocked his head with a smile. "Jimbo could afford to get the cameras fixed for a lot less green than hirin' someone to keep an eye on the place. You probably just stumbled across some guy takin' a trip from Alabama to California who was too cheap to get a room."

"No, no. I caught a glimpse, and they were Arizona plates on that truck."

"Then *they* were probably thinking about robbing the place!" Gabriel momentarily lost it but still spoke in a whisper. He quickly regained his composure. "You're the one who told me about your family. How you've done nothin' for 'em. How, when it's your time to go in a few short months, you will have nothin' to leave 'em. This is your one, single, solitary chance. You've got the keys. You *know* how much those knives and those rocks are worth. And you've gotta friend who can help ya sell it. These are signs, Clancy!

The cops won't ever catch ya. And even if they somehow did, it don't matter." Gabriel's voice turned compassionate. "The bottom line is brutal, but it's the bottom line just the same. You're on your way out. Or did the doctor call and say he made a mistake?"

Clancy shook his head, and Gabriel went on.

"Precious little time to give your family something, any-thing." Clancy tried to stop him again, but Gabriel needed to finish. "You'll do it tonight. You'll call when you get there. I'll meet you there and take you to the places myself. I want to help you, Clancy. It isn't a coincidence we met." Clancy had no idea how true that last line was. "When it's over less than twenty-four hours from now, send your family however much you want. You keep whatever you need. Now, drive safe. I'll look forward to your call. Okay? I need to go back up front and sell Jimbo a few things."

16.

BILLY WAS A HIGH SCHOOL CELEBRITY. He had made the varsity football team as a backup quarterback his freshman year. This was unheard of at the local high school back in the eighties. Despite his resulting popularity with the freshmen cheerleaders, along with virtually everyone else, his interest was exclusively focused on a girl who didn't seem to know he existed.

Ruthie Hawkins, although pretty, didn't flaunt it. In fact, Billy couldn't even help but wonder if she was aware of her beauty. She dressed in simple hand-me-downs and had no interest in cheerleading because she had no interest in football. Instead, she most enjoyed studying, piano lessons, and participating on the debate team. With all the hubris of a high school quarterback, Billy decided Ruthie would be his girlfriend. She just didn't know it yet.

One day, he walked right past his regular lunch spot and all his jock buddies to her sparsely populated table and sat down right across from her. While he hoped this grand gesture would win her over on the spot, her attention was so completely focused on her homework, she didn't even notice him for another four minutes until he pretended to choke on one of his chicken nuggets. Instead of getting her to agree to a date within five minutes, which was his plan, it took a full five months.

Billy and Ruthie were still going strong their sophomore year when Billy was called on midgame to replace the starter who had gone down with a broken ankle. Over the next twenty-four months, he led the Rockets to more wins than they had seen in years. Then, two years later to the week, Billy was knocked out of a game with a fractured collarbone.

Billy never returned to football, and Ruthie walked with him through the loss of his sport and identity. Slowly, with her help, he came to realize his injury was an opportunity for a new direction. While he had been a great quarterback, it wasn't only due to his impressive athleticism but his intelligence as well. In fact, it was his intelligence that had eventually won Ruthie over several years prior.

Two years into college, the two high school sweethearts decided they couldn't wait any longer. After all, they knew they were meant for one another. Even if everyone thought it was financially irresponsible, it was time to get married. Within a matter of months, they were married at Zion Lutheran Church in a beautiful ceremony complete with disapproving parents, drunken toasts, and a quick getaway to a bargain-basement honeymoon upstate.

They both took part-time jobs in addition to their full college loads. Billy began making deliveries for a local brewery at night, but the part-time work never took him farther than fifty miles. The cargo scored him bro credits with the buddies who hadn't abandoned him when the collarbone injury knocked him from the heights of teenage popularity.

Ruthie took a job as a waitress at a local diner. Her kind nature and good looks proved very lucrative, but a few unwanted advances convinced her to learn subtle methods of bringing attention to her wedding ring, which, in the end, helped a little less than she had hoped.

Their combined incomes proved just enough to pay rent for a rundown apartment while the student loans kept piling up.

The plan was simple. They would just get by for two years, join the world's workforce as newly minted college graduates, and attack their debt with ferocity. Once these three steps had been accomplished, and only then, it would be time to grow their family. The plan fell apart four weeks later.

Billy woke slowly on the day he would never forget. As the haze of too little sleep started to lift, he realized Ruthie was already up and frying some eggs in the kitchen. The apartment was small enough that a conversation could be held from any two locations.

"Good morning, sweetie. You're up early. Am I getting breakfast in bed?"

"Oh? You wanted some? I didn't get your order," she replied, then continued with mock sorrow. "That is just tragic."

"Oh waitress . . ." Billy singsonged.

"Don't you dare!" Ruthie came flying into the frame of the door wearing one of Billy's oversized sweatshirts and a pair of cotton shorts. "You do *not* get to call me that!"

Billy sat up in bed with his grin widening. "Well then, how exactly am I supposed to place my order?"

Ruthie ignored his last sarcastic query and disappeared into the kitchen.

Sure, the small apartment was in a less-than-ideal neighborhood, they only saw one another for an hour or two a day, and they spent every waking hour exhausted, but Billy knew their current circumstances were temporary. He just couldn't have known *how* temporary.

Billy decided to get moving.

He rose from bed, slipped a t-shirt over his strong frame, and wandered into the tiny hospital-white bathroom. Brushing his teeth over the sink, he felt Ruthie's hands slide forward around his hip bones and up over his ribs. Her lips softly kissed his shoulder blade through his shirt.

"Billy? Do you think I'll be a good mom?"

Happy to receive the unexpected visit, Billy responded with what he thought was obvious. "Of course, sweetie." He resumed brushing for a moment. Spit. Rinsed. "I have no doubt you will be the smartest, kindest, smokin'est football mom on the block in about ten years."

"Or maybe even this year?"

The words didn't register for a full three seconds that felt like three hours as Ruthie waited for a response.

Then, the grenade went off, and Billy spun to face his young wife. "Wait." His eyes locked onto hers. "Say that again."

"Or maybe even this year?" Her eyes looked up at his in the single most vulnerable moment of her entire life.

"Listen, Ruthie. If the answer to my next question is a yes, I could not be happier. Are you positive?"

Ruthie burst into the biggest smile her face could contain and wrapped her arms around Billy's neck as she kissed him. Between kisses, the words flowed. "Yes! I am positive! The result was positive! Everything is positive! We are having a little angel!" And then, after a very real pregnant pause, she pulled back and looked at Billy. "What are we going to do?"

"We'll be fine. I'll make it work. I'll take care of you both. Forever."

—

They nervously sat together holding hands waiting for the doctor to burst into the sparsely-furnished, white hospital room. Billy was certain the baby was okay.

The baby had to be. But why was the doctor taking so long? Or was this normal? No. The baby was healthy and normal. Everything was going to be okay.

Ruthie had decided to drop out of college as she wanted to get as much work in as possible before the baby arrived and then be a full-time mother to the little addition to the family. Billy was okay with it only after Ruthie convinced him it was what she wanted. Billy was still going to school but upped his delivery routes to full time. He always got home in the darkest hours of the early morning.

The door swung open, and Dr. Wood, a man with a face reminiscent of one of Tolkien's dwarves, entered the room. This dwarf was almost six feet tall though and gave off the impression he couldn't be moved against his will any easier than a mountain. His red face had fought the scars of adolescent acne, and his hands were thicker than most. Belying his mass, he sat gently on the wheeled stool across from the nervous couple and slid it gently toward them before taking a quick breath and exhaling into a warm smile.

"Ruthie? Billy? You look worried. There is no need to be. Everyone in this room is healthy." He paused for a brief moment. "Well, I can't vouch for you, dad."

The doctor looked at Billy and chuckled kindly.

———

The entire night was obscured in a foggy blur for Billy. He vaguely recalled the frantic call from Ruthie as he arrived at work.

The impossible tightrope of driving Ruthie to the hospital as fast as possible without crossing into recklessness.

Those precious seconds where he forgot if he should drive to the Synergy South County Hospital's door and abandon the truck or if he should drop her off at the door or if they should just park the truck and slowly make their way to the door.

Following the nurse who was pushing Ruthie's wheelchair toward the delivery room with an overwhelming sense of powerlessness.

Ruthie crying and gripping his hand.

Waves of screaming.

The first beautiful moment he saw Gabriel.

The very next moment when alarms started going off.

Dr. Wood booming orders and the frenzied scatter of medical personnel.

Being grabbed and pushed toward the door.

Searching for Ruthie's face in the chaos but never finding it.

The door shutting behind a nurse who was talking but not being heard.

The severity of the nightmare slowly becoming realized.

Time losing context.

Sitting in a chair alone.

A doctor approaching with an anguished face.

Billy was slightly buzzed as he drove north toward Fond du Lac. As always, some friends were watching little Gabriel while Billy ran his routes. He was eager to drop his last delivery and head home, but traffic was not cooperating. It was near a standstill in the middle of farm country.

Billy didn't want to engage in conversation, so instead of using the CB radio, he decided to check the news radio.

And nothing could have prepared him for this moment.

"*. . . the ramifications of Dr. Bradley Wood being convicted of involuntary manslaughter may just be the tip of the iceberg as we have uncovered another death that occurred on his watch. A representative for Synergy has already . . .*"

As the story continued, Billy's mind began to spin. He fought to refocus and ensure this wasn't the imaginings of a grief-stricken drunk-in-training.

"*. . . if it weren't for the testimony of a whistleblower who had personally witnessed several instances of the doctor working while* *under the influence, who knows how many more tragedies may have happened."*

Billy pulled to a stop in the gravel next to the highway, jumped from the truck, and threw up uncontrollably.

The next week of Billy's life was a circus. He knew he should contact a lawyer but kept putting it off. If he changed his mind, he could just use one of the multitudes that were trying to get him as a client. He also had a hard time avoiding media requests. Then, he got a letter in the mail from the company that owned the Synergy South County Hospital. It requested that he call them as quickly as possible.

Even though he knew he shouldn't do it without representation, he called the number.

After a number of transfers, a high-ranking representative of the company assured him that there was no proof of any wrongdoing on the part of the Synergy South County Hospital, but for the sake of public relations, they had every desire to "put this all behind them." They were offering a "deeply generous" sum if he would sign away his right to speak publicly on the matter.

If they would've treated him or Ruthie's memory with an ounce of respect, Billy would have taken the deal to help secure Gabriel's future and be done with it. But they weren't admitting to a solitary thing, and that would never be okay.

Billy finally went to a lawyer and had him draft up a counteroffer that consisted of two requirements. First, he wanted paperwork delivered within seven calendar days with an offer of twice the "deeply generous" amount. In exchange, he would not speak to any media sources. Secondly, there needed to be a corporate apology within one week of the signed paperwork being returned, or the media silence stipulation was void. A few days later, the same representative called and assured him this was far too big an ask.

Billy immediately hung up and didn't answer his phone again until the envelope arrived via certified mail. He opened the envelope to find a check with a whole lotta zeros at the end. It also included paperwork threatening him not to go public at any point in the future. Billy noted there was no public apology mentioned anywhere in the legal jargon. He headed to the bank that very day and made the deposit.

As far as Billy was concerned, the clock had started on that apology. They had seven days.

Maybe they were trying to figure out the wording that would cause the least blowback. Maybe they just hoped the one-two punch of the money and the threat would be enough to silence him.

On the eighth day, he realized there would be no apology and that they had chosen the second option. They miscalculated. Billy almost enjoyed calling every local news affiliate and telling them his story—the whole story.

It was time.

17.

GABRIEL SAW REBECCA WALKING ACROSS THE parking lot as he returned to his condo. He slowed down and casually drove by, enjoying the view, then pulled into a visitor's spot and slid out.

If the devil himself interviewed me to help create my ideal woman, I'd tell him to save himself the time and effort. It's already been done.

Every part of her was stunning, and it was obvious she had been made for him. Well . . . she was one of the women that had been made for him.

Gabriel had found most of his conquests in bars and clubs or in vulnerable states. He didn't know about bars or clubs, but he was pretty sure Rebecca had recently ended a relationship.

As Gabriel approached her from behind, she was removing something from the apartment bulletin board. He quietly drew near as she read over the piece of paper that was now in her hands. Not a single sound was made as he stood inches behind her now, breathing in the secret proximity.

She lowered the paper to her side, let out a deep sigh, and turned. Gabriel's chest was directly in front of her. She jumped back, letting out a squeak. Her eyes were wide while the paper she had been reading flittered to the ground, and her face began to flush.

"Gabriel! What the—? Why would you do that?" She was still breathing hard and was downshifting from shock to anger. She began to lean for the fallen paper.

"My apologies. Allow me to make amends for unnerving such a beautiful girl." He leaned down and snatched the paper, stealing a quick look. Rebecca reached for it, but Gabriel ignored the attempt and held on to the paper.

"What? You're going to stop teaching the classes?" Gabriel's voice quickly switched from surprise to flirtatious with a tilt of the head. "Is it because I didn't keep going?"

"Gabriel. I *asked* you to stop coming because you weren't taking it seriously."

"I was just trying to be conversational."

"You weren't taking it seriously, and you were taking away from Kathy's experience."

"That whale was just happy to have five minutes of real, authentic human interaction."

"Gabriel! Don't be ugly! Kathy is a sweet lady, a kind friend, and I won't have you talking about her like that!"

"Alright. Okay. Let me take you out for dinner to make up for it."

"No."

"Really? Even after I scared off those college thugs?"

"That was a month ago, and I already thanked you."

"I'd hardly call that a thank you."

"I said thank you."

"Yeah. Like I said . . ." Gabriel made his meaning clear.

"Anyway, I'm going to pass on dinner."

"And why would you do a thing like that?"

"Because, Gabriel, you are not my type."

Gabriel smiled. "So you don't like men who are tall, fit, handsome, drive a nice car, and have acquired wealth?"

"All those things are nice, but none of them are must-haves. You didn't mention kind, generous, or humble."

"I am kind to myself. I'm generous with people I care about. And humility is for people who aren't successful."

"See? Not my type." Rebecca, exasperated, began to walk away.

Gabriel grabbed her shoulder. "Rebecca—"

"Take . . . your hand off my shoulder." Her face showed she was done being pleasant.

Gabriel slowly removed his hand, and she walked away without another word.

Matter of time.

He took out his phone, did a quick search, and booked a flight to Orange County with a return flight less than half a day later.

18.

GABRIEL WAS STANDING IN FRONT OF his bathroom mirror going over every step of his impending trip. It wasn't extremely complicated, but that was precisely why he needed to be careful. The simplicity of the plan carried with it the danger of him becoming complacent. He couldn't let that happen.

He realized he had an extra fifteen minutes, plenty of time to do a bit of damage control before returning to California. He grabbed his go bag and took it down to his car. Then, he walked back toward Rebecca's unit.

He walked by a tall guy with dreadlocks who looked like he had just pulled a beanbag out of a dumpster.

Probably a big fan of Bob Marley and medical marijuana.

He had limited time and zero interest in making a new dumpster diver friend, so he avoided eye contact and made his way around the building containing Rebecca's unit.

The sound of breaking glass disturbed the quiet. He looked around the corner of the building to see some guy picking up a bag of groceries for Rebecca. Gabriel couldn't quite make out what they were saying to one another, but he didn't like seeing Rebecca smile at this guy.

Mercifully, Rebecca finally began climbing the stairs to her apartment when, without warning, the hippie behind him started shouting at his beanbag like a crazy person. Gabriel realized the idiot would draw Rebecca's attention in his direction, and he quickly stepped back behind the corner.

"Hey!" Gabriel whispered, trying to quiet the guy at the dumpster. It didn't work.

"Oh, Mr. Beanbag! You brought comfort on a daily basis while doing a thankless service! You saved my home from becoming a pretentious den of snobbery! In return, I treated you like an ass. You will *never* be forgotten! So long, good friend!"

The man held the beanbag in one hand while lifting the large dumpster lid with the other.

Then, in what appeared to be mid mental breakdown, he froze, looked at the beanbag, and let the lid fall while still holding the beanbag in his other hand.

"Hey!" Gabriel whispered urgently again. "Would you please shut the hell up?"

The hippie spun around and said in a ferocious whisper of his own, "How *dare* you?" Then, after quickly composing himself, "Have you no decency?"

"Listen, ya waste of oxygen—"

"*You* interrupt *me* in my moment of pain, so you can spy on Mikey? What kind of—"

"Are you intellectually capable of quiet? Or are you so fried that the small percentage of surviving brain cells you have left are working overtime just to comprehend the language I'm speaking?"

The hippie just stood there listening, and with his free hand, he slowly raised the dumpster lid. Without ever looking away from Gabriel, expressionless, he let it come crashing down again.

Gabriel could instantly think of ten ways to make this guy disappear, but none of them were worth his time. He might take care of him another day, but he had a plane to catch, and the trip *would* be worth his time.

As Gabriel stalked off, the hippie mumbled, "Lecture me on my brain cells when you don't show an ounce of compassion for a man battling his inner demons."

19.

SHORTLY AFTER HIS DAD'S DEATH, GABRIEL decided to escape his home-town and head west. He spent two weeks exploring Southern California before settling on the smallest place he could rent in the best neighborhood, which is how he ended up in his four hundred square-foot space above a two-car garage on Balboa Island. He was still over a year away from setting foot in Arizona for the first time.

During the winter months, the breeze off the bay could get a bit cool, but it was nothing compared to Wisconsin's winter where he wore Gore-Tex, heavy hunting gear, and thermal under-wear. Here, he only wore a hoodie and jeans as he walked to the ferry, took the quick ride across the bay to the peninsula, and walked across the thin strip of land to the Balboa Pier.

The beach was sparsely populated compared to the circus atmosphere that pervaded the sand from May through September. The water immediately before him held a family of seven from the inland empire, a vacationing family of five that hadn't realized how cold the water could get in the winter months, and a few local surfers in full-body wetsuits.

Gabriel took a seat on the sand and looked out at the ocean waves rhythmically pawing at the beach as he thought of his dad, the only parent he had ever known. He took in the enormity of the ocean, a perfect representation of how his father had abandoned him. He had basically told Gabriel to remain on the beach as he walked straight into an ocean of alcohol and dove deeply, never to be seen again.

"Take another headcount of the families." Gabriel had only heard the Voice once before.

He stood to scan the shoreline. He saw the family of seven.

The cute little kids aren't being watched very well as they play tag with the water, running down to touch the water between small waves, then running back as the next rolls in, but they seem alright. Mom is dealing with a complaining teenager, and Pops is a bit too into his sandcastle masterpiece. But they're all there.

The tourists were back on the beach and in the process of making a little picnic.

Both children are gobbling up PB&J sandwiches. Parents are now making their own. All four of them are happy enough to be seeing the beach for the first time. Probably from some part of flyover country that averages one family for every off-ramp.

Then, there were the surfers.

God, I hate surfers. I don't know why. I just do. I'm not a bad guy, but I can't help but root for the sharks. Okay. Maybe I'm not such a good guy. Wait. It was a family of five . . .

Gabriel instantly ran toward the shoreline between the family and the ocean, scanning the water. Behind him, he heard the mom begin to scream at her husband. The stocky sandcastle architect was now jogging to the scene. The surfers were looking toward the shore.

Gabriel continued to scan the water. Something wasn't right. Running past him directly into the water was the missing child's father. He swam out about twenty yards before pausing to look around frantically while screaming, "Kallee! Kallee!"

The Voice spoke. "Not in the water."

Where?!

The other dad jogged past him toward the edge of the water. He stopped and looked back. "Well, are you just gonna stand there or do somethin'?" He then took off jogging down the water's edge looking out at the ocean.

If anything, common sense dictated that Gabriel should have been the one in the surf searching for the girl. He had been a standout member of his high school swim team and had always loved the water.

"Turn around. Now."

He reluctantly turned and jogged toward the nearest building, a nasty public restroom used for intestinal emergencies only when absolutely necessary but mostly for changing into and out of swimsuits.

He jogged up to it and thought about going straight into the girl's restroom to see if that was where the girl had disappeared to but looked over to the boardwalk first. There, he saw a man holding Kallee's hand. They were walking in the other direction, but the girl kept looking back. Then, the man looked over his shoulder nervously. The man saw Gabriel and reacted by walking faster while pulling at the little girl's arm.

"Hey!" Gabriel couldn't think of anything else to say, but he knew he could outrun a man with a little girl. He broke into a sprint.

The man looked back again, and his face broke into a terror. He let go of Kallee's hand and ran up the path between two of the large beachfront homes. Gabriel ran past the now-screaming girl after the man. But with the sizable head start, by the time Gabriel emerged onto Balboa Boulevard—the peninsula's main street— the man had vanished.

Gabriel walked back to the beach where the mother had heard the screams and was now comforting her girl.

As Gabriel walked past them, he whispered, "Keep a better eye on your kids, lady."

"Excuse me?" The woman's eyes widened indignantly.

"I said keep a better eye on your kids." Gabriel wasn't whispering anymore. "While you were busy back there cutting the crust off your hubby's lunch, some perv waited 'til your baby girl wandered from the pack. What kind of mother lets that happen?"

The already upset mother burst into tears as she clutched her precious little Kallee. In the distance, dad was running up the beach, leaving Kallee's older two siblings who were upset by all the emotion they didn't fully comprehend. Neither parent was watching them. Gabriel shook his head.

These people are morons.

Walking back toward the ferry, he wondered about the Voice. He actually *heard* it. His whole life he'd had moments where he believed he was supposed to say something to someone about something random but didn't because he would've felt like an idiot. Or he felt he should take another way home and did. But this was different. He *heard* it. The only other time it happened was during that phone call he wished he could forget.

But he couldn't focus on that now. He had to book a flight to Wisconsin to finish up the last of the business that goes with being a sole heir.

20.

GABRIEL STEPPED OFF THE SHORT FLIGHT from Phoenix to Orange County and smiled. Familiar morning ocean breezes, beautiful people, and an easy mark. It was all he could ask for.

He went into the restroom, changed into a different shirt, and put on a Dodgers baseball cap and sunglasses. He made his way to the arrivals curb and looked for the jeep, having taken care of the first minor detail when he made sure his license was buried in his pocket.

He watched as a parade of luxury sedans and pristine SUVs drove up to retrieve their honored guests or returning loved ones. There didn't seem to be a dirty vehicle in the entire state until Clancy's mobile tribute to scrap metal appeared. Behind the wheel, the old man appeared to be on the edge of a nervous breakdown. Gabriel flagged him down.

As the jeep rumbled to a stop in front of Gabriel, it just got worse. Visible sweat dripped from Clancy's mop of gray-streaked hair and ran behind his thick glasses. His arm shook as he reached across to unlock the passenger door, voice quaking as he greeted Gabriel.

"Hi. Uh. Hi, Billy. Hope your flight went well." Clancy pulled away from the curb.

"Uneventful, my friend," Gabriel shot back. "Got the stuff?"

"In the back, boss."

"How was your drive? You got to see lovely, scenic Blythe, California, on the banks of the Colorado River!"

"Is there another part of Blythe?" Clancy stammered nervously.

"Relax, old man!" Gabriel smiled. "You saw everything there was to see from the freeway. I was just joshin' ya."

"Oh. Good. Good one." Clancy was at a stoplight waiting to pull out of the airport. "Santa Ana, right?"

"Actually, turn right. You are absolutely freaking out. We need to go somewhere you can relax for a few minutes. I know a spot that is completely deserted outside of a few summer months."

"No, Billy. I'm good. I swear."

"Oh yeah. You're great. You look totally relaxed. Like a guy who just drank four cups of coffee in a sauna. Keep going straight through the light."

"Aw, crud man. I'm sorry. Maybe we—"

"We are gonna go down to the ocean, relax, and weigh our options. Option one, we stick to the plan, and I introduce you to my contact. The problem here is that you need to get a grip on yourself. Option two, if you don't think you can calm down, I leave you at the beach and do the deal myself. The problem here is that you would have to trust that I'm not skimming off the top of your profits."

"Come on, boss. You know I trust you."

"And I appreciate that, Clancy. I do. But I would just prefer for you to be there so you don't *have* to trust me. Of course, there is option three, we forget all about it. The problem with this option is that you don't make any money, and you've already broken the law. Basically, that one doesn't make a bit of sense."

"Yeah. I know there is no goin' back for me. That isn't my

concern anymore. I just dunno if this . . . " MacArthur Boulevard crested a ridge revealing the splendor of the Pacific Ocean before them. Clancy had never seen the ocean in person before, and it caught him off guard for a tick before he went on. "I just dunno if this is the way."

"Hey, I get it. You're conflicted. I would expect nothin' less. Turn left at the next light."

Clancy turned left onto a congested stretch of Pacific Coast Highway that inched its way through Corona Del Mar.

"I'm startin' ta think my jeep sticks out a bit around here."

"Do ya think any of these rich folk got to where they are through honesty? Very few, my friend. Very few," he said to the man who had worked hard for every dollar he'd ever earned. "Some of their parents did what they had to do to get ahead for their kids. Turn right."

Clancy looked a bit skeptical while turning onto a skinny road lined with older trees and moderately large homes that cost small fortunes thanks to their proximity to the Pacific.

"Pull off here. We won't find parking any closer. Don't wanna let these bags out of our sight." Gabriel grabbed his go bag and Clancy's treasure.

By the time Clancy got out of the jeep, Gabriel was about a hundred feet down the road. "Wait up, Billy! I'm not as young as I used to be!"

He followed Gabriel down the sidewalk another two blocks to a cliff with a gorgeous view of the infinite ocean. Clancy started down a set of wooden stairs to Little Corona Beach, a pristine cove largely concealed from the cliffs above.

As Clancy finally got to the bottom step, Gabriel was nowhere in sight, and the little beach appeared to be completely abandoned. "Billy! Where the heck did you—*ugh*."

He felt a strong hand grip his shoulder as lightning sizzled across his neck. The warm lightning spread and made him gurgle for a moment before darkness obscured his vision. He tried to cough in a last futile attempt to clear his throat of the thick warmth and collapsed into the sand.

———

Okay. The clock starts now. Sixty seconds. First things first.

He dragged Clancy's body a few feet back to the base of the cliff and out of sight from above. He walked backward toward the ocean, using the bags to sweep his footsteps from the sand as he went. Once in the light surf, he slipped the heavy bags onto his shoulders, ripped off his gloves, and let them fall into the ocean water. Then, he headed up the beach as quickly as he could.

At the eastern edge of the larger and more popular Corona State Beach, he got out of the surf and headed back into the beachfront community. After a brisk two-mile walk through a neighborhood, he arrived at the Fashion Island Mall, where he boarded a bus and paid cash.

A few transfers later, he got off in Santa Ana and walked another six blocks to a park, where he sat on a bench next to a softball field and waited until Rodrigo (or whatever his *actual* name was) pulled up in his '69 Orange GTO. Gabriel got in the car and set the loot next to Rodrigo. Rodrigo ignored it for a moment, choosing to shake Gabriel's hand instead.

"Hey, amigo. Been a while. How've you been?"

"Life's a beach," Gabriel responded joylessly. "We need to move this along. I've got a plane to catch."

"Where's the flight headed again?"

"Kalamazoo. Can we move this along?"

"Calm down, my friend. Everything present and accounted for?"

"Rodrigo, if I ever try to short you, you have my permission to try and kill me. Okay?"

"Don't need your permission, and I won't try." Rodrigo punched his shoulder firmly. "I don't travel far with inventory, so we need to make a quick stop before the airport."

The GTO pulled out of the park and made a quick stop in the Bella Vista neighborhood before heading back to the airport just over seven miles away. Within two hours, Gabriel was comfortably back home in Arizona with a nice payout.

21.

GABRIEL FINALLY WALKED THROUGH HIS DOOR somewhere around 9:30 in the evening. He was soaked from the rain that had kicked up over the past hour, but he didn't care. It had been a great day. He worked out some aggression, made a profit, and guaranteed his local buyer would need as much replacement inventory as possible. Now it was time to relax.

He took a long shower, slowly washing the day away, dried off, poured a well-deserved glass of whiskey, and took up a spot on his leather couch. He grabbed the remote and flipped on his flat screen. A local reporter was earning her paycheck in the monsoon.

"Jill, how are you holding up out there?"

Jill was the one every news team sends out into inclement weather or to do puff pieces on new salt water taffy shops that will be out of business in six months as they are groomed to replace the female anchor every ten years, ignoring the fact the male anchor seems to hold on to his position until retirement.

"Sue Anne, I'm doing alright. The crew found me a dry spot in a picnic area here in Kiwanis Park in Tempe, but I wish I could say the same for a young woman who was found earlier tonight."

Gabriel leaned forward as he turned up Jill's voice.

"Unfortunately, the woman's body was found in the canal that borders this beautiful park where families had been spending the afternoon, oblivious to the horror that lurked just feet away until a local man, whose name is being withheld, made the grisly discovery."

The picture cut to a man Gabriel recognized being questioned by various police. Gabriel set down his wine in disbelief. It was the guy who had been flirting with Rebecca, and now he had found the body Gabriel had left behind. This would be quite a coincidence if Gabriel still believed in those. Didn't matter. Gabriel needed to take care of this guy.

"Police will not confirm whether the man is a person of interest at this time. They also refused to confirm the identity of the body until next of kin can be notified."

The police need to find a killer? Maybe I can be of assistance.

He waited for the segment to end before he pulled out his cell phone.

"Tempe Police Department. How may I direct your call?"

"Hello. I was just watching the news. I might have some information regarding the body that was recovered from the canal today."

"Oh. Okay. Please hold while I put you through to one of our detectives."

There was a short delay while the call was transferred.

"Hello. This is Detective Alvarez. May I have your name, please?"

"Gabriel Kane."

"Good evening, Gabriel. I understand you may have some information regarding the situation in Kiwanis Park?"

"Yes, sir."

"Go on, sir. What do you know?"

"Well, I was walking yesterday morning, and I saw the guy on the news . . ."

"I'm sorry. I need you to be clear. What guy?"

"Uh, the guy who found the body."

"Okay. Where did you see him yesterday morning?"

"He was at Our Lady of . . . of . . . uh . . . Fanta?"

"Fatima?"

"Yeah. Fatima. I think it's a Catholic church."

"Listen, Mr. Kane. I appreciate the information, but how is this relevant?"

"Well, the news said they couldn't get confirmation he was a suspect."

"That's right."

"Well, I thought you should know I saw him tossing something into the church dumpster."

Alvarez cleared his throat. Gabriel had just gotten the detective's attention, and he knew it.

"Okay. And what happened next?" Alvarez asked.

"No idea. I kept walking and didn't look back. Had no reason to at the time."

"Alright. Thank you, sir. I'm going to transfer you to someone who will take down your information in case we need to follow up, okay? Bobby! Line three! Three!"

"No problem, detective." Gabriel smiled.

The day just got even better.

22.

"**H**EY, DAD! IT'S SO GOOD to hear your voice!" Gabriel had been waiting for his father's call.

"Hey, son. It's good to hear your voice too." Billy's voice sounded worn and tired.

"Where are you?"

"Well, that's why I called, son. I had some mechanical issues that have put me behind. I might not be able to get home before Christmas. I hope ya can forgive me."

"No, dad. It's all good."

"He needs his rest. Tell him." The Voice startled Gabriel.

"Who was that?" he asked in surprise.

"Who was who?"

"Uh, never mind. I think we're both tired. Get your rest. I'll be here whenever you get here. No rush. Just do what you need to do and promise you'll be safe."

There was a thoughtful silence on the other end of the line.

"Know what? Ya just changed my mind. Yer my only boy and nothin' will keep me from being with you on Christmas," Billy said resolutely.

"No. Dad. Seriously—"

"Son, zip it!" Billy cut in. "Seriously. You never know how long you've got, and I refuse to miss a moment with you. Especially on Christmas. I need to get my priorities straight, push through, and get to my son."

—

Total darkness began to dissipate into hazy light, and silence was slowly replaced with the rising volume of muffled conversations and sirens. The light brightened as if Billy were swimming from the depths toward the surface. He sat up despite the protests of a few medical personnel.

They were asking him questions, but he couldn't make out a word. He looked past them to see his truck and the car he had smashed into. The two vehicles fused into a single entity of twisted metal.

Billy's mind was racing.

How did I end up in the westbound lanes? Did I swerve to avoid something in the road, and my path took me into oncoming traffic? Unlikely. I've fallen asleep at the wheel before although just for moments at a time and not since my sobriety streak. But is that what happened? Did I?

As much as he didn't want to think about whoever was in the other car, his mind kept circling back to it.

Oh Jesus. What have I done? How could I be this reckless? Or was the other guy to blame? No. I crossed the median. No way that driver lived.

Whatever happened, it was bad. There were wall-to-wall officers interrogating anyone with a pulse, and a police helicopter was circling overhead. Cars were slowly being guided past the wreckage in single file. Billy realized they were rolling by much slower than they needed to because they were all looking over at him.

Enjoying the show, ya idiots?

Suddenly, he realized they weren't looking at him. They were looking past him. Billy turned to see a body being loaded into an ambulance.

"William Kane? Mr. William Kane?"

"Billy. My name is Billy."

"Billy. We need to move you to the hospital to get checked out."

The medics moved him to an ambulance despite his objections. While Billy protested, more protests came from the patrolmen who wanted answers. They were told to follow the ambulance to the hospital and wait for the go ahead before talking to him.

As the ambulance accelerated away from the tragic scene, Billy was overwhelmed with sensory overload. He felt the road rumbling beneath him as he continued to be ever so slightly poked and prodded. He could hear the siren mingling with various beeps and communications between emergency workers, their words a mumbled hum. Then, two words broke through: "victims identified." These two words sparked an effort within him to swim toward the surface once more, straining to listen.

23.

GABRIEL PULLED INTO A HILTON ON the eastern edge of Houston. He was exhausted from the last eleven hours he'd spent driving across the width of Texas. Over seven hundred miles had passed without crossing a state line. More than a result of the past day, he was exhausted from the past two years.

He had been a full-time amateur superhero ever since the beach in Southern California.

With the majority of his inheritance still intact, he was beginning to deeply resent spending any of it for the sake of ungrateful strangers. Although he would never forget Kallee's name, there would be so many others he would never even know.

In Eugene, Oregon, there was the perky barista who was being watched by a teenage boy in the coffee shop.

"Don't let her leave unprotected."

The boy had his laptop open, but it wasn't even turned on. When she said goodbye to her coworkers, it was already getting dark. The boy immediately started packing up but not too quickly. Gabriel noticed him pacing her departure. So as she headed for the door, Gabriel got up at the same time as the boy and bumped into him at the door.

"Oh, excuse me. I'm sorry." Gabriel acted the part of a klutz.

"No worries," the boy mumbled without looking at Gabriel and scurried out the door.

Gabriel walked a few steps out of the coffee shop and made a fist before calling after the boy.

"Hey, kid! You dropped something!" As the boy hesitated and turned, Gabriel extended the fist as a tease. The boy walked back quickly to retrieve whatever it was, so he could resume his pursuit.

As the boy neared, Gabriel's hand sprung open, holding nothing, and grabbed behind the boy's neck. "Leave the girl alone." The boy moved to get away. Gabriel gripped harder and moved in. "Ya sick little piece of crap. Forget her. Try showering regularly. Quit the video games and learn how to talk to people. Shave. Random patches of facial hair don't impress anyone. And up the deodorant."

The boy broke free, but the barista was long gone by now. As the kid ran off, Gabriel hurled one more warning. "I'll be watching you! Don't make me hurt you!"

Gabriel left town the next morning.

In La Jolla, California, he kept an old man from standing on a rock. It was really nothing more than that.

In an effort to snap a picture of a seal, the man was slowly making his way down a precipitous set of rocks from the park sidewalk on a particularly windy day. He was only using one hand to steady himself in the rough weather while using his other hand to cling to his smartphone.

"Get him off the rocks before it's too late."

Gabriel called after the man several times only to be ignored.

He finally scrambled after the man, ripped the guy's phone away from him, and nimbly scampered back up to the sidewalk. The man yelled and began climbing back up. Bored, Gabriel sat down on the sidewalk while a small crowd gathered around him mumbling, but none were brave enough to confront him.

The old man finally got back to the top and wiped off his pants. Gabriel got up, walked over to him, and handed him his phone. The old man was about to yell at Gabriel when a large wave crashed into and over the rock below.

The old man appeared shocked for an instant before shifting to skepticism as he looked at Gabriel. "Oh, like you knew that was going to happen!"

In Gila Bend, Arizona, he heard what he needed to get and where he needed to take it. So Gabriel stopped at a gas station and bought five gallons of water. He then took Highway 85 south into the Organ Pipe Cactus National Monument. He took a side road and drove several more miles. When he arrived at his destination, he got out of the car and unloaded the water, setting the containers by the side of the road.

"Hey! The coast is clear! No soy policía!" Gabriel yelled into the expanse of seemingly uninhabited desert. "Agua aquí!"

No movement.

Whatever. Time to move on.

He got back in his car and began to drive off. As he did, he saw a mother and two small children stagger out of the brush and grab the water, quickly carrying it back to their shelter.

In Rocky Mountain National Park, just west of Estes Park, Colorado, there was the lone camper he was told to approach near Bear Lake. He parked two sites away and walked over. As he approached, he startled the man who was preparing dinner over a campfire.

"Hey, buddy. I'm a few sites down and just needed some advice. I've never started a fire before."

The man, roughly the same age as Gabriel, quickly relaxed into a smile. "I don't doubt that. Have you ever even camped before?" Gabriel realized he was dressed completely wrong for his cover story.

"Is it that obvious?" As he sat next to the fire, Gabriel scanned the site. There was no car or truck, but there was lipstick on a coffee cup.

"Sorry, pal, but absolutely. Try Eddie Bauer instead of Nordstrom next time you're at the mall."

In that moment, a car could be heard quickly approaching. The man turned, shook his head, and glanced at his watch before looking at Gabriel.

"Four hours to blow off steam. Think that's a new record for Little Miss Temper Tantrum. Our campfire lesson may have to wait."

The car skidded to a stop in the site's designated space that faced the fire pit. The woman looked furious and glanced at Gabriel before staring down the man while unleashing a torrent of inaudible curses. Gabriel knew the man was wrong. Four hours had not cooled her off. That was why he was here.

Neither man saw the gun sitting on the passenger seat next to her.

She violently shifted the car into reverse before slamming on the gas, peeling out of the parking spot, skidding, shifting again, and kicking up dust as she drove down the road.

The man was dumbfounded. "What in the blue hell . . ."

He was about to be even more confused.

"Well, my job here is done." Gabriel stood.

"Hold on. Do you think you could give me a ride into Estes Park in the morning?"

"Not happening. I'm out of here. I don't even like camping."

"Wait. What? Don't be an a-hole!"

Gabriel spun on the man. "Listen. I'm pretty sure I just saved your worthless life. You have a choice. You can thank me, or you can be upset because I won't give you a lift. Either way, I really don't care. I'm done with you."

He walked to his car, got in, and sped out of the park faster than Little Miss Temper Tantrum.

—

As Gabriel neared sleep in his hotel room on the road to another ungrateful stranger, he couldn't shake the feeling that this was a giant, cosmic joke.

I couldn't save my own dad but these idiots across America? Oh, by all means. They deserve saving.

24.

The WEATHER BETWEEN HOUSTON AND LAKE Charles was far from pleasant and getting worse by the mile. The rain seemed to be coming down in relentless sheets, but Gabriel pressed on.

As he passed Lake Charles, the Voice guided him. He began to see entire areas flooded on both sides of the freeway before exiting and heading down a virtually empty road to an even smaller, completely deserted road. The deluge dictated his slow crawl through the twists and turns of the road.

As he crept around a bend, the road suddenly submerged beneath a newly created lake. In the middle of the impromptu lake, Gabriel saw what he thought was the roof of a pickup truck with a young father, his wife, and a little boy. They were huddled up, soaked and shivering.

He backed up his car a safe distance from the growing flood and took a deep breath before stepping into the whipping winds and stinging rain.

Moments later, as he swam toward the family on their small metal island, he had a very unpleasant thought.

Doesn't this backwater hell hole have Lonesome Dove swimming snakes of death?

He swam faster.

As he gripped the metal, he raised his head to see the parents yelling to be heard over the pounding noise of wind and rain slamming into standing water. The man looked like a meathead with an expensive watch, and the petite woman had a better grip on her Louis Vuitton bag than her son. He shook the water from his ears and strained to hear two voices yelling very different messages simultaneously.

"We can't swim, and the water is—"

"—idiot thought his overpriced truck was able—"

"Stop calling me—"

"—overcompensating with a lift kit—"

"—because it has a Hemi, and with enough—"

"—so I can divorce the idiot—"

"I said stop calling me that, ya stupid—"

Gabriel had enough and pulled the five-year-old boy right off the roof and into the water. He quickly spun the shocked boy away from himself, swung his arm under one of the boy's armpits, and wrapped him close. He began swimming backward with the boy coughing atop his chest. The parents were both still yelling at him and each other, but the downpour was mercifully drowning them out.

As soon as Gabriel's feet touched the pavement beneath the water's surface, he straightened up and guided the boy to his car, revved up the engine, and cranked the heat.

"Listen, little man. I have to go try to save your parents. Stay right here. I'll be back in a minute."

"No! Don't leave me!" The boy reached out and grabbed Gabriel's hand. Gabriel stood in the rain waiting for the boy to calm down just the slightest bit.

Somehow, the rain seemed to shift into an entirely higher gear. Visibility was reduced even further. He could no longer see the flood's edge less than fifty feet down the sloping road. He had to go. Now.

"Listen, junior. Stay in the car. I'll be right back." He slammed the door and ran down the road until his feet began to splash. As soon as the depth hit his thighs, he dove forward and swam as hard as he could.

Out of the gray chaos emerged two figures who were seemingly standing on water. The roof of the truck was now more than a foot under the surface.

As he swam up, they were still yelling at each other until they noticed him.

"Took you long enough! And I thought *I* couldn't swim!" the man shouted.

"Shut up, idiot! At least he *can* swim! What kind of man can't even save his own?" The woman turned to look down at Gabriel still treading water. "Is my boy okay?"

"*You* shut up! Of course, Bobby's okay! Do you think this guy would just let him drown? He might be a moron, but he's not a murderer!" He then looked at Gabriel. "Well? Enjoying your dip? Or were you going to help us sometime before Christmas?"

Maybe little Bobby would be alright without these two.

"Don't do it." The Voice seemed to anticipate the dark thought.

"You're first!" Gabriel yelled at the woman. "Crouch down and sit on the edge of the roof!" She slowly did as she was told, putting every effort into keeping her purse out of the water.

Then, she leaned into Gabriel's ear and made an offer just above the roar. "Get me to my boy, and leave him here." Gabriel looked at her in disbelief. She locked onto his eyes. "Leave him here, and I'll give you a thousand dollars at the first ATM we see."

"Don't do it," the Voice repeated.

The man, unable to hear, but impatient with the chit-chat, crouched down. "Can you please get us to safety before you two have your first date?"

I'm done. The lack of gratitude. Saving horrible people. Serving people I'm better than. Done!

In one swift motion, he ripped the purse from the woman and pushed off from the truck's submerged roof. He slowed to a drift as he held the purse, watching as disbelief flashed in the couple's eyes.

"Whoa. What the hell, man?" the man yelled.

"No. No, no, no, no! Take me! You were supposed to take me!" The woman pleaded.

Nope. I'm not supposed to do anything. I'm not responsible for your poor decisions. What a load off! I am not responsible! You two deserve one another. And little Bobby back in the car deserves better.

"Debit card pin number!"

The woman's eyes flared with rage. "Excuse me?"

"Give me the pin or the boy dies."

White lie.

The man exploded. "You son of a . . ."

The woman slapped him so hard and with such ferocity, he stopped short.

She yelled, "Zero one zero three!"

The man turned his rage at the woman. "I can't believe you could be so stupid!"

"Shut up, idiot! He has our son!"

As Gabriel swam away, the couple's argument became drowned out by the deluge, and they were reduced back to gray forms in the rain.

There was a splash, and he turned to see the bigger form struggling back to the small submerged island that was now sinking deeper by the minute.

When Gabriel got back to solid ground, he searched the purse and removed every credit card and soaked bill. He stuffed it all into his drenched pocket, dumped the remaining contents into the water, and flung the purse as far back toward the invisible couple as possible.

Here's your precious purse.

He slid behind the wheel. The boy looked over at him, and

Gabriel shook his head. The boy tried to contain a sad whimper that persisted all the way back to Lake Charles.

Gabriel pulled to a stop about two hundred feet from a bank and pulled some gum from the center console, popping it in his mouth. He approached the ATM from the side and smooshed the gum right over the camera lens. Then, he flipped out the cards and searched for the debit. He popped it in and withdrew the max.

Upon returning to the car, he gave some of the cash to the boy before driving through the town making note of every bank. He began chewing another piece of gum. Eventually, he saw a hospital and pulled up to the entrance of Lake Charles Memorial. He looked over at Bobby. "You gotta get out little man."

The boy looked back over at him, his young eyes like saucers.

"Just walk in and tell them that your parents got stuck in a flood, and a nice man saved you."

The boy opened the door, got out into the rain, and began to shut the door.

"Hey!" Gabriel yelled, freezing the boy. "A thank you would be nice."

The boy managed a meek "thank you" before shutting the car door.

Gabriel pulled out and headed back toward the other banks.

25.

GABRIEL WAS A BIT UNEASY AS he arrived at the coffee shop. He thought he'd led the police directly to the suspect they needed with a quick phone conversation last night. Then, this morning, another detective called and asked if he could meet for coffee.

That call was impulsive. And stupid. I've got to keep from getting entangled in the investigation. Alright, this won't be a problem. It's not like you were asked to come down to the station. And it's a chick. You can charm the pants off the vast majority of them. Literally.

He walked through the door to the small, privately owned establishment and began to scan the place when a woman dressed in a professional blouse and dark jeans stood from a table and nodded with a hint of a smile. "Gabriel?"

He was about to turn on the charm, but was distracted for a quick moment by what he saw around her waist: a badge, a Glock 40, and handcuffs latched to a belt loop.

She caught that. Recover.

"Well hello, ma'am! You must be the most attractive law enforcement agent I've ever met!"

Too much.

"You must not have much contact with law enforcement."

"Thankfully not. Present company excluded."

She smiled a bit bigger now. "Grab a seat. Can I get you anything?"

"Uh, sure. A mocha breve."

As Gabriel sat, Gradillas stepped to the counter, placed the order, and paid while Gabriel enjoyed the view.

Dang girl. Work out much? You're strong, but everyone's got a weakness. And I've gotta find yours to keep us from going past my basic story. Every detail is another lie, and I'm guessing you're trained to spot them.

Gradillas sat across from him.

"Apparently, your drink will take a second."

"No worries. How can I help you, officer?"

"Detective."

"Of course . . . detective."

"I want to begin by thanking you for reaching out."

"Just doing my civic duty . . . detective."

"Of course. But my partner and I are grateful nonetheless. The more information we have, the faster we can resolve this case."

"Quite welcome. I would guess your job is incredibly difficult."

"It can be challenging, but it is also very rewarding," she replied matter-of-factly.

"Especially being a woman in a male-dominated field." He went on.

"Actually." Her face remained matter-of-fact. "That isn't the hard part. The guys are pretty great."

"So they treat you just like one of the guys?"

"No. They treat me just like another member of the force."

"Oh. Yeah. That's what I meant. Meant no offense."

"None taken."

Actually, it looks like a little was taken. Proceed with caution.

The barista walked over to the table and set down the mocha breve in front of Gradillas and the black coffee in front of Gabriel.

Gradillas looked up. "Try again."

"Oh! Sorry 'bout that. I just figured—"

"Yup." Gradillas just looked at her.

The barista quickly switched the position of the drinks and scurried off.

"So what *is* the most challenging part of your job?" Gabriel probed.

Gradillas took a slow sip and looked to be carefully considering her answer. "Let's just say there are a lot of single people in my line of work."

That didn't take very long. "I'm sorry to hear that. Except that means you're single."

"Not currently taking applications, but I'll keep you posted. For now, I'm mostly interested in what you saw."

"Well, now I'm a bit heartbroken, but I'll do my best."

Gradillas' phone beeped. She glanced down at it and maintained a perfect poker face before looking back up. "You were watching the news?"

"Yes. I'm single, and I own a condo in Scottsdale . . ."

Keep everything short. Offer nothing.

"We have your address on file."

"Well, don't *you* have the advantage?"

"You were watching the news."

"Yes."

"And you saw the man who found the body."

"Yes."

"You told my partner you recognized him. Remind me. Where had you seen him before?"

She's building a rhythm. Body shots before the uppercut. Be ready for it.

"A church parking lot."

"Which church?"

"The Catholic one near Old Town. I think it's the only one."

"Our Lady of Fatima?" Gradillas' face continued to look nonchalant as if this were a friendly conversation.

"Yes."

"What was he doing?"

"He was tossing some stuff in the dumpster."

"What was he wearing?"

"What?"

And there it was. The uppercut. Too few details and you were never there. Too many details and the fiction gets to be obvious.

"What was he wearing?" She leaned forward.

"Not sure I remember."

"I guess I'm confused. If he was tossing something in the trash, presumably facing the dumpster, how did you see his face but not his clothes?"

I gotta give her something.

"I was taking my morning walk. I looked over. I saw someone next to the dumpster. I don't remember the specifics except the guy turned around, and I saw his face. The guy from the news."

"You don't remember the type of shirt? Pants or shorts? Color of the clothes? Anything?"

"Sorry." He shrugged his shoulders and took a sip of his breve.

"How do you explain that, Gabriel?"

"I'm a guy. I don't take note of what other guys wear, but I don't forget a face."

That should suffice.

"What time was it?" she quickly asked.

He paused for a brief second. "Not sure."

"Come on, Gabriel."

"It was a morning walk."

"*My* morning walk," she corrected.

"Pardon?"

"You said '*my* morning walk' earlier. That is very different from '*a* morning walk.' The one you chose to say initially implies you take this walk regularly. If you take this walk regularly, you probably do it at the same time. If true, you should be able to answer the question precisely. What time was it?"

Another uppercut. Dammit. Gotta punch back and fast.

"Listen, detective. With all due respect, I'm just here to try and make your job easier. I'm here because I want to help the police figure out what happened to that person in the canal. I'm here to help make my neighborhood safer."

"And I get that."

One more swing.

"I'm certainly not here for the cup of coffee or to have my integrity put under a microscope."

Her expression softened slightly. "If you feel like I'm attacking you in any way, I apologize. That isn't my intent, but follow me for a second."

"Okay . . ."

"If what you told me is true . . ."

"It is."

"If what you told me is true, and we search that dumpster and find anything connected to the crime scene, but that evidence is void of fingerprints or any other forensic connection to the man from the news . . . if all that happens . . . and we are a long way from that . . . you are the only witness that can put him away. If you think this is abuse, you are in for a very rude awakening. Those lawyers will tear into you every single time you can't remember a detail, and they won't buy you a mocha breve."

Gradillas sat back and took a slow sip of her black coffee.

Questioned on the stand? Nope. Can't let that happen. Too many complications. I might just have to take care of the situation myself. Take matters into my own hands. Make it look like a suicide. Plant some new evidence that makes it look like the guy couldn't live with the guilt of killing the woman. Maybe that could work.

"I understand, and I'm sorry I don't remember more. But do you think there might actually be something in that dumpster?"

"Where do you think my partner is as we speak?"

As soon as Gradillas closed her car door, she called Alvarez. "Are you serious?"

Alvarez was also sitting in his parked car on the road just outside the church parking lot. He let out an exasperated sigh. "Picked up Monday morning. It was gone before the tip came in. I sent everyone home and contacted the Salt River Landfill. They know approximately where the load would be, and they're being cooperative. The thing is, it will take quite an effort. You met with the guy. Do you think it's worth it?"

"Far from a perfect witness. Memory is shaky and a bit of an ego," Gradillas responded.

"So he could be making it up because he has a Kardashian-level need for attention?"

"And I think he takes that walk regularly, so he might know when the trash is picked up."

"Well, he isn't the only one." Alvarez paused for effect. "While I was waiting for you to call back, I went back over the crime scene notes. Guess who got a job at Our Lady of Fatima this week."

"Shut up."

"Michael freaking Bale. When there is this much smoke, we either have a new pope or our suspect is guilty."

"Excuse me?"

"The pope. When a new one is chosen . . . or elected . . . whatever . . . there is white smoke that comes out of a Vatican chimney," informed Alvarez.

"What are you even talking about right now?"

"Our guy is guilty."

"It's possible," Gradillas conceded.

"Alright. We roll with the witness's story until proven wrong."

"But something doesn't sit right with me about the witness—"

"Hold up! Michael Bale just drove by me! Wait. He just pulled out of the church parking lot."

"Well, the guy has got to make a living."

"Yeah. Making a living precisely where a man saw him dumping something in a dumpster shortly after a woman disappeared. A woman he then somehow found where people had been walking by her all day."

"Like I said, it looks bad. Go ahead with that landfill search."

"I'll make the call."

PART THREE

CONFLUENCE

26.

GABRIEL NEEDED TO RELAX AND CLEAR his head, so he grabbed a cocktail and a steak at Durant's in central Phoenix. The noir decor and exquisite food lit in a decades-old red hue were precisely what the doctor ordered.

I'm losing my touch. In a matter of days, I murdered one person in Arizona and another in California. That doesn't matter. But then I voluntarily called a cop and introduced myself. Great plan. Because of that, I had a coffee date with another who barely stopped short of strapping me in a chair, aiming a light at my face, and interrogating me. What the hell is wrong with me? It stops here. I'm back on track. I'll take care of that tool from the crime scene myself. The police won't have any more interest in me, and I can get back to my life.

But the very nature of his life was unpredictable, so Gabriel had learned to prepare himself for anything. His tool kit always stayed in his car. His body was in peak condition. He had trained in various disciplines to ensure he would be able to dominate most physical confrontations. He never got drunk or high. In three words, he was ready. And his preparation was about to be put to the test yet again.

A member of the wait staff approached, placed a candle on his table, and began to light it.

"I'm dining alone tonight." Gabriel objected. "So no need for the romance."

"Oh, sir. My apologies. Each table is getting one in case we lose power."

"Lose power?"

"Yes, sir. Quite a wind storm has picked up outside. It happens occasionally during our monsoon season."

"I'm aware."

"Time to head north. Now. Do not continue to test me." It wasn't the waiter's voice.

Gabriel thought for a moment, then laid more than enough money for the meal and a tip on the table and quickly stood.

"Sir! You don't have to leave. I assure you, we are prepared for the weather."

"So am I."

He almost knocked the server over before exiting through the kitchen and heading into the building storm.

He made his way onto a freeway as the rain began to hammer the entire Phoenix metro area. He swerved a few times as he hit standing water, but lessons learned at a high-performance driving school helped him regain control of the Shelby Mustang without incident.

I am ready for anything.

The freeway led to the north edge of the Phoenix metro area and Cave Creek Road, where he was directed to exit.

He drove hard and fast into the teeth of a storm that was quickly becoming the worst he'd ever seen. Gabriel didn't know where he was going, but he was pretty sure that where he'd come from some pretentious snobs were now eating by candlelight.

As Gabriel continued to drive northeast, he finally seemed to come out the other side of the storm but remnants of its fury remained. Deep pools. Downed Palo Verde branches. Ditches full of rushing water.

"Turn."

He kept going toward an intersection about a quarter mile ahead.

"You missed it."

Gabriel hit his brakes, causing the Shelby to almost slide off the side of the road. He slammed it into reverse and gunned it about one hundred feet until he saw a small, two-lane road to his right. That was the way.

The small road wound toward an exclusive area of North Scottsdale known as the Boulders. Gabriel remembered the first time he drove through this area. The giant rocks looked like they were designed and constructed for Disneyland—Huge oval shells covered in stucco and painted to look natural—but they were solid. Some of them were as big as a mobile home. As he drove, more carefully now, making two more turns when prompted, he knew he had to be close. Then, straight ahead, the road curved sharply to the left to go around a behemoth of a rock about twenty-five feet high and more than sixty feet wide. Then, he saw a car that had missed the turn, carved a path through new mud, and smashed into the boulder's backside. Gabriel pulled into the gravel on the side of the road, got out, and looked in all directions.

First on the scene. No surprise there. Leave the tool kit until I get a better look. Might not even need it.

As he approached the car and looked through the window, he discovered exactly the scenario he'd expected. A senior citizen was trying to drive through the downpour, couldn't see, and missed the turn. A big collision that the Boulders won. No contest.

Alright, we got good news, and we got bad news. The good news is the driver was driving with his wallet on the passenger seat or center console because it is now flipped open on the passenger-side footwell. I don't even need gloves to grab it. The bad news is the driver is breathing and could come to at any moment. Face is pretty messed up and is getting all up close and personal with his steering wheel since the car is preairbag. Best to make this quick. No time to get the gloves.

Gabriel peeled off his shirt and wrapped it around his right hand a few times. He tried the door. Locked. He wrapped his hand with the remainder of the shirt, reared back, and smashed the passenger window. Glass exploded throughout the cab, but the driver didn't flinch. Gabriel manually unlocked the door with his wrapped hand and opened it. He reached down to pluck the wallet when he suddenly heard a man speak.

"Hey! Don't move him!"

Gabriel quickly retracted from inside the car, leaving the wallet. He straightened up to see exactly how complicated this would get.

There was no way he could've known.

It was the guy who found the body in the canal.

The guy who was hitting on Rebecca.

The guy he was trying to set up for murder.

Gabriel's mind couldn't decipher what this all meant. He just needed to respond. "Hey. I just busted the window, so I could check on him."

"You didn't move him at all, did you?"

"No. I know better." Gabriel was wondering how long it would take for a third person to roll up on the scene. That mystery was the only thing keeping Michael safe.

"Good. Good. We could cause more damage."

"Yeah, buddy. I understand that." He couldn't hide being annoyed.

"Okay. Cool. I have this first aid kit for the basics, but we shouldn't move him until help arrives."

"That could be a while," Gabriel shot back.

"Hope not. My friend already called 911."

"Where is he?"

"*She* is in my truck on the other side of this rock. We approached from the other direction."

"Okay. I'm going to check for gas leaks because I have news for you. If there is gasoline all over the place under this car, we *are* moving this guy."

Freaking nightmare for so many reasons. This was now a waste of a drive since the wallet is still sitting in the footwell. This guy just keeps showing up. There's a witness who might appear from around the corner any instant. Worst of all, an entire crew of firemen and/or police are about to roll up and find me with the guy I just implicated in a murder a matter of hours ago.

This could not get worse.

27.

I FINALLY FIND THE PERFECT GUY. *He's in amazing shape, he's single, and he rescues little children. Except . . . oh wait . . . he has a mental illness! Maybe. I mean, we did drive directly to an accident. But in this weather, if you drive long enough, it's bound to happen eventually. Right? Either way, I gotta call 911. This is all nuts.*

Rebecca slammed the driver-side door shut and cranked up the truck. She quickly turned the truck around and accelerated back toward Pima Road. As she was driving down the slick track, she whipped out her cell phone and dialed 911.

"Hello, 911. What is the nature of your emergency?"

"Yeah . . ." She was sliding a bit too much and needed a second to regain control.

"Are you there?"

"I'm at the corner of Mule Train Road and Stagecoach Pass. Good Lord! Is that for real?"

"Ma'am! What is your emergency?"

"There was a horrible accident. A guy ran off the road on Stagecoach and hit a huge boulder. We think he's unconscious."

"Are you there now?"

"No. My friend is. I drove back to the intersection because I didn't know what road we were on." That's when it struck her. They could've just tracked her location. She hated that she wasn't thinking clearly.

Rebecca turned the old rust bucket around again and began heading back.

"I want you to know that I've already dispatched help. May I have your name?"

"Rebecca. Rebecca Bishop."

"Alright, Rebecca. Please stay on the line with me."

"Okay." She was approaching the curve around the boulder and decided to slowly drive around to get closer to the accident itself. As she took the right bank followed by the sharp left turn, she saw the destroyed car that had run off the road to her left, passed it, and pulled off on the right across from a Mustang Shelby that struck her as familiar. "I'm at the accident."

"Please don't drive while you are speaking with me. Can you pull over?"

"Sorry. Already did."

"Okay. Emergency personnel should be arriving soon. You are pretty close to a fire department on Pima."

Rebecca got out of the truck and entered a world of chaos. She could hear sirens approaching in the distance. She couldn't quite place where she had seen that car. The rain was beginning to fall again, but it was barely registering compared to the storm cell that had already passed. She saw Michael standing on the far side of the crashed car.

As she ran toward him, another man stood up from behind it right next to Michael.

It was Gabriel.

"No gas as far as I could tell. I think we are good—" He saw Rebecca and froze.

"Gabriel! What the hell are you doing here?" Rebecca questioned.

Michael's face suddenly looked confused.

"I'm trying to help this guy!" Gabriel answered. He turned to Michael. "As I was saying, no gas as far as I can tell. We can wait 'til help arrives."

Rebecca looked very suspiciously at Gabriel then at Michael. "Do you two know each other?"

Michael quickly answered, "No. Why? Do you?"

"You could say that."

This cannot be a coincidence, but how could it be anything else?

The sirens went from distant to blaring in a flash as the fire truck rounded the boulder. And just as fast as the volume infinitely multiplied, it vanished as the truck shut off the siren. In that moment, the scene became even more chaotic as firemen poured out and began approaching the crash, questioning the three of them, as several police cars pulled up on the scene.

Michael, Rebecca, and Gabriel were each questioned briefly and had their information taken down. Most of their answers were honest. Gabriel claimed to be a storm enthusiast who was looking to grab some great shots with his cell phone camera. Michael said he was on a date. So did Rebecca. The only inconsistency was that Michael said they were just out driving and talking while Rebecca said they were lost. The police just chalked it up to a guy refusing to admit he'd gotten turned around in the storm.

━

Upon being told they were free to go, Michael and Rebecca climbed into the old truck. Michael went to put his key in the ignition, but Rebecca reached over, grabbed his hand, and stopped him.

I'd think she'd be eager to get back and be rid of me.

"Hang on a minute." She looked past him to Gabriel who was just getting into his car across the narrow street.

Gabriel revved it up, glanced over at the two of them, and spun a half-circle before rumbling out of sight.

"What is it?"

"I'm not sure," Rebecca admitted. "Let's just give him space."

"Alright. We'll head back the way we came."

"Only if the water has gone down."

Michael started up the truck, turned it around, and they slowly crept their way through the emergency vehicles as the sun was setting over the western desert sky behind them.

"So what is the story with that guy back there?" He broached.

"He has a thing for me. Bit of a slime bucket but mostly harmless. Until today."

"What do you mean?"

"There is no way he just ran into us."

"But he was there when we arrived."

She thought for a second. "I guess I really don't know what happened. Maybe it *was* just a coincidence," she conceded.

Coincidence?

The very word was like a canary chirping in a coal mine to Michael.

"It is a pretty random place to run into someone, you know, but I heard him mention something to an officer about trying to get a picture of the storm."

Rebecca shook her head. "He could've gotten great pictures of that storm anywhere within a fifty-mile radius. And did I mention, he lives in the same complex as us?"

"Wow. Thirty miles away."

Something about this is off, but what?

"So . . . still think it's a coincidence?"

"Those are rare . . . if they exist at all."

The topic of coincidences seemed to remind both of them about the abrupt end to their date. The silence became prolonged and awkward.

Rebecca decided to address the elephant in the truck. "So that, back there, you're telling me the accident wasn't a coincidence."

"No," Michael replied without hesitation.

"You knew where to go, and it led you to that accident."

"I knew where I was supposed to drive next." He searched for words. "Put another way, imagine you decide to take a hiking trail for the first time. It takes much longer than expected, so you find yourself on the trail well after sundown. All you have is the dim light from your cell phone."

"This analogy has a lot going on."

"Almost there."

"Okay. Hiking trail. Dark. Dim light. Go."

"Because the cell phone is so dim against the darkest night, you can only see the next step you should take. The good news is that the trail is very clearly marked. So you know that if you pay close attention each step along the way, you will get where you need to go even if you've never been there before."

"Okay . . ." Rebecca considered this for a moment. "So that kid in the pool back at the complex a few days ago?"

"Yes. Although it wasn't audible in that instance. Sometimes, I just feel it."

They rolled up to the area the police were blocking earlier. The police had left, and the water was very low now. Cars were cautiously traversing the remaining stream on the dark road. Michael looked to Rebecca whose face was now slightly illuminated by the old dash lights. She smiled gently and gave the slightest nod. He proceeded across.

Then Rebecca asked, "And me?"

"Pardon?"

"Meeting me. Talking to me. Asking me out. Am I like the accident? Am I like the boy in the pool?"

"I don't know."

"Michael, please be honest with me."

"I really don't know. I hope so." He considered for a moment. "Or I don't."

Rebecca shot him a look in the fading light. "What do you mean?"

"I think you are pretty special. Your intelligence. Your wit. Doesn't hurt that you are beautiful."

"You can go on."

"That's the thing. Even though I've basically just met you, I absolutely could. Your heart for those with special needs. Your understanding that there is more to a boyfriend than good looks. The way you refused to be left in the rain. The way you were probably certain I was insane, but you still helped me by calling 911 and didn't leave."

"Okay." Rebecca's face was turning a bit flush. "That's enough."

"And I haven't even gotten to your mad flute skills."

"You won't be cracking jokes when you witness them for yourself."

"And despite all that, I don't know how to answer your question, Rebecca. Did I just happen to run into you? Yes. Do I feel like I was supposed to? Yes."

"So does that make this some sort of cosmically planned arranged marriage? I'm not sure I'm down for that."

"Completely understandable." Michael considered his words for a moment before he went on. "When it comes to short-term interventions, it's clear. It's as clear as I hear your voice right now, but the long view is a bit more hazy. For example, I know I'm supposed to live where I live. But why? To stop a boy from drowning? To catch a murderer? To meet you? I still can't tell if it's one or all. Do I have specific tasks I've been assigned, or is it all intertwined? The dim flashlight. The next step. That's all I know. But here's the thing, it's still my choice. I still have free will. So we wouldn't be some sort of arranged marriage because we still have a choice every step of the way."

"And if, after the misadventures of the last few hours, you want to go on another date, will you only ask if you think you're supposed to?"

"No."

"Good," she said like it was settled.

"I'd ask if I wanted to, *or* if I believed I was supposed to."

"But you wouldn't ask if you believed you weren't supposed to?"

"I probably wouldn't." Michael realized how bad this could sound. "But like I said, I still have free will in all this, and so do you! We are both in this truck because we want to be."

"You might want to be in this truck with me, but that isn't why you are. You tried to leave me behind. You've given up your free will. We are in this truck together because I won't stand for being abandoned in a monsoon."

"And that is one of the thousand things that makes me think you are incredible."

"But the question remains. Do you want to go on another date with me because you like me or because you think we are somehow supposed to?"

"When you put it that way, it sounds creepy and a bit manipulative," he realized aloud.

"Glad you realize that."

"I want to go on a second date with you, Rebecca. Of my own free will. Does anything else matter?"

"I sort of want to make you promise to tell me if you ever get to a point where you don't want to keep dating, but you continue because you think you are supposed to—"

"I could do that." Michael volunteered.

"But I don't think that would work because I think that is the occasional norm for a committed relationship. For example, my parents don't feel like being married all the time, but they push through those times and come out the other end more in love than ever. And I don't think volunteering that they don't feel like being married every so often would help."

"I see your point."

"So here is my only ground rule. If you break up with me

because you think you are supposed to, even though you don't want to, you have to tell me."

"I will."

"Promise?"

"Promise. So are you my girlfriend now?"

"Slow down. That was all hypothetical." Rebecca smiled to herself, then abruptly changed the topic. "Do you think you are the only one who gets these feelings?"

"No. Of course not. I'm sure you've felt like you were supposed to do something before, like call a family member. Maybe you felt compelled to avoid someone who just seems a little off. You randomly decided to apply for a job. One day, for no apparent reason other than what you thought was whimsy, you took a different route home."

"Well. Maybe I should give it a try . . ."

Michael's thought was completely deleted from existence the moment he felt his right hand, which had been resting on the stick shift, covered gently by Rebecca's left hand.

"So *that* is how it works," she said matter-of-factly.

"Yeah. I guess so."

"Now it's your turn."

Michael swallowed. "Would you be willing to go on a second date . . . on Thursday night?"

"You will pick me up from my front door. That way, you won't try to ditch me again."

"Done. Can I pick you up at six?"

"I'll be ready. And if you aren't, I'll assume you are saving the governor. Or making a citizen's arrest. Or maybe—"

"I will do everything I can to be there."

"Good. So are you able to just find your way back to my car without my help?"

"It's not really something that happens on command, and it never happens if I'm just trying to impress someone."

After a bit of help from his copilot, Michael rolled to a stop.

He took a deep breath.

Should I grab a hug or go for the kiss? Either way, I should definitely get out of the car.

As he turned to unbuckle his seatbelt, Rebecca leaned over and gave him a quick hug. "Thanks for a memorable night. See you Thursday."

She smiled and jumped out of the truck.

28.

GABRIEL STUMBLED TOWARD THE DOOR. He had been up quite late the night before. A little time with some girls in the clubs of Old Town Scottsdale followed by a little more time with them at his condo helped get his mind off Rebecca and the man who seemed to be winning her affection.

Ding!

"Coming!" Gabriel snapped.

Wearing nothing more than boxers, he swung open the door to find Detective Alvarez and Detective Gradillas standing in the doorway.

"Good morning, sunshine," Alvarez said with a nod.

"Put on some clothes, Abercrombie," Gradillas added.

"You sure that's what you want?"

"I think she'll survive the trauma." Alvarez faked a smile.

"Okay. Okay. Ya woke me up. Give me a second."

He turned and wandered his way into his bedroom, shutting the door behind him, mostly to see if they'd let him.

Alright. What do they want? What do they know? He pulled on a t-shirt. *It might be time to relocate.*

He pulled on a pair of jeans that were a bit loose at the ankles. He strapped on his ankle holster and pulled his Glock 43 from under his bed.

You get a Glock. I get a Glock. Everybody gets a Glock!

He strapped it in and froze.

They'd spot it. This isn't their first rodeo. Dammit.

He unstrapped the holster and slid it back under the bed. The loaded gun, on the other hand, was set on the floor right next to the doorway.

Prepared.

He emerged to find Alvarez standing just inside the door while Gradillas seemed to be enjoying looking over his bookcase.

Alvarez wasn't in the mood for pleasantries. "What in the blue hell were you doing yesterday?!"

"Woah, buddy! What are you talkin' about?"

"Don't play with me!" Alvarez took a step forward, pointing at Gabriel. "Don't! I'm not in the mood!"

"I think my partner and I are a little confused." Gradillas turned from the bookcase. "Yesterday, you and I had coffee. Well, I had coffee. I have no idea what the hell you drank. And I'm pretty sure you left knowing that we were pursuing your tip."

"Yeah. We had it!" Alvarez was furious. "Thanks for your help, Mr. Witness Man. We got it from here. But no! You gotta go and screw the pooch!"

"I really wish you'd find a new expression," said Gradillas.

"It's the clean version, alright? I *am* being professional here!"

"If you're aiming to sound professional, try again." Gradillas shook her head.

They know about yesterday's accident. Doesn't matter how they know. What matters is the alibi. Coincidence isn't going to cut it.

"Well, I don't give a rat's tuchus if I sound professional in front of this moron anyway!" Alvarez was pacing and pointed right at Gabriel.

"Hey! I'm right here!" Gabriel protested.

"Oh, shut up!" Alvarez's small frame managed to bellow, silencing the room for a few moments.

I could end you.

"Tuchus?" Gradillas whispered.

"Please stop."

"Sorry." Gradillas was done poking fun at her partner. It was time to get serious. She turned to Gabriel. "Why were you there?"

"Where?"

"For God's sake, you idiot!" Alvarez was not in the mood. "Why, just hours after talking to Gradillas about implicating Michael Bale in a murder, were you at the same accident scene side by side with him? And so help me God, if you use the same lame storm chasing, picture-taking story . . ."

Gabriel's heart almost exploded in his chest. "What did you say his name was?" Gabriel needed to make sure.

"It isn't important," Gradillas immediately recognized the mistake Alvarez made and interjected. "We just need your answer."

Michael Bale. That is what he said. Need to get through this inquiry first. Think about the name later.

"When you and I talked, you made it sound like I wasn't a credible witness. Then, I saw him with Rebecca . . ."

"You know the girl he was with?!" Alvarez threw his hands in the air and spun away from Gabriel as if he just saw the entire case blow up in his mind.

"Then, I saw him with Rebecca." Gabriel continued. "We're pretty close. Given that he might have just murdered another woman, I couldn't just stand by."

"Does she know you're close?" Alvarez asked.

"Where did you see them?" Gradillas pressed, ignoring Alvarez's question.

Michael Bale. Michael Bale. Michael Bale.

"I don't know how many times I have to say it. I'm not under investigation! This Michael Bale guy is! And if you spent more time on him than on me, maybe I wouldn't have to follow him!"

Alvarez stepped toward him. "Oh, you stupid son of a—"

"Alvarez! We should go." Gradillas cut in as she turned to Gabriel. "And if you don't stay away from the man you saw at that church dumpster, I'll have you tossed in prison for interfering with an investigation. Am I clear?"

Could she even do that? Or is she bluffing?

"Fine. Just do your jobs and catch this SOB before he kills again."

Gradillas gently took Alvarez's elbow. "Let's go. This gentleman needs to reflect on how his interference could jeopardize our investigation."

Alvarez stood his ground a moment longer, staring. "Why do we always get the brain surgeons?"

"Let's go." Gradillas tried again.

Alvarez relented. They turned and walked toward the door.

As Gradillas opened it for Alvarez, he muttered, "Every witness we get . . . intellect of a kumquat."

Gabriel watched him go.

Yeah, I'm definitely going to end you.

29.

Inside the ambulance, two simple words broke through and sharpened Billy's senses: "victims identified."

Then, he heard the names that changed his life, ". . . Ezekiel and Phyllis Bale of Milwaukee County."

Ezekiel. Phyllis.

Those names.

". . . efforts are being made to locate their child, Michael."

The letter he still kept in his bottom drawer.

"Must've swerved to avoid something."

"Probably just an unfortunate no-fault accident resulting in multiple fatalities."

This wasn't real. This couldn't be real.

He let himself fall back into the deep.

30.

BILLY DIDN'T HAVE A DRINK ALL DAY. In fact, it was his first sober day since being released from the hospital twelve months ago.

Gabriel had picked him up once the doctors were satisfied with his medical evaluation and the state patrol was satisfied with his account of what had happened.

Gabriel said he wanted to stay the night and refused to leave his dad, but it only took Billy ten minutes to lose his patience and yell at Gabriel to get lost. Five minutes after his son finally left, Billy walked to the nearest bar.

He almost didn't make it home. He fell into a pile of snow left behind by a plow and passed out one block from his front door. He was woken up by two buddies walking home from another bar. They quickly realized he was in a bad way and helped him make it the final stretch home.

Now, twelve months later, he was approaching the spot where it all began.

Began. That was the wrong word. Ended. That was the word.

He was almost to the precise location.

He pulled his pickup to the side of the highway and took a deep breath.

This might keep me from Ruthie, but she deserves better than eternity with a man like me anyway. Gabriel will inherit a small fortune from the payoff, and he won't have to deal with a drunken disgrace of a father anymore. And Michael deserves justice. There needs to be a reckoning.

He reached into the glove box, pulled out the cold, unforgiving steel, and sat it on his lap. He apologized to Phyllis, Ezekiel, Michael, Ruthie, and Gabriel one final time. His body shuddered, rejecting his decision, but his mind was set.

His body was found on the side of the freeway by a patrolman twenty minutes later.

31.

A LVAREZ AND GRADILLAS DECIDED TO PICK up some burritos less than a quarter mile from Kiwanis Park. The location was intentional. In the shadow of the crime. Haunted until the case was solved and a child could sleep knowing the person who killed their mother had met justice.

They dumped their trash, leaving the table between them clear of everything but their drinks.

"At the end of the day, what do we have?" Gradillas asked.

"Well." Alvarez considered. "We have a man who found a submerged body that at least fifteen to thirty people passed without noticing."

"He's observant. What else?" She pressed.

"He has no girlfriend, no close friends, no steady job."

"A loner. Or shy. Or troubled," Gradillas voiced the possible reasons.

"Or my life in high school," Alvarez offered another.

"What else?"

"We are rushing his DNA against a small sample taken from beneath one of the recovered nails. Not sure if anything usable survived the weather." He shook his head, less than hopeful.

"Probably a long shot. What else?"

"He was witnessed tossing something in a church's dumpster between the time she went missing and when she was discovered."

"Maybe he is a volunteer, or maybe he works there." Gradillas enjoyed playing devil's advocate even when she knew the answer. It was a useful exercise that helped her and Alvarez make certain they had every base covered.

"He does. But he didn't when he dumped mystery items in that dumpster. The woman was murdered. He is seen dumping something. Days later, he begins working there," Alvarez responded.

"Is the individual who witnessed him dumping something a good witness?"

Alvarez shook his head in contempt at the thought of Gabriel. "He is an idiot who has already attempted to intervene in the case."

Gradillas thought silently for a brief moment.

Alvarez took notice. "Where did your mind go?"

"Inserting oneself into a case is sometimes a sign of guilt. Is this witness actually a suspect?"

"I don't see it in this case. The only connection is the girl."

"I tend to agree. We can always circle back. As a witness, do you think his testimony is truthful?"

"I do. The dumpster and his new job would be too great a leap."

"That brings us back to the primary suspect," she led. "What did he put in the dumpster?"

"We don't know, but we will within the week." Alvarez nodded with optimism returning.

"Maybe. The dump keeps trying to say it's a long shot. And even if we find something, it could be completely unrelated."

He sighed. "I sincerely hope not."

"Let's assume it is. What else do we have?"

"When we first met Mr. Psycho, he had been accused of stalking another woman."

"Definitely makes him a suspect, but it doesn't make him guilty. Other than our friendly, neighborhood witness, do we have any other alternative suspects?"

"Well, let's see." Alvarez was frustrated because he knew Gradillas was right. "Spouse was out of town on business, and we've verified it with hotel and restaurant receipts. No life insurance. Nanny was with the child. No enemies. No bitter exes to speak of. No enemies at all really. Short answer? No. No other obvious suspects. If it wasn't Michael, it most likely was a stranger."

"Unless we get a DNA miracle or the epic landfill treasure hunt pays off, we've got plenty of sizzle but no steak," she concluded.

"If we collect enough smoke," Alvarez said, almost pleadingly, "a jury will know it is coming from a fire even if we can't show it to them."

"It's possible but far from a lock. And the district attorney's office likes to maintain a winning record."

"But do you think he did it?" he finally asked.

"That's the thing. I really don't know," she admitted.

"I think he did it." Alvarez seemed to decide on the spot, nodding slowly as if to convince himself.

From somewhere beneath the table, *"Bailamos"* by Enrique Iglesias burst forth. Alvarez pulled out his phone.

Gradillas facepalmed and said, "You have *got* to change your ringtone."

"What? You've seen me dance. Everyone needs a theme song, my princess."

"You call me your princess again, and I'll punch you in the neck."

Alvarez ignored her and answered the call. "Alvarez here."

He waited a brief moment.

"Yeah. Okay. Great. And what did you find?"

As Alvarez continued to listen, his eyes went wide, and he couldn't hold back a smile. He covered the cell phone for a second and whispered, "We've got the son of a bitch." He removed his hand from the phone. "Okay. Here's the deal. We cannot afford any contamination. Seal it up. Then, lock it up. Then, guard it with your friggin' life. Am I clear?"

He waited for confirmation.

"Great job, Santorini! Gradillas and I are on our way over now."

32.

THANKS TO MONSOON SEASON, WORKING OUTSIDE was zero fun whatsoever. The Phoenix area was not only insanely hot but humid as well. The humidity wasn't rising to the levels the Deep South sees with regularity, but it only took a little moisture to make life quite miserable when temperatures reached over 110 degrees Fahrenheit.

The other pain this particular monsoon season brought Arizona was debris. Last night's storm was the worst of the season, and Our Lady of Fatima's entire campus was littered with fallen palm fronds, small branches, and a wide variety of trash.

John, the facilities manager, seemed more than happy to give the distinct honor of cleaning it all up to Michael. About four decades younger than John, Michael was making quick work of the enormous task.

Michael was excited just to have a paycheck again, and this time, his boss actually knew about his unique lifestyle. It gave a certain bounce to his step as he filled and lifted heavy trash bags with exceptional efficiency. He was lugging two of the enormous bags when it hit.

"Time to go. Now. You need to vanish."

Seriously? On week one? Unbelievable.

But the Voice persisted, more urgently than usual. "Leave. Disappear. NOW!"

Michael dropped the bags where he stood and went looking for John. He found him in the maintenance storage room in front of the computer ordering more bathroom supplies.

"John? You got a sec?"

Looking up from the dusty monitor, John replied, "Son, please tell me you need more garbage bags."

"No." Michael paused for a second. These conversations never went well. "I need to cut today short."

"Come on, man! Seriously?"

"I can't really explain—"

John got up from the desk. "Don't bother. Father warned me that you might have to leave at random times and said I was not allowed to ask why. I trust my pastor, so you'll get no questions about where you have to go."

"Okay . . . thanks." Michael turned to leave.

"Hold up. Do you know when you'll be back on duty?"

Michael paused, turned, and pressed his lips for a moment before shaking his head slightly. "Afraid not."

"Great. Wonderful. Well. Skedaddle. I'll let Father know."

As Michael ran to his truck, home didn't seem like the right place to go. Without further direction, there was really only one destination he could think of.

Michael pulled out of the parking lot, and at the precise instant he turned the corner and his truck accelerated out of view, Gradillas drove up to the church from the other direction.

⸺

Gradillas walked onto the church campus with purpose but wasn't sure where she was headed. She had tried to convince

Alvarez he should've been the one to go to the church since he had just been there, but he thought Michael might try to run. He'd need to pick a few things up before going into hiding, so Alvarez wanted to head straight to Michael's condo.

Gradillas saw an older guy wearing a polo shirt, jeans, and a big set of keys hanging from a belt loop. She hollered over to him, "Sir! Sir! Do you work here?"

John smiled widely and answered, "Sure do."

Gradillas approached and asked, "A guy named Michael works here, correct?"

"Sure does."

She took out her badge and flashed it at the smiling man as she continued. "Where is he right now?"

"I've got no earthly idea, officer."

"*Detective* Gradillas. Has he been here today?"

"Yes, detective." John was not going to lie, but he wasn't going to make the process efficient either.

"Did he leave?"

"Yes, he did."

"Come on, sir! When did he leave?"

"Just as you pulled up."

Gradillas pulled out her phone and quickly texted Alvarez. *Barely missed him. Might be headed your way.*

Alvarez's reply came three seconds later. *Ok. Rdy. Thx.*

Gradillas shot back, *Questioning ppl here. If he doesn't go home, we need to know where else he would go. You good?*

Alvarez responded, *Suit yourself. I'll collar the ahole solo :) waiting on warrant. Dumb 4th amendment.*

Gradillas turned her attention back to John. "I need you to tell me what happened before Michael left. Specific details. Every action. Every word."

Gradillas listened intently as John slowly recounted every action and every word. Just as Fr. Fitz had instructed him to.

"So the pastor of this church told you in advance Michael

might randomly have to leave, and you weren't supposed to ask questions?"

"Precisely." John's eyebrows lifted.

"And that doesn't strike you as odd?"

"Sure as hell does." He looked up and did the sign of the cross as he said, "Sorry, Big Guy. Sure as *heck* does. But Fr. Fitz is the greatest man I've ever known, and if he tells me to do something, he has his reasons."

"That sounds suspiciously like the kind of blind trust in the clergy that got your church into trouble recently."

"Hey!" John lost his cool in an instant. "Fr. Fitz warns every employee that if they hurt a child, he'll personally take a baseball bat to their kneecaps and gladly go to prison for it. And ya know what? I'd hand him the bat."

"Sure you wanna be telling a detective that?"

"Yup. Father would need backup in the slammer."

"Where is the pastor now?"

"Happy to take you to him."

—

John knocked lightly on Fr. Fitz's open office door.

"John! How goes the cleanup?"

"Father? This is a detective. She would like to chat with you about Michael."

Fr. Fitz quickly got up from behind his desk and extended a strong hand. "A pleasure to meet you, Detective . . ."

"Gradillas. Pleasure to meet you, Father . . ."

"Fitz." He motioned Gradillas to a chair and rolled his own from behind the desk and looked at John. "That will be all. We'll be able to take it from here."

"Okay, but Father?"

"Yes, John?"

"She knows he left just before she arrived."

"If that is what happened, that is what you tell her." Fr. Fitz smiled comfortably at Gradillas.

"And she knows you warned me Michael might have to leave unexpectedly and not to ask him why."

"You told her the truth, which is precisely what my instructions were. Thank you, John."

He nodded at John, who finally got the hint and saw himself out.

Fr. Fitz settled into his chair and laid his left foot across his right knee. "Would it be rude of me to ask to see your badge?"

"Certainly not." Gradillas grabbed it from her belt and handed it over. Fr. Fitz accepted and examined it for a brief moment before handing it back.

"Well, everything appears to be in order, Detective Gradillas. How may I be of service?"

"As I'm sure you know, I don't have much time. Where is Michael Bale?"

"I do not know, nor did I know he wasn't on the property until John informed me in your presence."

"But you had warned John that Michael may have to leave his job on a moment's notice, and you instructed him that he wasn't to ask why."

"That would be correct."

"So you were aware the police might come looking for him?"

"Detective? My Church, the Catholic Church, has endured a horrible season of self-inflicted pain . . ."

"With all due respect, it seems to me that the Church was the one inflicting the pain," Gradillas interjected.

"Like I said, self-inflicted pain. I mean it quite literally. We did the inflicting, but we were also the victims. What I mean to say is this, the clergy who perpetrated evil on the young and vulnerable, as well as those who enabled it through cooperation or indifference, were certainly members of the Church. But those young and vulnerable who were victimized were no less members of the church. Have I explained my expression adequately?"

"Still don't follow, but this really isn't pertinent to—"

"Understandably, people who are not Catholic somehow see the clergy as the Church but not the people in the pews. They are just as much the Church. Therefore, some members of our Church horrifically wounded other members of our Church."

"I have no idea what this has to do with anything. Let's get back to the original question. Did you know the police might show up, and he might have to leave quickly in order to escape?"

"And back to where I was going originally. My Church has inflicted enough pain upon itself through a minority of the clergy who were complicit in pure evil. These men lied to authorities and made it far more difficult for good people to catch bad people. Therefore, Detective Gradillas, I will not lie to you. I do *not* believe Michael to be a bad man, but it is not my job to determine his guilt in the eyes of the law. Having said that, I had no idea the police might come looking for him. Although, if what he told me is true, I suppose I shouldn't be shocked."

Gradillas shook her head and said, "Let's make this simple then. What did he tell you that would make any of this make sense?"

Fr. Fitz couldn't help but rethink his decision to continue his conversation with Michael outside the seal of the confessional. It would have made this conversation much more simple.

And brief.

"You said you didn't have much time, detective."

"Oh, I have time for *this*." Gradillas sat back.

Fr. Fitz proceeded to tell her everything Michael had shared. It took some time, with Gradillas occasionally asking for clarification.

"And you believe this insane story?" she finally asked.

"I believe one of two things is taking place with young Mr. Bale. Option one, he is mentally ill, and it is the church's job to take him in and help him. Option two, what he is saying is true.

Based on the good he is doing, he is probably being led by the Holy Spirit even if he doesn't realize it, and it is the church's job to take him in and assist him."

"But again, with all due respect, keeping in mind I don't share your belief system, if those two options are on the table, aren't there two other options?"

"Which would be?"

"Option three, he is mentally ill and doing horrible things because he is unstable. Option four, what he is saying is partially true, but he isn't telling you the whole truth because what he is being led by . . . isn't the Holy Spirit."

Gradillas, armed with today's fresh evidence, actually believed option five. The option she chose not to share with the old man. Michael Bale was a complete psychopath capable of acting completely innocent and almost naive.

"If it is option three or four, I pray you catch him quickly," the priest responded.

"Then, help me. Where could he have gone?"

"As far as I know, there are only two other people in his life. A new friend by the name of Ron . . . or Rob. I believe it was Rob. The girl's name was Rebecca."

"Do you know anything else about them?"

"He is quite fond of Rebecca. And they both live in his complex."

Gradillas immediately texted Alvarez. *Only 2 friends both live in his complex. Rebecca & Rob.*

The response was instant. *Rebecca was at last night's accident. Rob is new. I'll call it in & get her info & find out how many Robs & Roberts live here.*

Ok. Be careful. Good chance he's there. OMW.

Gradillas stood up quickly, extended a business card, and said, "If you can think of anything else."

Fr. Fitz stood, took the card, and lifted a small package off his desk. "Can I offer you some fresh brownies for the road?"

33.

GRADILLAS ARRIVED AT THE CONDO COMPLEX to find Alvarez leaning against his car and talking on his phone.

"Alright. I'll knock on his door. Send a unit to his work. If Michael is there, arrest him on the spot. If Rob is there"—he looked up and saw Gradillas walking toward him—"keep him there until either Gradillas or I arrive. We need to ask him some questions."

"Bring me up to speed." Gradillas knew they were closing in.

"I have a uniform on Michael's front door. We are still waiting on an emergency warrant before we can enter. Got Rebecca's info right away thanks to last night's police report. Knocked on that door and got bupkis. Rob took longer but just found out there is exactly one Rob here who is under the age of sixty, so I'm going with him. Sent a unit to his workplace, and we are headed to his front door."

"Great work."

"Thanks. Let's walk and talk. What did you find out about our neighborhood nutcase?"

As they walked toward the side of the complex en route to

Rob's condo, Gradillas began telling Alvarez the legend of a man who always ended up where he needed to be.

192

34.

MICHAEL'S TRUCK SKIDDED TO A STOP in the alley behind Humboldt Camping Supply. He made his way around the building and burst through the front door.

"Woah, kemosabe! Easy on the hinges, my man!" exclaimed Rob from behind the register.

"Sorry, man. I didn't know where else to go."

The look of desperation on Michael's face was not lost on Rob. "What's up, dude? Talk to me."

"I'm not sure. I need to disappear for a bit."

"It's happening, isn't it?" Rob's eyes lit up.

"Rob! Not the time."

"Okay. Got it. How long do you have to vanish?"

"Don't know."

"Okay." Rob looked down at the counter and seemed to formulate a plan. "I've got this, Mikey." He turned toward the back of the store. "Bossman!"

"What?!?" rang out a grumpy voice from the back.

"I need you to cover the register! I've got to pick out a few rental items with a customer!"

"Anyone in line?"

"No, sir!"

"Well, let me know when there is!"

"Copy that!" Rob yelled before turning his attention to Michael. "Let's go."

In the next few minutes, Rob had picked out a two-person tent, a sleeping bag, and a collection of used camping supplies. He grabbed about eight MREs and stuffed them in a bag. He found the multi-tool Michael had turned down two days before and tossed that in the bag.

"Rob. I can't pay for all this stuff."

"The rentals are free for employees, and I'm renting them. The purchases will be on an employee discount, and Brindy is buying."

"You mean your mom, right?"

"That would be the Brindy."

"Does she know?"

"Well, okay. Fine." Rob smirked. "I wasn't going to tell you, but I get an allowance."

"Sometime in the future when we have a minute, you are going to explain that to me."

"Whatever. Where are you parked? Didn't see you pull up."

"In the alley out back."

"So this *is* serious. Okay. Let's start carrying this out. There is an exit through the storage room. I'll carry everything from here to there. You carry it from there to the truck. Deal?"

"Deal."

"Go unlock the truck, and I'll be right behind with the first load."

As Michael propped open the door from the storage room to the alley, Rob's boss noticed him.

"Wait! You're not a customer. You're his friend from the other day." He looked at Michael, visibly ticked.

Michael froze briefly. "Uh, he said Brindy is payin'."

Rob walked into the room as the boss declared, "Well, Brindy doesn't work here, so she can pay for the rentals too."

It didn't take long before everything was out to the truck. Michael was walking through the back room toward the front to thank Rob when his friend came running at him.

"Dude! Five-O, Five-O! Cops just pulled up! Put Woods Canyon Lake in your phone's map and head there! When . . ."

"Rob! Stop. I don't have a phone."

Rob dug out his phone and pressed it into Michael's hand. "Take mine." He whispered, "Woods Canyon Lake. When you get to the campground, ask for Skye. Tell her you are my friend. She'll take care of you."

"Woods Canyon Lake. Skye. Got it. But I need you to find Rebecca. Unit G14. She knows about me. Tell her I'm sorry I missed our second date."

The bell attached to the front door rang. Someone just entered the store.

"Oh!" He reached in his pocket and pulled out a small wad of cash. "Brindy wants you to have gas money too. Now go!"

"Hello? Anybody here?" A voice called out from up front.

"One sec, bro! Finishing a bit of inventory back here!" Rob replied.

"Rob. I don't know how to thank you . . ."

The boss came up behind him and gave Michael a big plastic grocery bag that was tied shut at the top. "Take this with you," he whispered. "In case they search the place."

Rob looked incredulously at his boss. "Seriously?"

Michael didn't have time to argue. "Got it." With that, he ran out the door. Rob shut it behind him just as two officers walked into the room.

"What can I help you find, officers?" Rob asked.

"Stop right there!" yelled the boss randomly. "Do you boys have a warrant?"

"No, we don't," the older policeman answered. "Because we—"

"Then, get out of my storage room before I start calling my favorite attorney and telling them a grand old tale about an illegal search!"

"Then, please join us in the storefront. Now."

The older officer was not playing around.

But Rob's boss was. "I'll think about it."

Rob followed them out and tried to diffuse the situation. "I'd be happy to answer any of your questions, gentlemen."

"Good. Is there a Robert Safranski on the premises?"

"That would be myself."

"Thank God," said the younger officer. This meant they wouldn't have to deal with the old conscientious objector in the back.

The older officer remained a bit more focused. "Do you know Michael Bale?"

"Sure do. He's my best bud. Somethin' happen to 'im?"

"When was the last time you've seen him?"

"Ahh . . . two nights ago. We ate some pizza. Talked about life. I led a rousing group rendition of a Lionel Ritchie song."

"Lionel Ritchie? Which song?" asked the younger officer.

"Chip. You can't be serious," said the obviously annoyed older officer.

"'Dancin' on the Ceiling,' Officer Chip." Rob offered. "'Hello' would not be a good choice for a group sing-along, obviously."

"Obviously," agreed Officer Chip.

"Enough!" Officer Big Shot restored order. "Are you sure you haven't seen him since then?"

"No, I have not, officer."

"Okay. Well, if he makes contact, call us."

As he handed Rob his card, it occurred to Rob he should be more curious. "Is he in trouble?"

"Sir. I know he is your friend, but if he makes contact again and you don't reach out to us immediately, you will be the one who is in trouble."

"Woah, woah, woah. Easy officer. No need for threats. Just wanted to make sure my brother from another mother was a-okay."

"I'm sure he is. Just focus on the fact that the next time he reaches out or shows up, you'll call the number on that card."

"I will go straight to my cell phone. You have my word."

"Thank you. We appreciate your time."

As the officers left the store, the younger one started humming "Dancing on the Ceiling," and the older one punched him in the shoulder.

Hard.

35.

GABRIEL HAD BEEN SITTING ON HIS couch for hours. He was just staring at the old, weathered travel trunk that now sat in the center of the living room floor.

The moment the detectives left, he had ripped apart his closet to unearth it and dragged the heavy monstrosity to its current location. But now, he couldn't bring himself to open it.

He didn't want to let the ghosts out.

This is stupid. This is who you used to be. This isn't you now. Open the dang thing.

He got up and walked over to the trunk, lowered himself onto the floor, and sat inches from it, legs crossed. Then, he reached out and raised the latch that hadn't been touched since Gabriel left Wisconsin for the final time. Lastly, he creaked open the ancient chest itself to find a carefully folded red and black flannel shirt next to an intimidating tower of papers and folders.

The shirt had been his father's favorite. Gabriel slowly unfolded it to reveal a framed picture it had been protecting. He refolded the shirt with reverence and set it on the armrest of his leather couch. After looking closely at the happy picture of Billy and Ruthie Kane, taken on their wedding day, he took the framed picture and leaned it directly in front of the bottom of his television. He peered back into the trunk, and there it was. It had been obscured by the wrapped picture of his parents—the gun Billy used to end his own life, laying at the bottom of the chest with the deep pile of paperwork to its right. He left it in the trunk . . . for now. Finally, he transferred the substantial stack of paperwork to his dining room table before closing the trunk and pushing it against a wall.

His task for the day was enormous, and he knew it. He returned to the table with the largest coffee cup he owned, filled to the brim, and a plastic garbage bag in tow. He took in the hundreds of pages he could never bring himself to throw away without reading, and had no intention of ever reading, until today. He began at the top in his search for the name Michael Bale.

Gabriel had no idea that thanks to him, less than one hundred yards away, there were two detectives looking for the same man.

36.

"**Y**OU KNOW, AS A CATHOLIC, I CAN tell you I believe that God *can* speak to people. He can move people to do things. He can move people to say things. He can help people in need. What that priest told you . . . it isn't that far-fetched," Alvarez said as they approached Rob's front door.

"How many years has it been since you set foot in a Catholic Church, Alvarez?"

"Well, that depends." Alvarez smiled. "I was in the parking lot yesterday."

"*Inside* a church."

"How long has it been since I got married?"

"Which time?"

"The first time. The second go-round was just in a courthouse."

"My point is, I find myself for the second time in an hour asking the same question. You don't believe this insanity, do you?"

"Like I said . . . things like this happen in the world."

Gradillas rolled her eyes heavenward. "Oh my—"

"But I don't think they are happening to this guy. He's just a deranged freak show. I've got the door."

Gradillas walked to the corner of the unit where she had a visual on both exterior sides and every possible exit while Alvarez boldly walked right up to the door and knocked loudly.

"Police! Open up!"

He's always so subtle and cautious, Gradillas thought to herself.

Alvarez pounded on the door a second time. "Will you open up if I say I've got Girl Scout cookies?" He sauntered over to a window and cupped his hands to the sides of his face to look inside. "Can we *please* just say we heard a noise in *any* of these three units?"

"That would be a negatory, Detective Vigilante," Gradillas responded quickly.

Gradillas knew Alvarez was just venting. He was as by-the-book as she was. He just had a significantly shorter ramp-up period before hitting a ten on the frustration scale.

Alvarez's phone beeped. He pulled it out and read an incoming message with a smile.

"*Now* we are getting somewhere! Rob is at work. Let's go have a chat with the guy."

37.

THE DETECTIVES ROLLED TO A STOP in front of Humboldt Camping Supply. As they exited their respective cars, the boss immediately saw the badges and guns on their belts.

"Scruffy!"

"What?!" Rob's voice called from the back.

"You've got more friends!"

The bell above the door rang as the detectives entered.

"We are looking for a Robert Safranski," Alvarez said, skipping introductions.

"So you are just gonna use me to get to him, huh?" the boss muttered. "Not even gonna pretend like I meant anything to you?"

Rob sauntered out of the back, threw his arms out wide, and smiled broadly. "More cops! How exciting for me!"

"You are Robert Safranski?" asked Alvarez with a look of confusion.

"Yes. I'm black. Ever hear of adoption? It's this cool system where wonderful people raise a child who—"

"Yeah. I'm familiar with the concept. I'm a detective, so a hint of respect might be nice."

Two Woodstock time travelers—the only two customers in the place—looked at one another, trying to mask their alarm. They quickly made their way out the front door and into their van.

As it rambled out of the parking lot, the boss vented. "Come on, people! Ya just scared off half of my customers for a typical Wednesday!"

"Apologies, sir," Gradillas spoke up. "We just have some questions for your employee here."

"I know. I know," the boss grumbled. "I'll be in the back."

"Actually, we'd love it if you could stay. It'll only take a few minutes." Gradillas stopped him.

"What's stopping me from going on my lunch break right now?" The boss snapped.

"Absolutely nothing, sir." Gradillas remained cool. "But since we are looking for a suspect in a major case, if we don't get full cooperation, we'll be forced to get a warrant—"

"Go ahead!"

"—and if we have to get a warrant, I will personally live in one of your tents with my badge on full display until every square millimeter of this entire premises has been searched."

The boss wasn't a good actor and couldn't avoid looking like he was concealing something. Plus, the few customers he had didn't appreciate spending quality time with "the Man."

Alvarez chimed in with a grin, "Dude? She is not playin'."

"Fine. Lunch can wait."

"Good," Alvarez declared. "Now that we have two people to talk to, when did you last see Michael Bale?"

Rob was quick to protest. "I already told the officers—"

"Tell *me*," Alvarez interrupted.

"Two days ago."

"And you?" Alvarez turned to the boss.

"I don't even know who that is." The older man gestured.

"You both realize," Gradillas chimed in. "That since he is

wanted as a suspect in a murder . . . that if either of you lies to me, that makes you, at the very least, guilty of obstruction of justice? Quite possibly more."

"Come again?" The boss tilted his head.

Alvarez looked at him, smelling blood in the water. "Obstruction of justice at a minimum.

Accessory to murder if he's convicted. Neither of those are good, my man."

"What does this Michael kid look like?"

"Dude!" Rob yelled.

"What, man?" His boss turned on him. "Brindy ain't gonna pay my legal bills. Your buddy is a murder suspect? Naw, man. That is way above my anarchy tolerance level."

"Not cool, bro," Rob whispered.

"Rob!" Alvarez roared. "Shut your pie hole before I have to cuff you right now!"

Gradillas brought up a picture on her phone and showed the boss.

"He left just as the cops got here. He was parked out back. Picked up stuff to go camping."

"You dirty rat," Rob whispered.

"You're fired, scruffy," his boss replied sharply.

"Guys! Shut. It. Down." Alvarez was fantasizing about using his taser on both of these numbskulls.

"Where is he going?" Gradillas asked.

"Come on guys . . . it wasn't him." Rob pleaded.

"Where?!" Alvarez demanded again.

"Dead Horse Ranch. North side of Cottonwood," Rob quickly answered.

Alvarez spun and headed back outside dialing someone on his phone.

"Is he telling the truth?" She held the boss in a glare.

"Well, I don't—"

"I told you," Rob interjected. "Dead Horse Ranch. Don't hurt him."

"If you are lying, we'll know within the hour, and you'll be in jail before Mr. Bale."

"I know the odds of that happening in this country."

"That is *not* what this is about." Gradillas didn't appreciate the insinuation.

"Just don't hurt the guy. He's innocent."

Gradillas turned and left as quickly as she arrived.

Within moments, both cars were gone, and Rob headed for the back exit.

"Hey! Where do you think you're going?" the boss called after him.

"You fired me. On top of that, I've got less than an hour before the cops are looking for me again thanks to you, ya nark!"

"Wait, what? He's *not* at Dead Horse Ranch?"

"No. He's headed for Fool Hollow Lake. Or Lake Tahoe. Or freakin' Mongolia. Like I'd tell you!" Rob turned and headed into the back storage room.

"Awe, come on! I didn't—"

The door to the back alley slammed shut.

38.

ABOUT NINETY MINUTES OUTSIDE OF THE Phoenix area, Michael found himself grabbing some peanut butter cups in the town of Payson. He asked the guy behind the register if he'd ever heard of Woods Canyon Lake when a woman who was grabbing a few bags of chips said her family happened to be heading to the area to camp for the night before fishing tomorrow away. Michael followed her SUV the remaining 40 minutes. While not likely, Michael realized there was a chance the police had already found Rob and had begun a trace.

Even at this late hour on a weekday, the parking lot was more than half full with cars, trucks, and SUVs all trying to escape the summer heat back down the hill in Phoenix, more than six thousand feet below the pine-nestled lake. The only building within sight was a small general store selling boat rentals, bait, and over-priced camping supplies frequently forgotten by parents in their rush to escape their homes and work responsibilities.

Michael walked in and saw several people milling around and making important decisions. Did they really need s'mores bad enough to pay ten bucks for a small bag of marshmallows?

He grabbed two gallons of water, went over to the counter, and asked if a "Skye" worked here. He was told she was the camp host for the Spillway Campsite and was given a small map of the area. He was also charged five bucks for the water.

He drove his truck up and around to another road that descended through dense pine before it opened up into a large camping loop on a different shore of the lake.

Tents and RVs were scattered throughout the loop. Campfires were already lit, surrounded by adults laughing and talking away while their children ran free. As Michael gazed at this wonderland of friendship and family, a cute blonde girl of about twenty-three, wearing denim shorts, a small tank top, a campground baseball cap, and boots walked toward the driver side of the truck. Michael rolled down his window as the girl approached. He noticed the tiny piercing on the side of her nose and the wolf tattoo on her right shoulder.

"I'm Michael, and I'm going to guess you're Skye."

The girl leaned on his open window frame a bit flirtatiously. "And I'm gonna guess you are a cute psychic. Except . . . one thing. Spillways full." She stood back up. "Reservations only. But you can head back up that hill, hook a left, then a right, and there is a bigger campground right there. Not lakefront property but only about a mile from here. You can visit the lake from there to your heart's content."

"I guess that can work. Except . . . one thing. I'm supposed to tell you I'm Rob's friend."

"What?!" Skye jumped off the ground, throwing everything above the waist through Michael's open window to hug him. She didn't let go while he heard her muffled voice say, "I am so excited to meet you! If Rob is your friend, well, then you are my friend! What do you need, tall, dark, and Rob's friend?" Skye finally extricated herself from the truck.

"Well, I've never put up a tent before. Can you leave your post and follow me to the other campground to lend a hand for a few minutes?"

"Not going to happen." Skye shook her head earnestly. "Because you are setting up camp right here on my site."

"Oh, that really isn't necessary."

"Shut your face!" She leaned back through the open window and looked around. "Got anything to eat?"

"Some MREs from where Rob works."

"I thought you said he was your friend?" Skye smiled, amused at her own joke. "Okay, dude gorgeous. Here's the plan, pull off the road right over here. I'll help you unload. Then, you drive your beastly truck back to the general store. Tell Irma I want two of my steaks and a six-pack of Four Peaks. Scamper back as quickly as you can. Once the sun goes down, it gets real dark, real quick. Don't worry your sweet suburban head. I'll help you set up camp."

As they unloaded the truck, Michael realized Skye was grabbing heavier loads than he was, which was particularly damaging to his male ego considering she probably weighed less than half as much as he did.

He picked up the steaks and brew and was just pulling back into the campsite, worried they wouldn't have his tent up and a fire going before it became pitch black. Turns out, there was nothing to worry about.

In his short absence, Skye had set up his tent, loaded all his belongings into it, and had a campfire roaring. She was pulling some tinfoil, spices, and a huge pan out of the back of her old Volvo wagon.

"Oh, *there* you are!" she said through a wide smile.

"How did you . . .?"

"I'm not your average girl."

"Guess not."

"Now, get out those steaks. I'm only a non-vegetarian one night a week!"

39.

GABRIEL'S TRASH CAN WAS OVERFLOWING, and his patience was wearing thin. So far, he'd gone through what felt like a million pages, and they all added up to nothing. There was no mention of the name. That name his father would whisper repeatedly in his deepest moments of depression. The name Gabriel only knew as the child of the couple his dad's truck had killed when it malfunctioned.

The guilt his father couldn't shake.

All that was left was a single manila envelope tied with a single string of twine.

He opened it slowly. This was it.

The top page was an accident report. He skimmed down the page and saw the words "No-fault."

That doesn't add up. Dad won that major lawsuit, which was where all the money had come from. If the accident was "no-fault," then . . . then where did the money actually come from?

He reread the names to make sure it was the right accident. It was.

Gabriel wiped at his eyes and looked again.

"No-fault."

As a result of those two simple words, for the first time all day, he reserved a sheet of paper instead of tossing it in the trash. He placed it off to the left end of the table.

The next paper was a clipped article about a Dr. Bradley Wood.

And what the hell does this have to do with anything? He was found guilty of wrongful death in two cases. Two people died on his watch because he was an out of control addict. One of the victims was Mrs. Ruthie Kane.

So this is where the money came from? Someone murdered my mom. Kept me from ever knowing her. Someone named Dr. Bradley Wood. But why would dad intentionally mislead me? Why make me believe an entirely different narrative?

He set the clipping on top of the no-fault accident report. He planned on coming back to the esteemed Dr. Wood.

Then, there was an envelope from Synergy South County Hospital. In it, he found a bank deposit receipt for half a million dollars made out to his father. It also included paperwork saying his dad would not go public at any point in the future in exchange for the payoff.

What the hell?

As Gabriel restuffed the envelope and was setting it aside, he heard a voice singing horribly out of tune somewhere outside his window. It sounded exactly like that moron who threw a funeral for his beanbag. That idiot who slammed the dumpster lid when he first saw Michael with Rebecca. That simpleton who called Michael "Mikey." Gabriel jumped up from the table, grabbed his keys, and was out his front door.

—

Rob was on a serious high and not the kind people always accused him of being on either. He had a new friend, and he had just proved how far he would go for him. He equipped Michael to hide until they could prove his innocence. He threw the police off the trail. He was even willing to make himself a wanted man to help his brother. Now he was racing the clock to tell his buddy's girl why he wouldn't be able to make his date tomorrow night.

I'm a freaking hero.

As Rob was walking toward Rebecca's front door, he began singing "Holding Out for a Hero" by Bonnie Tyler. Poorly.

He bounded up the steps and knocked on her door. He waited a moment before knocking again. When no answer came, he reached into his pocket and pulled out a pen and an old fast food receipt from his wallet. On the back of the receipt, he wrote, *Michael can't make it tomorrow night. Not his fault. He'll be in touch.* He looked at the note, smiled for a moment, and added, *He really likes you.* He lifted Rebecca's doormat and used it to weigh down a corner of the receipt-turned-note. He then turned and skipped back down the steps as Gabriel quickly ducked under them.

As Rob was walking away, Gabriel slid around the rail, quietly ascended the stairs, grabbed the note, and read it. He turned to see Rob walking away.

"Hey!" he shouted at him from behind.

Rob turned to see Gabriel standing at the top of the steps, holding the note he just left for Rebecca.

"Whoa, dude! That ain't for you, bro!" Rob began walking back toward the stairs with machismo.

Meanwhile, Gabriel stuffed the note in his pocket while rapidly descending the steps. Just as Rob placed a foot on the bottom step, Gabriel placed his hands on each handrail, lifted himself off the steps, and kicked Rob squarely in the chest, launching him backward through the air until he landed on the sidewalk below with a sickening thud.

Before Rob could recover, Gabriel flew down the last few steps and kicked Rob in the ribs with enough impact to crack at least two of them. Rob rolled onto his side, curled, and wheezed in an effort to find a breath, but before he could, Gabriel had circled Rob and unleashed another ferocious kick to Rob's lower back, landing with such force that Rob's curled form sprang from its position as he cried out in shocked pain.

"Where is he?!" Gabriel demanded.

Rob couldn't speak. He could hardly move.

"You think he is the only one?!" Gabriel shouted as he taunted Rob by grinding the heel of his foot into Rob's side. "It happens to me too, except I'm different. I've evolved."

Rob summoned the will to gasp out, "Would you please . . . just . . . shut the hell up?"

In a rage, Gabriel scrambled down to straddle Rob's battered body and savagely gripped him under his chin. "Hey! Hey! Look! At! Me! Who do you think murdered that woman in the canal? Huh? Who?" He gathered himself with an alligator grin. "And here's the fun part. No one will believe you. Your word against mine. You are friends with a murderer. Of course you would try to discredit a witness. And just look at our lives. Who's gonna believe you? Now! You are going to answer me. Where is Michael Bale?"

"Dead . . ."

"Not yet, jackass, but I'll get you there soon enough if you don't answer me."

"Dead Horse . . ." was all Rob could say through Gabriel's grip on his throat.

A voice shouted from behind Gabriel, "Is everything alright over there?"

Gabriel looked over his shoulder to see a middle-aged businessman about twenty feet away walking toward him. Gabriel jumped to his feet and walked directly toward the man.

He put on a slightly panicked voice. "I think that guy just got mugged! Call the cops! I'm going to get a first aid kit!"

Gabriel went straight to his unit and carried his trunk over to the table. It still contained his father's gun. He tossed in all the papers from that final folder, everything he'd read and everything he hadn't gotten to. Then, he took his father's shirt off the armrest of the couch and placed it inside. Lastly, he grabbed the picture of his parents and tucked it safely in the trunk as well. With that done, he latched and carried the trunk out toward his car.

"Stop!" a voice called out from behind him.

He turned to see the businessman standing there with his cell phone out, taking his picture.

Gabriel slowly lowered the trunk to the ground. "Now, what are you doin'?"

"He told me you attacked him," the man answered nervously. "So I'm taking your picture for the police!"

"Well, let's make it a good one."

Gabriel smiled broadly for a brief moment. The flash of a smile was just enough to confuse the man and caused him to let his guard down. Gabriel went from a standstill to a dead sprint in the blink of an eye. The man stumbled backward for a second before trying to turn and run, but by the time he was able to regain his balance and make a break for it, Gabriel was on him. Gabriel shoved him hard, sending him tripping into a face-first slide. The phone skittered out in front of him. Gabriel stood over the shaking man, waiting for him to stand.

Slowly, the man rose and looked at Gabriel face to face for an instant before Gabriel grabbed the phone and deleted the picture. Then, he unleashed a nasty right hook, knocking the man out. He looked around at all the windows surrounding him. Deleting the photo was one thing, but there were too many potential witnesses for anything more. He pocketed the man's phone and was on his way.

40.

ALVAREZ HAD TOLD GRADILLAS HE WOULD wait for local backup out of Cottonwood, but he lied. If Michael was camping somewhere in Dead Horse Ranch State Park, Alvarez wanted to find him and make sure he didn't hurt anyone else. Besides, he had limited time before sundown, which would make searching the park infinitely more difficult.

He had methodically driven from campsite to dusty campsite, asking each person if they had seen anyone matching Michael's description. No one had, and his mood was quickly deteriorating. Although the park was situated about one hundred miles north of Phoenix, it was nestled in a valley where the temperatures were hardly cooler than the sweltering Phoenix heat. The name alone should have tipped him off.

All was not lost. There were two sites set up whose occupants had been gone all day. One obviously belonged to a family, as evidenced by miniature camping chairs and toys tossed about. He didn't give that one a second thought.

The other site, on the other hand, had his full attention.

It contained a single tent and a single burner stove set up on the provided picnic table. Alvarez didn't enter the tent but peeked through the mesh ventilation to see a single sleeping bag. It fit the profile perfectly. Alvarez approached a site a bit closer to the park entrance than Michael's possible site, flashed a badge, and let them know he would be parking next to their RV.

"You have nothing to worry about. Just a guy way overdue on his child support." Alvarez lied. "I'll never get out of my car. You won't even know I'm here. Although, if you bring me one of those hot dogs I'm smellin', I wouldn't complain."

As night fell, Alvarez settled in and waited for Michael to return.

41.

THE BUSINESSMAN, WHO HAD INTRODUCED HIMSELF to Rob as Jack Doyle, was squatting next to Rob's battered body. Jack had gradually helped move Rob onto the bottom step below Rebecca's condo.

"Friend? I know you told me not to call the cops, but I really think—"

"Dude! No! Please! I am trying to practice the ancient art of forgiveness!"

In truth, Rob didn't know if the police had already discovered his lie. If they had already gotten to Dead Horse Ranch and Michael wasn't there, he might end up beaten senseless *and* in a jail cell. He needed to get to Michael and warn him. This guy was after him and was much more dangerous than the police, but Rob's ribs were now throbbing in pain.

"Fine. Can I at least call someone or help you get somewhere?"

"No, Jack. I appreciate you more than you know." Rob grunted at a surge of fire in his side. "A lot of people would've just kept walking. Thank you. Seriously. Thank you so much. You're a good man."

"Well . . . alright. If you need anything, call me. Here is my card."

Jack extended his business card. Rob slowly took it, wincing slightly, and glanced at it to see the words "Jack Doyle, Doyle's Fine Books." With that, the conflicted Jack Doyle, against his better judgment, slowly turned and left the wounded young man on the step.

Rob stuffed the business card in his pocket and strained to sit a bit more upright.

"Oh my God! Are you alright?"

Rob looked up to see a dark-haired woman standing before him, holding her textbooks with a laptop bag over her shoulder.

"Rebecca?"

Rebecca looked at the beaten man with suspicion. "How do you know my name?"

"Michael sent me to give you a message."

"Uh, okay." A combination of confusion and relief swept across her face. "But if you are able, let's get you up these steps, so I can take care of you. Give me one second. I'll be right back."

Rebecca ran her things up the stairs and into her home. She came back down and slowly helped him up to her living room, step by step.

She tried to gradually lower Rob, but he collapsed onto a couch in the beautiful but simple room filled with Ikea furniture. The room had been given delicate, feminine touches Rob would never think to add. Fresh sunflowers. Lush, green plants. Framed pictures of family laughing. It would've been a beautiful place to recover if only there was time. Rebecca was around the corner in her small kitchen prepping a cold pack.

She returned to her living room, knelt before Rob, and pressed the pack against his ribs, gently moving his arm to hold the pack on his own. She vanished into her bathroom and emerged with a small homemade first aid kit. She wiped a bit of blood from the back of his head that he didn't even realize was there.

"You might have a concussion. We need to get you to a hospital to get checked out. You can tell me whatever you need to on the way."

"No. I can't go to a hospital, or I might get arrested."

"Excuse me?" Rebecca took an instinctive step back.

"You are gonna wanna sit down for this."

As Rebecca sat in a chair directly across from Rob, he proceeded to tell her everything he knew. Michael was wanted for murder—a murder Gabriel had committed. Gabriel was claiming to possess the same ability as Michael. Both the police and Gabriel were hunting for Michael, but he was hiding out in a campground east of Payson. And Rob had lied to both the police and Gabriel and told both parties that Michael could be found at another state park two hours west of his actual location.

As he wrapped up, Rebecca was no longer looking at him. She was just staring out her window processing it all. She needed a moment to catch up.

Rob waited until he decided the message had officially been delivered. It was time to grab a few things from home and head for Michael. "Well, there you go. Thanks for patchin' me up. I guess I should get goin'."

Still not looking away from the window, Rebecca murmured, "When are we heading to his campsite?"

The question froze Rob in place. "Huh?"

Snapping out of it, she looked at Rob and asked more firmly, "When are we heading to his campsite?"

"Whoa. Hey there, I dunno what you are talkin' about."

"As I see it, Michael is wanted by the law and a psychopath, and if you aren't wanted by the law and the same psychopath, you will be soon enough. The psychopath has a thing for me, so I'm not sticking around. The three of us need to figure out what to do next."

"Wait. The nutcase likes you?"

Rebecca fidgeted in her chair. "Yeah. You could say that."

"Oh. That's not good. He knows you two had a date scheduled for tomorrow night, and he was spying on the two of you when you were talking on the steps outside the other day. Bet that didn't make him happy either."

"Well, obviously if he is trying to pin a murder on Michael."

"But now he wants to find him. Why? I don't get it."

The question only hung in the air for a brief moment.

"He's gonna try to kill Michael," Rebecca said as it became clear.

"No, he won't." Rob stood and winced again as he took a slow breath. "I've got one friend who gets me, Rebecca, and some nut job ain't gonna hurt 'im."

"Sit back down. I'll be packed and ready to go in five minutes. You just turn off your phone and remove the battery in case the police are already onto you. I'll do the same just to be overly cautious. I'll help you to your place, and we'll get you packed. We'll head there tonight. I wish you could rest up a bit, but we can't be here when Gabriel gets back."

"Does removing the battery actually work?"

"No idea. Saw it in a movie. And one more thing . . . and this isn't up for debate. I'm driving."

"But I know where we are going, and some of my gear is already in Bosco."

"Bosco?"

"Bosco is my sweet Bronco's name."

"Ah. Okay. So I'll drive Bosco, and you'll point me in the right direction."

"No one drives Bosco but me."

"Except tonight." Rebecca got up and got packing.

42.

GABRIEL PULLED HIS SHELBY MUSTANG INTO a well-lit gas station on the north end of the Phoenix metro area. As he began pumping the gas, his finger pulled the lever to keep the flow going, so he could leave it there and open the trunk of his car.

There, he unlatched his father's wooden chest, pulled out the paperwork, and tossed everything he'd already seen back into the trunk.

He paged through several legal papers that showed his father had sold anything of value before his suicide. Receipts. Bank statements. A paper showing the consolidation of accounts.

Following these papers, Gabriel found a copy of the last will and testament of William Kane. He had seen another copy of it shortly after his father's body had been found. It was straightforward. His father left him everything. Everything but a dad. Everything but what he had needed the most.

Next, there were two newspaper clippings stapled together. The first was an article that gave the results of a regional high school cross country meet. The winner was Joshua Jenkins. Second place was an athlete named Vince Benniker. The runner who finished third was highlighted. The athlete's name was Michael Bale.

The second clipping was a list of high school honor roll graduates. Again, one name was highlighted. Michael Bale.

Only a single sheet of paper remained—the single sheet of paper that changed everything.

43.

THE DOOR SWUNG OPEN, AND DR. WOOD entered the room. He sat gently on the wheeled stool across from the nervous couple and slid it gently toward them before taking a quick breath and exhaling into a warm smile.

"Ruthie? Billy? You look worried. There is no need to be. Everyone in this room is healthy."

Ruthie's tensed shoulders dropped visibly in relief.

The doctor then looked at Billy. "Well, I can't vouch for you, dad."

With everyone's ongoing health established, Billy's mind immediately moved on to the next mystery. He wanted to know if it was a boy or girl. Truth be told, he didn't have a preference, but the curiosity was killing him.

Only seconds had passed as the doctor let the young couple enjoy a few moments of peace. Billy wasn't feeling very patient. "So doc, have anything else you'd like to share?"

"Yes. As a matter of fact, I do. You are having boys."

Billy leapt to his feet, pumping his fist as he quickly imagined raising a son. "We're having a boy! A boy!" He bent over to speak directly to his son still residing within Ruthie who remained frozen—not that Billy noticed. "Junior! Can you hear me? You're my boy! Wooh!"

Billy went back to his private touchdown celebration.

Ruthie reached up and fumbled for Billy's arm without looking away from the doctor. "Can you repeat yourself for my husband?"

Billy's party abruptly stopped when he realized Ruthie's hand was trembling. "What? Didn't you hear the man? He said we're having a . . ."

His brain seemed to replay a freshly recorded audio track at the same instant the doctor repeated the word, "Boys."

Billy Kane showed his character. Despite the earth-shaking panic welling up within him, his voice managed to say nine words with complete calm. "Twins. So we get two angels instead of one."

44.

AFTER THE STEAK AND TWO BEERS, Michael was done. His mind and body seemed to realize he was safe. Every part of Michael Bale was completely spent, and it was time to shut down. He crawled into his tent and was snoring within minutes.

Outside, Skye kept the fire going. This was her favorite part of her camp hosting gig. The vast majority of the campers on her loop were down for the night, and the only two things she could hear were the crackle of her fire and the sounds of the forest. The massive canopy of stars mingled with silhouettes of towering trees overhead.

In the distance, she heard the rumble of a truck approaching. She cocked her head a bit and listened a bit more closely. "Bosco?" As soon as she was sure, her joy could've lit up the night. "No freakin' way."

As headlight beams began to shoot through the trees from up the road, Skye jumped up from her camping chair and ran into the camp road. She waited impatiently as the Bronco slowly crept into the campsite. As soon as the headlights moved around the last turn and struck her, she jumped up and down waving her arms in the air for a moment before pointing the truck into a spot next to Michael's.

Skye ran up to the driver-side door and pulled it open. She didn't find who she expected in the driver's seat. Her heart traveled from flittering to confused in a single moment, and it showed.

"Uh, who are you?"

Rebecca looked over at her and let her turned head fall against the headrest. "I'm exhausted."

"Um, I'm Skye."

In that instant, Skye saw Rob sitting in the passenger seat. He managed a half-smile and a single wave of his hand. "Hey."

The small movement caused an involuntary grimace.

"Hey." Skye's voice sounded concerned. "What's wrong?!"

She flew to the other side of the truck and opened Rob's door.

"I got beat up by Bruce Lee."

"Is that Bruce Lee?" Skye asked as she looked beyond Rob to Rebecca, ready to rumble.

Rob laughed in pain for a moment before he shook his head. "No. No. This is Rebecca. She's a friend of Michael's." Rob swallowed for a moment and looked over at the truck. "Is he asleep?"

"Full, buzzed, and passed out in his tent."

"Thanks for taking care of him. He's one of the good ones."

"You are most welcome. Now, let me get you out of Bosco, so I can take care of you." She looked over to Rebecca with a twinkle. "Are you a *really* good friend of Michael's?"

Rebecca just looked back at her, slightly baffled.

"She is asking if you want to sleep in Michael's tent." Rob explained without turning to face her.

"Oh. Uh, what are my options?"

"Well." Skye tilted her head. "Rob will be staying in my tent, so we can either set up Rob's tent for you, or you can sleep in Michael's tent. I'd rather not set up Rob's tent because I'd like to be able to take care of him right away. Plus, it's really late, and I don't wanna wake up other campers."

"Skye?" Rob interjected. "We are not dating."

"Yet, Rob." She exhaled with an air of frustration and a look heavenward. "We are not dating, yet."

Rob smiled just a bit.

"I'm not sleeping with you, ya big lug!" Skye continued. "Listen. Michael is hibernating, Rebecca looks like she needs to be, and you need a beautiful camp host to nurse you back to health. So relax. I'm not going to seduce you . . . yet."

Rob's smile grew. "As long as we're clear. I'm an honorable man after all."

"I know, Robby. And that's why I love . . . hanging out with you."

Rebecca was feeling a bit more awkward by the moment. She didn't want to be in Michael's tent. It was too soon. It would be weird in the morning. Everything about it seemed inappropriate or presumptuous. But she didn't want to rock the boat either.

"It's fine. I'll just grab a sleeping bag and crash in Michael's tent."

"Okay!" Skye chirped and immediately began helping Rob out of the passenger seat.

As Skye helped Rob gingerly into her tent, Rebecca opened the back of Rob's Bronco. Skye reappeared, extinguished the remnants of the campfire by stirring nearly a barrel of water into it, and walked over to stand next to her to get Rob's things out.

"Hey," she whispered. "I don't want you to get the wrong impression of me. I know I have the name of a free love goddess, but I just want to take care of Robby."

"I get it," Rebecca said briefly, wanting nothing more to do with this topic.

"No. Seriously." Skye wouldn't let it go.

"Oh I didn't think—"

"I think we'll get married one day. But I'm not crazy, ya know."

"Oh." Rebecca tried to keep a poker face. "Wow."

"Yeah. I know. But I'm not crazy. I know he has to get the message too."

"That's very—"

"But he will. I know he will."

Rebecca finally decided to wait in silence.

"You know what?" Skye pointed at her. "You are a great listener."

Rebecca waited an extra beat before responding, "Thank you."

Skye turned her petite shoulders to face Rebecca directly and wrapped her arms around Rebecca, hugging her. "I can see why Michael would like you."

As the hug subsided, Rebecca looked down at Skye and asked, "Just curious. Did he say something about it?"

"Listen, sister. My heart might belong to Robby, but Michael doesn't know that . . . and most guys seem to think I'm pretty hot."

Rebecca shrugged a bit as she said, "You are a beautiful girl."

"Thanks! I really do like you! Anyway, Michael definitely acted like a taken man tonight."

"How do you mean?"

"A woman knows when a guy is checking her out. Most guys check me out, but all night, the entire time we spent together I felt like I was spending time with my big brother."

"Maybe it's just because he is a really good guy." Rebecca reasoned.

"I think he is. But let me ask you a question. The last time you two were together, did you feel like *you* were spending time with your big brother?"

"No . . . no, I didn't," she confessed.

"Then he *is* taken. Taken by you." Skye put a sleeping bag in Rebecca's arms and reached back into Bosco to pull out the rest of Rob's stuff. She turned to Rebecca, winked, and said, "Behave yourself."

In a flash, Skye was back in her tent, and Rebecca was left alone under the enormous blanket of stars.

She took the sleeping bag and crept toward Michael's tent, unzipping it as slowly and quietly as she could manage. The way Michael was snoring, she doubted she would wake him, but she didn't want even the slightest possibility of that happening. She stepped in and then slowly rezipped the flap. She turned and realized it was far from pitch black inside.

Because the forecast showed no possibility of rain in the area, Skye had not attached the canopy to the screen at the center of the roof, and as a result, the stars were giving the interior of the tent a slight illumination.

She looked down and saw that Michael had shifted and was sprawled out diagonally, leaving two triangles of available real estate, neither large enough for a grown human to sleep comfortably. She chose the one closer to the entrance and unfurled the sleeping bag. Over the next five minutes, Rebecca did a dance of awkwardness as she wriggled herself vertically into her sleeping bag. From a standing position within the sleeping bag, she slowly lowered herself into a ball in the corner she'd chosen.

As she tried to relax, she took stock of her current situation. Wearing her clothes in her sleeping bag. No indoor bathroom. Teeth that hadn't been brushed. Cold. Unable to lay down comfortably and stretch out fully. Stuck in a small tent with a tall snoring man.

How did I get here? Less than a week ago, I hadn't even met the man sleeping right next to me. Less than a day ago, I hadn't met the other guy I just drove into the wilderness with. And less than an hour ago, I hadn't met the girl who just gave me relationship advice. Granted, what she said made sense. If Michael gave someone who looked like Skye every impression that he was her brother, but everything about him compelled me to reach over and place my hand in his, there must be a reason. Maybe Michael is taken by me.

She realized she hoped so.

She listened to him snoring, smelling a combination of his deodorant, sweat, and campfire smoke. She could see the outline of his chest rising and falling. Memories of the past few days filled her mind. Looking out her window to watch him walk away after she'd first met him. The way he smiled at her when they met up outside of the restaurant on their date. How he described a life lived for others, not his own. How her hand felt when it touched his.

She was suddenly overwhelmed with the desire to sidle up against Michael's side. To feel his warmth against her own. To move closer, feeling safe and cared for.

Nope. This is not happening.

Rebecca quickly unzipped her bag and stood, bunching her bag back up in her arms, and got out of the tent as quickly as she could muster. She walked over to the Bronco where she intended to sleep, opened the driver-side door, and slid in. As she spread her sleeping bag out like a blanket and reclined the seat, she heard a grunt. She spun around to see Rob stretched across the backseat.

Yeah. This is so much better.

She did her best to relax, closed her eyes, and was out in less than five minutes.

45.

AS THEY MADE THEIR WAY BACK into the little apartment that suddenly seemed even smaller, Billy remained stuck in a silence he couldn't seem to shake. The feeling of imprisonment was so strong, he hardly moved beyond the doorway and into the apartment.

He knew it wasn't fair to Ruthie, and she probably needed reassurance in a time like this, but he couldn't muster the strength. It was as if he'd used up all of it in that initial moment, but the drive home took too long and left a window for the reality to set in.

"Billy?"

Billy wasn't ready for this conversation. He needed to think. He needed solutions. His brain kept trying to run through different ways he could possibly make enough money for this new reality.

Selling a kidney? Drug smuggling? Moving the four of us into my beer truck?

"Billy! Come here!" She was summoning him to the bedroom where she was on the bed seemingly staring up to heaven.

Billy laid down next to her and stared upward as well. Might as well. God only knew how they'd get through this.

After a few moments of deafening silence, Ruthie spoke again. "I still can't believe it. I mean, you would think I'd be able to tell."

Billy turned his head on the pillow to look at his young bride. "Are you okay? I know we didn't plan on this happening so soon."

"Yeah. We definitely didn't plan on this." Ruthie laughed, looking back at her young husband. "I don't think we could've. But somehow . . . and maybe I'm in shock . . . I couldn't be happier." She smiled that radiant smile that first hooked him during their freshman year of high school.

He never understood how a young woman so beautiful from the jump could multiply her beauty with a smile. That smile ignited a light of hope in Billy.

"I'm happy too," he tentatively began, but as is often the case, the smile of a strong woman can instantly refresh the reserves of courage in a man. "I'm going to be such a cool dad. I mean, I guess you'll be okay too. But those boys will have the coolest dad in the world."

"Since you brought them up." Ruthie turned onto her side and leaned against her man, her head on his chest. "I decided what our kids' names will be."

Billy said, "Oh, really?"

"Yup."

"Well," Billy began, amused by the strong woman he had married. "Do I have any say in this?"

Ruthie reached up and tenderly touched Billy's cheek with her hand. "You are the one who gave me the idea."

"And just how did I do that?"

Ruthie turned over completely and began to kiss Billy ever so softly. And as their lips still mingled, she whispered, "When you said, 'We get two angels instead of one.' So . . . I want to name them Gabriel and Michael. Our little angels."

46.

ALVAREZ'S POSTURE WAS GETTING WORSE BY the minute as he continued to gradually slide lower and lower behind the steering
wheel, losing the battle to remain awake in the darkness of the
state park. About an hour ago, he was mercifully brought a hot
dog and a s'more from the nearest campers, but he had to turn
down the wine cooler they offered. His refusal was more about
trying to remain conscious than being on the clock.

Although he was all alone, he did have backup. Local police
weren't willing to man a stake-out location on such a long shot,
but they *were* willing to be on call. If Alvarez saw Michael drive
by, the plan was for him to call them and wait until they arrived
in an unmarked car before approaching the suspect.

*If that smartass from the camping store told me the truth, this has
to be his campsite, and it is only a matter of time before he returns
for the night. If the guy from the camping store lied and this was just
one big goose chase, or if he called and tipped off his buddy, I'll arrest
the guy myself. And I'll make sure I slam the guy's head into the police
car's door frame on "accident." Okay, probably not. But a healthy
imagination is . . . healthy.*

He was getting nervous because, at some point, he'd have to relieve himself. Knowing his luck, that would be the precise moment his friendly neighborhood killer would return home from his daylong bird-watching expedition.

Alvarez didn't actually think Michael was taking up ornithology, and that made him significantly more nervous than the state of his bladder.

Where has this guy been all day? The two most likely scenarios are both nightmares. Either I'm just sitting around while he's victimizing someone else, or that Safranski kid warned him, and he's two states away by now.

Alvarez was roused from his thoughts by two headlights creeping into the camping area. As they neared, Alvarez was discouraged as he realized the headlights belonged to a car instead of Michael's truck. So unless he'd switched vehicles, this wasn't going to be Michael.

As the car neared, Alvarez was able to identify it as a classic Shelby. The car was a beautifully crafted piece of machinery, and Alvarez had only seen one other car like it in person. It belonged to . . . it belonged to their primary witness.

"What the hell are you doin' here?" Alvarez mumbled aloud from behind his steering wheel. "You'll either ruin this whole thing, get yourself killed, or both."

The car was crawling by as Alvarez jumped from his vehicle and began walking after it in the darkness, shrouded in a dim red shadow behind the growl of the slow-moving Mustang. Alvarez watched in momentary interest to see if the car would stop at the site he once again thought must be Michael's, but it just kept rolling. Alvarez stopped and stood in the middle of the camp road as he waited. If he pursued Gabriel, that would probably be the precise moment Michael would show up. Besides, the Mustang was only a few sites from a dead end and would have to circle back within two minutes.

As he stood in the darkness, Alvarez wondered whether he

should let Gradillas know that Gabriel just joined the party. The last text he'd sent her was to inform her that he thought he might've found Michael's campsite and was going to wait for his return. He promised to get backup when Michael arrived. He pulled out his phone and was about to text her when the headlights made their way back. As they hit Alvarez square in the face, he clicked off the phone, stuffed it in his pocket, and walked quickly toward Gabriel.

I never promised to text if an intellectually-challenged witness showed up.

Gabriel pulled to a stop and quickly exited his car to face Alvarez.

With an angry whisper, as to keep from waking up the campers in the nearest sites, Alvarez ordered, "You need to get the hell out of here right now!"

"Where is he?" Gabriel whispered.

"Listen, kid," Alvarez said with added urgency. "You need to get out of here! Now!"

"Okay. But first, I have to show you something that proves he's guilty." Gabriel turned and started walking back toward the trunk.

"No!" Alvarez whispered in anger. "You need to listen to me!"

Gabriel looked to be an over-eager witness too excited to retain an ounce of common sense. He seemed nervous as he opened the trunk of his car. He reached in and pulled out a pair of gloves.

"I've been careful not to disturb the chain of evidence," he said as he slipped on the gloves. Then, glancing over at Alvarez, he asked, "That is what it's called, right?"

"Gabriel!" Alvarez was done. "We have everything we need. We have your testimony. We have DNA placing him at the scene of the crime. So unless you've got a signed confession—"

"But detective, I do have a confession!" Gabriel unlatched the wooden trunk and opened it with a creak. "Look for yourself."

Alvarez was bewildered.

What could he possibly have?

He stepped forward and looked into the trunk. All he saw was a pile of papers, a flannel shirt, and a gun.

Without warning, a strong arm wrapped around his neck from behind and cut the air from his throat. Gabriel hissed, "It wasn't Michael, and it wasn't his mom. It was his brother."

As Alvarez's head began to throb, shock overtook his training. He reached up and scratched away at Gabriel's arm, trying in vain to find air.

"Who's the idiot now? You arrogant little prick!"

The taunt snapped Alvarez back to his training. He reached up and gripped the back of Gabriel's head, preparing to use his lower center of gravity to wrench Gabriel's head forward and flip him over his shoulder.

Gabriel quickly countered by thrusting his left foot between the detective's feet to increase his leverage.

A mere ten seconds into the struggle, Alvarez knew his time was limited as the grip on his neck kept tightening.

With his last thread of consciousness, he reached down for his sidearm. Gabriel used his brute strength advantage to lift Alvarez off the ground and spin him, slamming him face-first into the hard, unforgiving dusty road, never letting go of his chokehold. The oxygen deprivation to the brain quickly finished its work. When the body beneath him went completely limp, he snapped Alvarez's neck with a quick, merciless twist.

47.

REBECCA WOKE UP WITH A STIFF neck that only an uncomfortable night spent sleeping behind the wheel of a truck can produce. She wiped the sleep out of her eyes to see Rob standing directly in front of the truck, shirtless, with an enormous mug of coffee and a big grin. His side was wrapped, and his friendly face was covered with three Band-Aids.

"Hey, everybody! Sleeping beauty has awakened!"

Skye came running up to the door and swung it open. "Good morning, big sis! Want some coffee? Oatmeal? Beer?"

Rebecca was used to waking up a bit slower than this but did her best to hide it. "Coffee will be fine."

"Cool!" Skye bounded back toward the campsite picnic table with Rob.

Michael approached. "I don't want to be presumptuous, but you seem pretty determined to get that second date."

She stiffly stepped out of the truck. "Good guess, but I really just wanted to be alone with Rob for a long drive in the woods."

Michael looked over at Rob who was talking to Skye by the relit campfire and flapping his arms like a chicken for some reason . . . or for no reason at all. "I can see the animal magnetism."

Rebecca suddenly remembered she had on yesterday's clothes and yesterday's makeup.

How is it Michael looks like he's just showered? It isn't fair.

Michael looked back at her. "Just to make my intentions clear, know that I intend to fight him for your affections." He turned and walked back toward Rob and Skye.

Rebecca walked over to join them, and Skye handed her a mug of coffee as large as Rob's. "It'll kickstart your heart."

"Sorry." Rob sat slowly into a camping chair. "This won't be a typical, chill camping expedition. We need to figure out our next step."

Skye placed three other camping chairs near Rob's. "Yeah. I think you're all swell, but I can only harbor fugitives for so long. Most of the people who camp here are from the valley, and if your pictures have been released to the press, someone will recognize you within a day or two at most." She sat in the chair closest to Rob.

Rebecca sat and sipped her coffee. "So this guy is a raving lunatic and wants Michael dead. The cops think Michael is the killer. And Rob is wanted by the police as well. How can we possibly point the cops toward Gabriel before they catch Michael?"

Rob looked at each of them. "Any of you professional interrogators?"

Michael took the fourth seat and looked at Rob. "Sure. A confession would be nice, but based on what he said to you, he hears the same way I do, so the real trick is catching someone who is always one step ahead."

"Well, dude, you are always one step ahead, so which came first, the chicken or the egg?"

"Rob? No offense. I don't even know what you're saying."

"Are you the rock, paper, or scissors? And which is he?"

"Not sure he wants to sit down for a game of roshambo to determine who goes to jail."

"The question remains." Rebecca interrupted, getting every-one back on track. "How do you get ahead of the guy who is always a step ahead?"

Michael shook his head. "If we stick with the game analogies, that's a tough game to win."

"I was a soccer player!" Skye volunteered out of the blue.

"Never told me you had Tourette's," Rob said with a wink.

"One, Tourette's is a serious syndrome. Two, there was a point. So extend me the same patience you seem to expect of me." Rob closed his mouth and looked away while she went on. "When I played, I got in trouble because whenever my team started getting rocked by the other team, I would just start tack-ling everyone on the other team."

"Was this in high school?" asked Rebecca.

"I wasn't even ten yet."

"Now that isn't surprising." Rob laughed.

"Again, still a point."

His smile disappeared again. "Sorry."

"Even as a little girl, I believed that if you can't beat someone, change the game."

Michael sat up a little straighter. "Okay, what are you suggesting?"

"If Rebecca and I were going head-to-head in a fire-making competition, she should pull out a lighter."

"Hey." Rebecca looked at Rob. "Got one I could borrow?"

"I'm offended by your insinuation." He grinned at her.

"I cannot believe I'm the focused one here," Skye said with a hint of actual frustration.

"No." Michael objected. "I'm with you. We need to find an advantage."

"He likes you, right?" Skye looked to Rebecca.

"He does." She shifted uncomfortably.

"No," Michael interjected. "That is not going to happen."

"I'm just saying. Men will drop what they're doing and follow a beautiful woman wherever she wants." Skye continued.

"Since when?" Rob faux-protested.

"Since Adam and Eve." Michael was gently shaking his head. "Doesn't matter. Not going to happen."

"You sound pretty confident in a woman's ability to influence a man." Rob looked at Skye, obviously still in pain but trying to hide it.

"You know I am." She looked right back at him.

Michael didn't like where this was headed. "So you expect her to just walk up to a killer and ask him to confess to murder? It's reckless, and on top of that, if he is trying to win her over, he probably won't try to win her over with, 'I'm a murdering murderer who likes to murder. What do you do in your free time?'"

Rob shook his head. "No. That's not what Skye's saying—"

Rebecca looked into the fire. "I'm the only one who can draw him out."

"He's the rat." Rob nodded.

"What?" Skye asked.

"There was a rat in the workroom. We couldn't catch it. Not until I put peanut butter, bacon bits, and a touch of honey—"

"Are you guys listening? Doesn't matter. It's not worth it." Michael looked at Rebecca. "We aren't serving you up to this guy on a silver platter."

Rebecca still hadn't looked away from the fire. "I'm not enough."

"Girl. Do not underestimate your hotness," Skye said.

Still not looking from the fire, Rebecca continued. "I'm not enough. I am the only one who can draw him out, but I won't be able to get the confession. Only Michael will be able to do that."

Rob leaned forward. "Go on, Ms. Mastermind!"

"The trap has to be irresistible enough to overcome any warning he gets. His confidence will be enough to make him want to meet me anywhere. But once he's there, his hatred of Michael might be enough to make him confess."

"You're the peanut butter." Rob looked at Rebecca. "And you are the bacon bits." He looked at Michael.

"What about the honey?" Skye asked.

"Well, that's clearly you. But that has nothing to do with catching this Gabriel guy."

"Aw." Skye was glowing.

"You might be right Rebecca," Michael conceded. "But I don't want you anywhere near him when he's in a rage."

"I might be able to convince him with a phone call, but I don't want you to be alone with him either. When he shows up somewhere to meet me, and you are there waiting for him, how will you get a confession and not get yourself killed?"

"He won't be alone." Rob sat straight up and shielded the pain it caused.

"Listen, brother." Michael smiled softly. "I appreciate everything you've already done, but you aren't in any condition to be of much help in a physical confrontation."

Rebecca had an idea. "Maybe he doesn't have to be. Skye, would you be able to take a few days off on extremely short notice?"

Skye smiled and coughed two little pitiful coughs. "I think I might be coming down with something."

"Oh, I'm sorry to hear that." Rebecca winked at Skye. "Rob? You down?"

"You know it. What're you thinking?"

48.

L IKE A PICTURE THAT IS ENTIRELY out of focus, with the exception of a single subject, there was only one singular moment of clarity. It consisted of a few brief seconds and a nurse saying, "Your first boy is healthy."

"Gabriel." Billy managed to mumble.

"Gabriel. Gabriel is healthy. But during your second baby's . . ."

"Michael."

"Michael. Michael is going to be okay. But during Michael's delivery, there was a complication . . ."

Complication.

That was the word she used. For the nurse, this word seemed to explain away everything that happened that day. And it was that simple word that demolished Billy and drove him to the hospital floor in a pile of shattered pieces that used to add up to a man.

49.

GRADILLAS WAS TOLD TO STAY AWAY, but it would've taken an army to keep her from seeing for herself.

As her car skidded to a stop in the dirt just short of the police line, she saw a mixed bag of law enforcement types milling around comparing notes. Some she knew from the Tempe Department, some local uniforms, some state, and quite a few mystery guests in plain clothes.

Gradillas walked toward the line like she knew where she was going. She flashed her badge and smiled at the boys. Then, she ducked under and walked as close to the center of the action as possible before someone recognized her. As expected, it was her direct supervisor, Sergeant Hutson, who also happened to be the man who told her to stay back in the valley.

"Gradillas!"

She kept walking.

"Gradillas! What the hell are you doing here?"

Gradillas pulled up, took a deep breath, and turned to the barrel-chested man chasing her down. "Boss. I just—"

"No." He closed his eyes, shaking his head vigorously. "No. Walk back to your car."

"Just hear me out. No one else has been in this guy's house. No one else has talked to his best friend or reviewed his family history. Who else has talked to his boss? And I've done it all this week! It's fresh. I know this guy better than anyone else here. Let me help you catch him."

"And nobody else here just lost their partner, detective. You won't be thinking clearly."

"Just let me look. If I can't help you, I can't help you. Just let me look around for a few minutes. Stick someone to my hip if you need to. I don't care if someone is watching me."

"Gradillas."

"Sergeant."

Hutson nodded his head toward the center of the scene. "Go. And give me your thoughts before you leave, but so help me, if you go all vigilante, you'll be on desk duty until you have dentures."

"Thank you, sergeant."

Gradillas walked past several different law enforcement personnel talking about media requests, coordinating further with state park officials, and jurisdiction issues. Past all but a few of them, there seemed to be a second, invisible line. It was an area where only crime scene units had entered two hours before. Gradillas stopped and inhaled in an effort to steady herself. She looked at the ground ahead, full of small yellow marker flags. Near one grouping, there were a few tire prints in the dirt.

"Hey, Gradillas." She heard an awkward cough. "Detective Gradillas." It was Santorini, a nervous redhead whose brilliant analysis was only equaled by his lack of natural social skills.

"Hey, pal." Gradillas looked up and saw him avoiding eye contact. "Hutson send you over?"

Still not looking up, he said, "When I was eight years old, my sister's pet rabbit passed away. It caused profound emotional instability for several days."

"Santorini."

"I am sorry for your inevitable emotional instability."

She took a deep breath. "Thank you, San—"

"I understand Michael drives a rather large truck." He took a step toward the tracks. "Wide track. Certainly wider than most cars. Bigger tread too. These tread marks aren't small by any stretch, not a compact car, but not a truck either. The killer is—"

"Michael."

He looked up and cleared his throat. "The killer is driving a sedan or sports car with big tread."

Did he abandon the truck? What is he driving now? Stolen or provided by an accomplice?

She walked toward another cluster of tiny flags. There were several dark spots on the hard dirt. Blood that had dripped in the dark.

It was Alvarez's or Michael's. Alvarez, I hope you put the hurt on him before it was over.

She took two more steps.

Another flag, just a few feet away from the ones marking the blood, was the worst. Scribbled hastily in the dirt were the words, *The witness is next.*

She looked back at Santorini with misdirected disdain. "Innocent until proven guilty? Who else would want to take out our only witness?"

"As you know, definitive handwriting analysis is impossible in dirt as—"

"Sergeant!" Gradillas was done with Santorini. "Sergeant Hutson!"

Within moments, the gruff man emerged. "What is it?"

"Was someone going to tell me about this?"

"What?"

"The witness is next? Seriously. The man killed my . . . he killed a detective. Now he is threatening to kill our witness?"

"I know. We are working—"

"How does he even know we *have* a witness?!" The surrounding personnel stopped their conversations and were openly listening. "Is he in protection yet?"

"Lower your voice! Now!" Hutson waited for Gradillas to remember she was talking to a superior, but in that moment, she didn't much care. "We are in the process of searching for him right now."

"Oh, good God! One detective is dead. The killer somehow knows about our witness and is going after him. Or . . . or he is saying that so we focus on protecting the witness, but he is actually coming after me?" She paused to give Hutson a look implying she was waiting for him to catch up. "Don't you think this is all vitally important intel for someone in my position to have?"

"I was going to call you when you showed up against orders, detective! Now, stand down."

"Fine! But for the record, I hope he comes after me and gives me an excuse."

"Lower your voice," Hutson whispered. "I'll pretend I didn't hear you say that." He looked around to see the other conversations had resumed. "Now, do you want protection or not? I can spare a uniform."

"Why would I? The evidence right here says the killer is going after the witness, not me." And with a sarcastic smile, she turned and headed toward Alvarez's car, parked in a nearby campsite.

Think it through. Michael was now driving a different vehicle. He had driven past where Alvarez was parked. Alvarez must've seen him drive by. When he did, he got out of his car and walked after him. He didn't call for backup. He engaged Michael on foot.

According to the fellow officer who broke the news to her earlier in the morning, he had bruising around his neck, skin under his fingernails, and dirt ground onto one side of his head.

She had seen Michael. Sure, he was taller than Alvarez, but he wasn't particularly muscular.

Alvarez might not have called for backup. He'd always been the impulsive one. But he wasn't downright stupid, either. So how had

Michael gotten out of his vehicle and managed to get behind Alvarez without some kind of struggle? Alvarez wouldn't have turned his back on someone he was convinced was a killer. And how would Michael know about our witness? Come on. Think.

She struggled without her favorite sounding board. Without her partner.

She almost choked on her loss. The permanency of it. She forced herself to push it away and tried to understand what had happened.

Eventually, Hutson noticed she was still there and decided he had given her enough rope. She needed to leave for the sake of her sanity. He quickly assigned two officers to escort her from the scene.

50.

"**Sir? do you want to see** your boys?" Billy heard the kind voice that could never know the world in which he now existed. "Sir?"

He never looked up from the chair he had gently been moved to from the floor. "I want to see Gabriel."

"Gabriel. Okay. Well, the good news is that both your baby boys are healthy, and they are next to each other."

The good news? How stupid. How idiotic. How vacuous could this waste of space be?

"I only want to see Gabriel."

Gabriel was born without issue.

Gabriel was his son.

Michael took away Ruthie.

Michael's birth caused the death of Ruthie.

Michael could go to hell as far as he was concerned.

"Um . . . but sir . . . they are in the same room being cared—"

Billy sprang out of his chair. "Then move the little bastard! Or move my son! I don't care either way! There are multiple options I could write out for you if it helps!"

"But sir . . ."

"Just do it!" The nurse scurried off in confused fear. A few moments later, another representative approached with a large orderly at her side.

Billy was now seated again but coiled and ready to throw chairs through every window in sight.

"Mr. Kane? It is my understanding that you only want to see the child who was born first?"

Looking at his hands clenched as if in prayer, although prayer was not remotely on his agenda, Billy managed to say, "Yes. I want to see my son."

"Mr. Kane? Thank you for your patience as I clarify your wishes. You've been through quite an ordeal. When do you want to see the child who was born second?"

He let the inadequacy of the word "ordeal" pass. "Never. He killed my wife." Still no movement beyond muscle twitches.

"We understand you have been through quite . . ."

Understand? They really need to stop talking. Understand is now the second most insulting word of the day.

Billy stood slowly, a controlled inferno. The orderly stepped forward. Billy was amused that this mountain of a man thought his size stood any chance against the rage spinning and multiplying by the second within him, but he had no intention of violence in this moment. The only thread of sanity he still had within his grief was telling him that if he crossed the line into a single violent act, there would be no stopping.

Billy ignored the orderly and addressed the lady who was proving as inadequate at human communication as her predecessor. "You understand nothing about what it is that I'm feeling, about what I know. I want to remain with Gabriel in this hospital for as long as I am required by the law. Not a single moment longer. As far as the other bastard is concerned, I don't care what you do. You can have him. Big Boy here can have him. Doesn't matter."

The large orderly couldn't hide his look of disgust as Billy continued. "I'll sign whatever paperwork needs to be signed. I don't need or want time to think it over. I won't change my mind. Is that clear?"

51.

Leaving Woods Canyon Lake, Rebecca rode with Michael, and Skye rode with Rob in Bosco the Bronco. They stopped several times so Rob's body would have a few minutes to recover from the constant jostling. Just outside of Fountain Hills, both trucks pulled off Highway 87 into the far reaches of a reservation casino parking lot. Rebecca pulled out her cell phone, replaced the battery, powered it on, and looked up Gabriel's number.

Michael silently wondered why she had his number.

As if able to read his mind, Rebecca took a moment to say, "He took my phone and put in his number. Trust me. I didn't ask him to." Rebecca then looked straight ahead, took a series of three deep breaths, and dialed.

"Hello?" Gabriel was soaking in an oversized tub in his Scottsdale resort suite.

After driving back from Dead Horse Ranch the previous night, Gabriel drove directly back to his neighborhood bank and

"

withdrew the maximum allowable amount from the ATM next to the front door. He made sure to look worried for the camera. He then repeated the process at five other branches. Finally, he drove to the resort and checked in under an assumed name, paying in cash with a significant sum in reserve for possible charges. Exhausting work, but necessary for good optics if he was going to claim he was afraid for his life.

"Gabriel?"

"Who is this?"

"It's Rebecca. We need to talk." Her voice sounded shaky.

"Rebecca? What's going on?"

"I'm scared. There's this guy . . ."

Gabriel sat up in the tub. "Did someone hurt you?"

"No. Well, not yet."

"Okay, Rebecca. Calm down. Tell me what's going on."

Rebecca's voice continued to be noticeably shaky. "There's this guy, Michael. He's the guy you saw me with at that accident."

Gabriel put his phone on speaker, got out of the tub, dried off, and tossed on a resort robe. "I remember."

"Well, we were on a date."

"Rebecca . . . " Gabriel made his voice sound like a disappointed confidant.

"I know. I know. I think he's dangerous."

"Why?"

"Some detectives just told me he killed that lady who was found in the canal a few days ago."

His eyes widened. "Yeah. I think so too."

"Really?"

"Rebecca? I'm not supposed to tell anyone this, but I've been working with those detectives."

"I don't understand."

"I told the two detectives on that case that I saw him dumping some stuff in the dumpster behind a church the morning after the murder."

There was a significant moment of silence. "Okay. I still don't understand."

"Rebecca! This guy happened to find a body no one else found all day. Then, he's dumping stuff in a random dumpster the next morning."

"But that all sounds circumstantial. They seemed so certain when they talked to me this morning."

"The detectives?"

"Yeah. They seemed so certain. How could they be so sure?"

"I overheard they have DNA evidence. Maybe that's it."

"So he has to be guilty." Rebecca paused again. "Can we meet somewhere? I don't feel safe on my own."

"Great idea, but I can't meet you until later tonight. Can you lay low until then?"

"Well . . . yeah . . . I guess."

"Okay. I have the perfect place. There is a tiny pawnshop on the corner of Broadway and 30th Avenue. Meet me at eight. The place will be closed and there will be less than five people within a square mile at that hour."

"But Gabriel. Do you think—"

"Lay low until then."

He hung up.

———

Rebecca turned off the phone, slid it into her pocket, and turned to Michael. "Ready for an update?"

"You should roll down your window first."

Rob and Skye were standing there, hoping the call went well.

"He's pretty determined to frame Michael. He told the detectives he saw you dumping something in a dumpster the morning after the lady was found in the canal."

"Are you kidding?" Michael was shaking his head.

"I'm sure that's where he dumped the evidence himself. It

gets better. He said they are in possession of DNA evidence. How is that possible?"

"It isn't possible." Michael looked dumbfounded.

"Sure, it is." Rob jumped in. "If 'the man' needs a conviction, DNA evidence magically appears all the time."

"You know I'm crazy about you," Skye interjected. "But you have got to stop watching so much TV, Robby."

"Then how do they have our man's DNA?"

Michael was methodically trying to retrace his steps since the canal. "They had two different opportunities that I can think of. After I found the victim in the canal, an officer offered to throw away my water bottle. Then, two officers were in my home at the same time. I wasn't able to watch them both the whole time."

"So you really think they are trying to frame you? Just like Gabriel?" Rebecca asked.

"Honestly, I don't know what to think. Maybe the police are positive I did it. They have a witness, and they just need a bit more to put me away, so they manufacture it."

Rob nodded proudly. "Like I said."

Rebecca held up her hand. "If he is telling the truth, there is nothing we can do about it. So more than ever, we need that confession."

"So how are we gonna do it?" asked Skye.

"He wants to meet me in a parking lot in an industrial area of south Phoenix at eight."

Rob got out his phone. "Did he give you the name of the place or an address?"

"Just the cross streets, Broadway and 30th Avenue."

After powering up his phone followed by a five-second search, Rob said, "In the words of the great Elvis Presley, 'In the ghettooooo.'" He quickly powered off the phone.

"Yeah. He said there wouldn't be anyone around. The three of you will need to arrive at least thirty minutes early." Rebecca looked back to Skye. "Remember, you stay hidden no matter what."

"Yeah, yeah. I know my role. Where will you be?"

"I'll wait near Tempe Town Lake," she suggested. "That way, once you get what you need, I'll be a couple of blocks from the Tempe Police Department. We can all go in together."

Michael finally spoke up from behind the wheel. "Every part of this plan is dangerous."

Rob looked through the open window at him and swallowed hard. "Aw crap, man. You're gettin' a bad feeling about this?"

"I don't like it, but I haven't gotten any warnings."

"Then it's a go!"

Rob looked at Rebecca. She nodded.

He looked at Skye.

"Let's do this." She slapped the open window.

"So," Michael began. "Until all three of you recklessly throw yourselves into harm's way for someone you didn't even know a week ago, where should we hide out for the afternoon?"

"Uhh . . ." Skye grinned. "I've got a rich friend, and I can practically hear the slot machines all the way across the parking lot."

"My mom." Rob clarified. "My mom is rich. I just mooch off her."

"As much fun as that sounds, we should probably avoid big crowds." Michael turned to Rob. "Does mom have enough cash to book us a room for the day?"

Rob raised his eyebrows. "Like I said, she's rich."

52.

S YNERGY MUST'VE FIGURED THE MONEY WOULD be enough to keep Billy quiet.

They miscalculated.

He casually called every local news affiliate and told them his story, sure to include every gritty detail. He told them how much he loved his wife. How he raised a boy on his own. How in his delirious grief, he blamed his second son and gave him up. How he now understood it was never that little baby's fault. How he now understood it was the fault of the doctor and the hospital that hired him. How he knew this because they sent him a large check with the intention of squashing the story. How these people, who were responsible for the death of his high school sweetheart and the ensuing grief that caused him to blame the wrong person and lose his second-born son, may even sue him for telling his story.

Every news outlet ran at least one segment on the story.

53.

AS GRADILLAS DROVE AWAY FROM DEAD HORSE, she made a decision. For the first time in her law enforcement career, she would go against a superior's wishes and wasn't going to pursue this case using traditional means.

Hutson is a good man, and he's correct in his assumption that I'll have a hard time keeping my emotions out of the case. But the fact remains, I have more firsthand knowledge of the suspect, the witness, and the crime scene than any living soul. Alvarez knows more, but he isn't talkin'.

Gradillas hadn't driven twenty miles before she decided to make a few calls. She pulled her car into the parking lot of the Copper Star Indoor Shooting Range and dialed a number. A woman she hadn't spoken to in over ten years picked up the phone.

Gradillas began the conversation in the most unusual way. The woman was intrigued. After all, it isn't every day that someone who went on to work in law enforcement calls an old friend who went on to work in a newsroom and begins the conversation with: "This call never happened."

Gradillas gave the woman a few details about the case. Hutson might know it was her, but he'd never be able to prove it. Gradillas also gave her the name of the prime suspect. Her friend would be able to get pictures of him from social media.

She hung up and immediately made the second call.

"Humboldt Camping Supply. How may we help you avoid the concrete jungle?"

"I'd like to speak with Zane McKean."

"Never heard of the guy." The grumpy voice lied.

"Are you sure you aren't Mr. Zane McKean? Owner of Humboldt Camping Supply?"

"Who's this?"

"This is Detective Gradillas. We met recently, and I deeply considered testing one of your tents by camping in the store for several days."

"Yeah. You're great for business. Thanks for that, by the way."

"Here is the short version, Mr. McKean. I need you to know three things. One, I need to find your employee Rob Safranski. Two, the last time I was there, I had a partner. He was murdered last night by a friend of Rob's. Three, if you know how to get a hold of Rob or you know anything you haven't told me, you are going to prison for a long time—"

"Just hold on a minute—"

"—because when a member of law enforcement is murdered, you can bet your ass that anyone who obstructs, *in any way*, the capture of the murderer, well, God help them. Because no member of law enforcement, no government official, no one in a courthouse, no one in prison will."

"He lied!"

"Who lied?"

"Rob."

Alvarez used to lose his mind when people gave the minimum answer instead of just being entirely forthcoming. Gradillas remained outwardly calm. "Elaborate. Now."

"Detective, do I need a lawyer?"

"That is certainly your right. But there is a murderer out there. If you tell me everything you know and do everything you can to help me catch him, I give you my word you won't need a lawyer."

"Rob was hooking the guy up with supplies like a zombie outbreak just hit Arizona."

"And as far as you know, he was headed to Dead Horse Ranch?"

"Or Woods Canyon Lake."

"Excuse me? Woods Canyon Lake?"

"As Rob was shoving him out the door, I might've heard him mention it. He never brought up Dead Horse until you two were here."

Gradillas cleared her throat as she prepared to clarify what she'd just heard. "When I was here with my partner, we were told Michael was headed for Dead Horse Ranch, which is nowhere near Woods Canyon Lake."

"That's what Rob told you. I was going to mention it, but Rob cut me off, and I trusted him."

Gradillas' mind was racing.

Woods Canyon Lake? Had Rob intentionally misled them? Entirely possible. Alvarez was murdered in an entirely different location. Unless . . . unless Michael was hiding at Woods Canyon and Dead Horse was just a prearranged ambush. That would mean Rob is more than a supportive friend who has been fooled. He's Michael's partner in all of it! Hell, Rob could've killed Alvarez himself. That would explain Alvarez being caught off guard.

Gradillas might only be alive because she had stayed behind in Phoenix bringing Hutson up to speed and building the case file in anticipation of handing it over to a prosecutor.

"Last time I'll say it. If you are anything short of entirely honest with me right now, you will find no mercy at any point in your prosecution."

"You've made that clear, detective. The kid was here with Rob. Rob gave him everything he'd need for a camping trip. Said something about Woods Canyon Lake and shoved him out the back door. Then, when you pressed us, he shut me down and said Dead Horse. I don't know why. I don't even know what's going on."

"As soon as we end this call, I need you to text me all the contact information you have for Rob. Phone, email, alternate addresses, emergency contacts. Am I clear?"

"I can do that."

"The second we hang up."

"The second we hang up."

Gradillas decided she needed a bit more on Robert Safranski first. "Rob seems to live without clear direction or consistent motivation. Probably a recreational drug user. Is that appearance accurate to who he really is as far as you can tell?"

"Honestly, you've got me questioning my own judgment."

"How would you have answered my question if I'd asked it a week ago?"

He took a moment to consider this. "I guess I would've said you aren't even close. I'm probably a lot closer to that description than he is. He's never done any drugs as far as I can tell. He may have an occasional drink, but I've never seen it. And no clear direction? He once mentioned his mission in life is to leave everyone better than he found them. No consistent motivation? He talks about his mom all the time. She's filthy rich. Dunno how. And he loves her but doesn't want to be anything like her. He is a kid who is trying to figure out how to do adulthood right. He is intelligent and rich, two ingredients that add up to power. He hasn't figured out how to use that power yet, but he's working on it."

Doesn't sound much like a willing, active accomplice to a serial killer.

"Okay. Send me that info, and stay by your phone."

"I will, but what do I do if Rob comes back?"

"Text me as quickly as possible, but don't tell him. If he is who you think he is, he has been fooled and is in immediate danger."

"And if he isn't who I think he is?"

"Then, you're the one in immediate danger."

54.

"**I**F YOU WANT MY BODY AND *you think I'm sexy, come on baby let me know . . .*" Skye was in the bathroom shower washing off a week's worth of campsite soot and grime, singing in a surprisingly beautiful voice.

Rebecca, sitting on the edge of the hotel room bed, laughed quietly. "Rob, is she doing that to you on purpose?"

While Michael was standing at the window, Rob was relaxing on the bed, hands clasped behind his head, feet crossed, watching a recorded poker tournament. "I dunno what you're talkin' about."

"Actors," Michael said, ignoring the other conversation Rob was suddenly drawn into by Rebecca. "Michael Keaton."

"Robert DeNiro," Rob shot back, keeping up with both conversations.

Rebecca turned to him. "You know exactly what I'm talking about."

Rob responded without moving his eyes from the television. "Yeah. She knows exactly what she's doing."

"Musicians." Michael continued, sounding triumphant. "The King of Pop, Michael Jackson."

"The King of Reggae, Bob Marley."

"Then, why don't you do something about it?" Rebecca jumped back in.

"I'm not ready yet."

"Athletes. Michael Jordan."

"I concede the category of athletes," Rob said with his eyes still on the television.

"Rob?" Rebecca clarified. "I'm not talking about marriage."

He turned his head to look at Rebecca. "I am."

"Oh, wow. Hey. Listen. I hardly know you, but you two have never even gone on a date, have you?"

"Don't need to. I know. She knows. She is just a bit impatient."

"Head coaches!" Michael thought he had another winner. "Mike Ditka!"

"Since you said Ditka, I can't help but think you meant 'coaches with hot tempers,' and that would cause me to say Bobby Knight."

"How long are you going to make her wait?" Rebecca interjected again.

"Until I'm the man she deserves."

"Okay, pal. Next category. Artists. Michelangelo."

"I see your Michelangelo, and I raise you Bob Ross."

Michael burst out laughing. "I love happy trees as much as the next guy, but Bob Ross cannot be considered a better artist than Michelangelo!"

"Dude? You are so wrong." Rob pulled out his phone and turned it back on.

"What are you doing?" Michael asked. "Only for emergencies."

"And your completely false assertion is an emergency. I'm going to search 'best artist ever' and see what comes up."

"I don't know much," Rebecca finally said. "But that beautiful girl seems to think you're already the man she wants."

Before Rob had the opportunity to respond, his phone buzzed, and all conversations ceased. Rob looked up, eyes wide.

"What should I do?"

"Your call now," Michael said with detectable frustration.

He put the phone to his ear. "Señor Roberto. How may I be of assistance?"

"Where are you?" A woman's voice asked with no preamble.

"Well, thank you for making me feel popular, but may I ask who's calling?"

"This is Detective Gradillas. Where are you?"

Rob cleared his throat before responding with a formal, "Hello, detective." This caused both Rebecca and Michael to spin around. "Unfortunately, while I am unable to disclose my current location, I'll be coming to you within twenty-four hours. Cross my heart and hope to die."

"Is that a threat?"

"What? A threat? No—"

"We asked you where a suspected murderer was. My partner went there in pursuit. My partner was then murdered. Do you have anything else clever to say? Or can we just cut the crap? Are you complicit in these murders or just plain stupid?"

Rob placed the phone on the bed for a moment, unable to catch his breath. Michael and Rebecca glanced at each other before Michael asked, "What's up, buddy?"

Rob swallowed hard and lifted the phone back to his ear to hear Gradillas saying, "Rob? Hey! Rob?"

"I'm here."

"Which is it, Rob?"

Rob was slowly shaking his head. "Detective . . . detective. I'm so sorry. It's all my fault."

"Explain! Now!"

"I told you. I told him."

"I don't understand."

"I told you. Then, I told Gabriel. I thought you'd catch him. Or it would at least stall you until we could prove it was Gabriel who did it."

"Hold on. I need you to be clear with me. What are you suggesting?"

"It wasn't supposed to happen like this."

"Rob? Where are you?"

"I'm so sorry." Rob's voice cracked with emotion. "God. I am so sorry . . ."

"Rob? Where are you!?"

"I promise you, we'll get you the proof you need. Until then, don't trust Gabriel."

"Who's 'we'? I need to—"

Rob hung up.

Michael and Rebecca just looked at him in silence. They didn't know what happened, but they knew it wasn't good.

"Uh, guys? What's going on?" It was Skye peeking around the corner wrapped in nothing but a towel. "Guys?"

Rob still couldn't meet anyone's eyes. "I need to go for a walk." He started to get up gingerly.

Michael moved toward him and placed a hand on his shoulder. "Not without me, brother."

Together, they walked past Skye, who was trying to read Rob's pained face.

The two friends let the hotel room door slam shut behind them as they walked toward the casino floor.

"What was that all about, buddy?" Michael inquired after about thirty feet of silence.

There was no response.

"Can I at least ask where we are going?"

Rob kept walking, looking straight ahead like he was seeing a ghost. "I just need some air."

"Okay, my man. We can do that. No problem."

They continued on in silence as they reached the casino floor and walked along its edge toward a large automatic double door exit where the gamblers dropped off their cars for the valet service. Business was slow on a hot summer weekday. They continued past an isolated group waiting for their cars to be returned, but that was as far as they made it.

"Oh God, Mikey. I feel sick." Rob doubled over, hands on his knees.

Michael put his arm around his friend and scanned the people nearby. Nobody was even looking in their direction. With all the encouraged drinking that took place just inside the doors, even in the middle of the day, seeing a man getting sick probably wasn't that out of the ordinary.

"You gotta talk to me, brother. What happened?"

Still looking at the ground, Rob muttered, "I got someone killed."

Michael bent over to Rob's level. "What was that?"

Rob straightened up painfully. "I got someone killed."

"I seriously doubt that, brother."

Rob seemed incapable of catching his breath. "Detective Alvarez. He's dead. He's dead because of me."

"Rob? I need you to tell me what happened."

"When they came by the store—"

"Who?"

Breathlessly, Rob went on. "The detectives. When they came by the store, they wanted to know where you were. They asked my boss. I didn't know whether or not he knew where you were, and I couldn't take that chance. So I interrupted and realized they probably already guessed you might be headed to a campsite because my boss already said you took camping supplies. I'm not sure. I don't remember. All I know is that I needed to think of a campsite nowhere near you. I needed to keep you safe. So I told them you were headed for Dead Horse Ranch."

"Where is Dead Horse Ranch?"

Still breathless, Rob shook his head. "Not important. Near Cottonwood. Not important. Anyway, I sent them there. Then, yesterday, when I got attacked by Gabriel, he kept trying to force me to tell him where you were. Well, that wasn't going to happen.

So I thought . . . two birds, one stone."

"Oh, Rob. No."

"Yeah, man. I told him Dead Horse. I thought the cops were there, lookin' for ya. If he showed up, it would seem pretty shady. At a minimum, it would keep them tied up while we figured out our next step. But that wasn't what happened . . ." Rob turned away from Michael, both hands gripping his hair in disbelief.

"What *did* happen, Rob?"

"That was Detective Gradillas on the phone. Detective Alvarez went up to Dead Horse to find you. She doesn't know exactly what happened, but Alvarez was murdered. She thinks you did it. And she's not sure, but she thinks I might be in on it because I told them you were there."

"Okay. Okay. It sucks that Alvarez was killed, but he was murdered by a psychopath. That isn't your fault."

"Aw, come on, man!" Rob protested loudly. "You know I pretty much set it all up! I might as well have killed the cop myself!" Rob had gotten louder than he realized.

Michael looked around.

Everyone seemed to be pretending not to have heard Rob's outburst except one person.

He was looking at them like he was working out a math problem, and then he solved it.

Pointing straight at Michael, he shouted, "Hey! That's the guy who's wanted by the police for the canal murder! I just saw him on the TV in the bar!"

Michael grabbed Rob by the wrist and jerked him back past the onlookers toward the sliding double doors. "Let's go!"

The doors slid shut, and instead of taking the perimeter of the casino floor, Michael pulled Rob through the center, dodging left and right through the throng of machines and gamblers until he found the hall back to their room.

"What the hell was *that*?" Rob was reeling from emotional whiplash.

"Looks like we've made the news, my friend."

The friends broke into a sprint back down the hall to the room. Michael slammed his fist against the door.

Rebecca swung it open. "What's going on?"

"We were recognized! Grab your stuff! We gotta get outta here!"

Skye came out of the bedroom, this time fully clothed. "Rob, I'm so sorry . . ." She went to hug him.

"Not now, Skye!" Michael didn't have time for tact. "We need to get out of here now!"

"Got it. Run from the law now. Console the stud muffin later."

"Crap! Didn't turn off my phone!" Rob found it, powered it down, and slid it into his pocket.

Within thirty seconds, the four of them were out the door running down the hall toward the casino floor.

"Wrong way, Michael. Turn around." The Voice startled him.

He had been leading the other three and threw his arms out to the side to stop everyone. "Other way, folks!"

The four friends skittered to a stop and ran back down the hall past their room. Behind them, casino security staff flooded the hall.

Now running behind his friends, Michael reached out and knocked over a housekeeping cart to slow the stampede behind them. They reached the far end of the hall and burst into the blinding Arizona day.

All four tried to get their bearings as Michael said, "This way!"

The four began weaving through parked cars with Michael leading the way.

"Drop down."

Without hesitation, Michael yelled, "Get down!"

All four dropped to their knees just before a security truck sped by.

"Okay."

They all got back up and kept scurrying through the expansive lot while a small fleet of security was spreading out behind them. Finally, on the fringe of the lot, they came upon Michael's truck and Bosco the Bronco. Michael and Rebecca piled into his truck while Rob and Skye headed for the Bronco.

Rob pulled out his keys, which Skye quickly snatched from his hand. "Passenger seat, big boy. You're still trippin'."

Michael called out to Skye, "Stay right behind me!"

"Aye, aye, Captain Do-Gooder!"

The trucks thundered out of the lot, blended into the passing traffic, and quickly headed directly west toward Old Town Scottsdale while casino security continued to scour the lot behind them.

Wide-eyed, Rebecca looked over at Michael. "Where to, Mikey?"

Michael nervously smiled while checking the rearview mirror. "That's Rob's name for me."

"Fair enough. Where to, Michael?"

"Well, Rebecca, unless I hear otherwise, I think it's time for me to introduce you to my church."

55.

T WAS A MONDAY NIGHT THAT could chill a person to the bone. Ezekiel and Phyllis were cuddled under a blanket watching Monday Night Football when Michael started to cry in his nursery.

Phyllis started to get up, but Ezekiel jumped up quickly. "I got him."

His least favorite team, the Cowboys, was absolutely crushing the Falcons, and the game was almost over anyway. Spending a little time with his little man seemed a much better option.

Phyllis stayed cozy and watched the Boys finish the game 41–17.

"Tonight, we bring you a local story of a disgraced doctor and a horrible tragedy that has become even worse just weeks later."

Phyllis waited intently for the story. It was about the doctor who had been all over the news after two separate, unrelated deaths had occurred on his watch. Thanks to Donna, her friend at South County Hospital, she had heard that this was probably the doctor who was responsible for the death of her baby boy's birth mom.

Minutes later, Phyllis watched helplessly as the rumor became reality. A man named Billy Kane had lost his wife and given up his second boy, Michael. He had been paid off by Synergy (or the company that owned it, Phyllis didn't care). He had thought it was his second son's fault. He realized how insane this must sound, but the loss of his wife had made him a bit less than sane for a while.

As soon as she heard Ezekiel coming back, she flipped off the television. She had already made up her mind this was not something he needed to see.

56.

FR. FITZ WAS GETTING IRRITABLE IN the afternoon heat. His black pants and long sleeve black shirt with a Roman collar were not made with this weather in mind.

He was standing next to a middle-aged man with a clipboard who was wearing jeans and a polo shirt. They were on the west side of his parish office, looking down to where the wall met the landscaping.

"I'm not sure what *your* definition of pest control is, but I tend to think of scorpions as pests. Since we are looking at several of them and they are just outside my office, I don't think you are actually controlling them."

The man looked back at the pastor with a big grin and said, "Well, at least they aren't *in* your office, *amiright?*" and slapped his shoulder.

The pastor and former amateur boxer had long ago learned to restrain his machismo instincts. His face remained like flint, and he looked at the man just long enough to melt the guy's grin before saying, "So respraying today will be covered under our original contract . . ." He paused for effect before slapping the man's shoulder. "*Amiright?*"

The man froze for a moment before responding, "Yessir . . . I mean yes, Father. I'll go get the equipment right now."

The man was walking away as Fr. Fitz's cell phone buzzed. It was a text from John.

Where r u Padre?

Shaking his head, he texted back, *Just outside the office, and please take the time to spell words out. You aren't a twelve-year-old.*

A moment later, Michael came running up to him. "There you are!"

Fr. Fitz was happy to see Michael again. "I'm sorry I wasn't standing around in the church lighting candles. Do I want to know what you've been up to?"

"I need your help."

"What's the problem?"

"What I'm about to say will sound like a joke, but it's real. I've been framed for multiple murders, but I'll be able to prove my innocence tonight. I just need somewhere to hole up until then."

"Oh God."

"Father—"

"Help me. Amen . . . Now, Michael, I believe you are an innocent man. I do. But I won't lie to the police to shield you."

"That's fine, Father. If an officer of the law happens to come by before dinner and asks where I am, go ahead and tell them. Deal?"

"Fair enough."

"Great! Where should we hide the trucks?"

"Wait a minute. Who's 'we'? As in plural?"

"Remember Rebecca? The beautiful girl you encouraged me to ask out?"

"Of course."

"And there is Rob. The guy you encouraged me to befriend. Remember him?"

"Yes, I do."

"Well, Rob has a girlfriend. At least, she *will* be eventually. Her name is Skye."

"And they are all here?"

"Yup."

"And somehow, you've dragged them into this?"

"Yup."

"Oh, Michael." The priest pondered something for a moment. "How many trucks?"

"Two."

"Okay. Go get the trucks. I'll open the gate to the athletic field. Drive them slowly to the far end, and park them next to the shed. They won't be visible from outside the property. Then walk back, and the rear entrance to the rectory will be unlocked."

"Okay! Thank you, Father!"

Michael turned to jog off when Fr. Fitz called after him, "But if you rip up the grass, I'll turn you in myself!"

57.

THE YOUNG MAN SITTING ACROSS FR. FITZ'S dining room table had just poured his heart out. Fr. Fitz was doing his best to explain that while the kid may not have made the smartest choices, what had happened wasn't his fault.

The young man was refusing to let go of the role he had played, somehow more afraid to duck responsibility than to accept some of it. ". . . and I guess the concept of culpability is what is trippin' me up—"

Michael burst into the room. "Hate to break this up, but we gotta go. Now!" He quickly headed back into the living room.

"Everything okay?" Fr. Fitz asked, concerned.

Rob was already moving toward the door. "If Mikey says it's time to go, it's time to go."

Fr. Fitz's phone buzzed with a text from Rob's phone, but the message was from John. They had swapped phones thirty minutes ago since Rob's was the last phone the police had contacted.

The cop who was here a few days ago just pulled up. I thought YOU should know.

"Rob!"

"Yeah, Padre?"

"That detective just rolled up." He paused to collect his thoughts. "She might peek around the outside of the property for a minute before heading to the office. I'll go over to meet her. The only chance you'll have to get away with your trucks unseen is while she is inside the office."

"Let's continue our deep thoughts another time," Rob concluded.

"I'd like that very much."

The two of them rushed into the rectory living room where the other three were waiting.

"Thanks for visiting, but you really must be going now!" Fr. Fitz proclaimed. "A certain lady detective seems very determined to find you. Follow me."

All five headed out the back door, and as the other three took off across the field, the priest grabbed Michael's shoulder.

"What is it?"

"Son, be discerning. God isn't the only voice that speaks to us."

"Father? If the devil starts growling in my ear, I promise I'll tell him to take a hike."

"That's just it. He's the great deceiver. And I read somewhere that he likes to disguise his voice as our own."

"Well, that's horrifying."

"Quite. Now get going."

"Thanks, Father. For everything," said Michael before running after the other three.

Fr. Fitz made his way behind a stucco wall connecting the rectory and the offices when he heard the detective talking with John.

"Oh, he's a very busy man with many responsibilities, so he could be in a meeting. If he is, he might not be able to reply."

John was definitely going to be getting a raise.

"Just call him. Meetings can be interrupted."

"Okay. Hold on. My eyesight isn't as good as it used to be," John stalled.

Fr. Fitz scrambled to pull his phone out of his pocket and switch it to silent while at the same time shuffling toward the back entrance of the offices as quickly as possible. Before he got to the door, he saw the phone lighting up. He unlocked the door and answered as the door shut behind him.

"Hello, John." He walked the hall past two other staff offices to his own and shut the door.

"Excuse me, pastor. This is Detective Gradillas. I need to speak with you again."

"Absolutely. When would you like to meet?"

"I'm at your parish now. Where are you?"

"I'm here as well. I assume you are out front?"

"Yes, pastor."

Fr. Fitz was already walking out the front door of the building and saw Detective Gradillas and John off to his right. "Detective! Good to see you again." He reached out his hand.

Gradillas took it. "You as well."

"Why don't we chat in my office?" He motioned Gradillas back to the front door. Then, he glanced at John. "The gate to the athletic fields needs to be unlocked right away. I've got a few things I need to move."

"Right away." John turned and headed off.

Through the front door of the offices, Fr. Fitz stopped for a moment to ask the receptionist how her baby was sleeping.

"Oh. He is going through the four-month regression. Waking up at all hours. But he's so darn cute! I feel like a zombie every time he wakes up, but then I look down at his smiling face and all is forgiven. You know?"

"Actually, I don't. I'm an uncle, but that never required middle-of-the-night feedings. In fact, when I visited, I always rented a hotel room until they were sleeping through the night."

"Oh! Right! Of course, I—"

"Father." Gradillas finally had enough. "I don't mean to be rude, but my questions are a bit pressing."

"Oh! I'm sorry I slowed you down, ma'am," the receptionist said with more than a hint of attitude, not pleased that the center of her universe wasn't the center of everyone else's.

"Now, now, Sally. The detective is right. I shouldn't keep her waiting. But I am overwhelmed with joy that your little baby boy has such an incredibly loving mother." He turned to Gradillas. "My apologies. Now, on to my office."

Once Gradillas took her seat and Fr. Fitz settled behind his desk, he pulled some tinfoil back and smiled. "Do you like monkey bread, detective?"

"Father? Do you know the whereabouts of Michael Bale or Robert Safranski?"

"Oh, this sounds quite serious." He set the paper plate wrapped in tinfoil down.

"Do you?"

"Not at the moment, no."

Gradillas shifted in her seat. "What does *that* mean?"

The priest cocked his head and decided it was time to shift gears. "It means that I respect you. I believe you are trying to catch a murderer. I will help in any way I can. I will not lie to you. And I will answer every question honestly. And honestly, I do not know where those boys are at this moment."

Gradillas leaned forward. "Have you seen either of them since we last spoke?"

Fr. Fitz nodded. "I have."

"Michael? Rob? Or both?"

"Both of them."

"Together?"

"Yes."

"When was this?"

"They were here about ten minutes ago."

"Are you serious?! Pastor! You said you wouldn't lie to me!"

"Right."

"Are they on foot or in vehicles?"

"Last I saw them? On foot."

"Which direction?"

"Toward their vehicles. Michael's old rusty truck and another truck. It was an old Bronco or an International if memory serves."

Gradillas sprang up from her chair and called someone.

"Michael Bale and Robert Safranski are in two vehicles. Mr. Bale is in his registered truck. I believe Mr. Safranski is in his as well. They are within ten minutes of Old Town Scottsdale. Alert the state as well as Scottsdale, Phoenix, Mesa, and Chandler PD. Ask for the Salt River Reservation's cooperation. Yes. Possibly armed and dangerous."

Gradillas hung up the phone and began dialing another number.

Fr. Fitz was going to plead their innocence. "Detective—"

Gradillas shot out her free arm and pointed in the air as if to say, "Not now!"

"Hey. Gradillas here. I just missed Michael Bale and Rob Safranski by ten min—" She waited as she took a verbal lashing. "I know." Another pause. "Fire me later, but they are within ten to twelve minutes of Old Town Scottsdale. I called it in. All surrounding cities and state patrol have been notified." Another pause. "Yes boss . . . I'll stand down." A final pause. "Fine. I'll wait to hear from you before I do anything else."

She hung up and Fr. Fitz quickly tried again. "Detective—"

She made the same hand motion, but this time, her eyes flared. She finished dialing one more number.

"It's me again. Bale and Safranski are in the Scottsdale area and on the run. I'm texting you both vehicle descriptions." She listened to the response. "No. It's confirmed. DNA evidence at two scenes. Confirmed they were traveling together but are in their own vehicles. Every local department is looking for them. But the more eyes the better, right? And it's always good to be the network that aided in the capture, correct? Go with this, trust me. Gotta go."

"Detective!" Fr. Fitz's baritone brogue wouldn't be denied a third time.

"What?!"

"I need to tell you something, and since you are standing down, it sounds like you don't have anywhere to be."

"Fine. But not lying isn't enough. No more deception, evasion, or omission! I've tried to be respectful, but I'm just about done with you. And I'm considering some very serious obstruction charges!"

"Fair enough." Fr. Fitz motioned to the chair. "Will you take a seat?"

Jaw clenched, Gradillas stared down Fr. Fitz as she sat slowly. "Talk."

"When the boys were here, Rob told me about your partner. I am so very sorry."

"Really?" Gradillas bristled. "You aren't going to hide behind the seal of confession?"

"The boy isn't Catholic." Fr. Fitz clarified. "And even if he was, he didn't confess to murder. He needed to make sense of the tremendous guilt he's feeling."

Fr. Fitz went on to tell Detective Gradillas everything he had been told and everything he believed.

58.

THEY DIDN'T KNOW IF THE GENERAL public was looking for Rebecca and Skye, but they now knew Michael and Rob were wanted men. So while Rebecca drove Bosco the Bronco toward Mill Avenue in Tempe, Skye drove Michael's crowded truck. Michael was in the passenger seat, slouching as low as he could manage, peeking out over the dash. Meanwhile, Rob was stuffed into the middle, curled uncomfortably on his left side, his head resting on Skye's lap. As the truck made its way across the expansive Phoenix metro area in a carpool lane, Rob was quietly groaning with every bump.

"I'm sorry, Robby. I'm doing the best I can." She checked her rearview.

"No. You are amazing . . . I mean . . . you are doing amazing."

"I'll take the unedited version." She smiled as they transitioned from one freeway to another, heading for the Deck Park Tunnel that snaked below over a half mile of downtown Phoenix.

"Get a room, you two." Michael cracked.

Skye raised an eyebrow. "Well, technically, we had one just a few hours ago."

"And how did that work out for ya?" Michael teased.

"Be respectful, man." Rob put an end to it.

Without warning, Skye tapped the brakes even though their lane was flowing just fine. Michael was about to ask what she was doing until he saw the police SUV on the left side of the freeway up ahead.

"What should I do?" Skye asked nervously.

Then, Michael noticed the car with a single driver that had been pulled over in front of it. The patrolman was out of the car and occupied with the carpool violation. They'd lucked out.

"Just drive right by. We're good."

Skye pulled the truck into the small, dusty parking lot about forty-five minutes early. The sun had just dropped beneath the western horizon, and with only a single neglected light pole to be seen, it would get very dark soon.

Michael quickly looked around the abandoned lot and recognized it. He'd been here before. That night when he scared off the old man in the jeep. In the daylight, there was a startling lack of cover. Chain-link fences were on both sides of the red dirt parking area that ran from the road to ninety-degree angles and directly into the sides of the small pawnshop on both sides. On the left side, the fence hit flush with the front corner of the building. Nowhere to hide. On the right side, the fence line was about four feet behind the front of the building.

Rob looked around and realized the futility of their plan. "This is not good, man. Not good at all. Where are we supposed to hide, bro?"

"We can do this. Rob, you have to stand around that corner. Hide in the shadows until you hear me talking. Then, use John's phone and get that camera around the corner. Zoom in as closely as you can, but make sure every setting is silent. Do *not* give away your position."

"Okay. I can do that, but that doesn't leave anywhere for Skye."

"Skye. I need you in the bed of the truck."

"No way, dude!" Rob objected.

"Why the bed of the truck?" Skye seemed to be game if it made sense.

"The truck is the only other place to hide. When his headlights sweep the lot, you'd be exposed under the truck. If you're in the bed of the truck, I'll be able to direct his attention away from you. Just wait 'til the headlights sweep over you to turn on your phone."

Skye looked up at Rob. "Makes sense to me."

"I don't like it, man, but if you tell me it's gonna work . . ." Rob just shook his head.

"We're good." Michael grabbed Rob's shoulder. "This has to work."

"Alright. But don't think for a second that I can't distinguish between 'This *will* work' and 'This *has* to work.'" Rob turned to Skye. "Please be careful."

Skye gave him a sparkling smile in return. "*You* be careful. If it goes south, I'll just pretend like he's on the other soccer team." She climbed up onto the back tire of the truck and hopped into the bed, disappearing in the process. "And *poof!* She's gone!"

Michael placed his hand on Rob's shoulder. "Come on, brother. It's time."

Rob hugged Michael, almost against Michael's will, smacked him on the back, and walked off to his position behind the only exposed corner of the pawnshop. He pulled out John's phone and turned it on. The phone buzzed with a text. *At Rula Bula on Mill. Let me know when it's done.*

Rob texted back, *Will do.* Then, he texted Gradillas a link to a live streaming site with the simple message, *If you want to catch your friend's killer, someone needs to watch this site for the next hour or two.*

Suddenly, Michael was left standing alone in the middle of the dirt parking lot, completely exposed. No gun. No defense.

Hey. Feel like letting me know if I'm gonna live through this? He silently asked the Voice.

There was no response.

———

Michael didn't know how long he had been standing there in the dark, but it seemed like hours had passed.

Is he gonna show? Will he still stop when he sees me instead of Rebecca? If he expects Rebecca, he won't be carrying a gun, right?

There were a thousand details, and if any of them didn't go smoothly, this whole thing could end in disaster.

In the midst of this uncomfortable thought, a faint deep sound slowly rose in volume. Headlights became visible through the chain-link fencing, ever so slowly rolling up the road.

It was Gabriel's Mustang, and it was barely moving. As each tire slowly rotated, Michael could hear the crackling of small rocks and loose gravel under the growling of the engine. The car continued its slow, methodical approach.

The possibility that Gabriel would see Michael and accelerate away was becoming very real. And if Michael was being honest, that wouldn't be the worst possible outcome.

The car's front wheels angled, and the car slowly rolled into the lot. The beams swept past the truck and struck him square in the face.

Michael raised his arm to shield his eyes, squinting to see past the light.

The car kept inching directly toward him, parallel to his truck, until the headlights moved below his sightline.

Ominously, the car continued to roll ever so slowly until it gently bumped his shins and grunted to a stop. The engine turned a few more times before it clicked off.

It was so quiet, Michael could actually hear the dust settling.

As his sight slowly adjusted, he saw Gabriel sitting behind his steering wheel. Surprisingly, he looked frightened. The driver-side door slowly opened, and Gabriel stepped out, looking like he was about to be executed.

"What are you doing here?" Gabriel's voice shook.

Michael took a deep breath. "Gabriel Kane. I know who you are."

"Yeah. I bet. Listen. I'll make you a deal." He stumbled back half a step. "If you let me live, I'll refuse to testify!"

"You are a murderer. You murdered that woman in the canal. You murdered Detective Alvarez. I'm sure you've murdered others—"

"Wait! No!" He raised his hands, palms down as if to negotiate. "I said I'll refuse to testify, but if you're gonna try and frame me, you might as well just shoot me."

"Gabriel! This isn't going to work!" Michael took a step toward him.

Gabriel turned and nervously scrambled around his car's open door and pulled out a gun. He shook as he pointed it at Michael. "Back off! Back off! I've carried this ever since I realized I was a witness against a murderer!"

"Woah. Easy there." Michael slowly raised his hands to the sky.

Gabriel kept the gun trained on Michael as he slowly stepped toward the truck. "Don't think I didn't hear your friend in the bed of the truck. Is it Rob? Does he have a gun? What did you two do to Rebecca?"

Just before Gabriel saw Skye, Rob stepped out of the shadows in the far corner of the small lot, keeping his camera phone aimed at Gabriel. "You didn't hear anything! I'm right here!"

Gabriel swung his aim to Rob, then back to Michael. "Do you have a gun?! Does he have a gun?!"

"Naw, man. Just filming you," Rob said with defeat as he took a few steps closer.

"No gun," Michael said quietly.

"So you thought you could threaten me into a confession and just go on killing people? That ain't happening! Get over here! Right next to him! Now!"

Rob slowly and painfully walked his way across the dusty lot. He looked at Michael and said, "Sorry, brother."

"Toss the phone on the ground at my feet."

Rob grumbled but complied.

"Now. Both of you. Hands above your heads."

They slowly raised their hands.

"Happy now?" Rob asked with venom.

"Yeah. Sure. Except I *did* hear something in the truck." His gun was quivering. "Whoever you are," he yelled over his shoulder. "If you've got a gun, toss it out! If it's another phone, turn it off and toss it out. I don't want you telling more lies about me! Bottom line, if I don't see something fly out of that truck in the next five seconds, I'll shoot one of these nutcases in the knee! I don't want to, but you'll make me!" He lowered the unsteady gun. "Five! Four!"

"Listen man!" Rob lost his patience with the charade. "There isn't anyone else!"

"Three! Two!"

A cell phone came flipping out of the truck bed. Gabriel stomped on it, smashing it with his foot.

"I knew it! Now stand up slowly with your hands up!"

There was a moment of metallic rustling in the back of the truck before Skye slowly got up and stood above them all in the bed of the truck. Gabriel's eyes widened almost imperceptibly at the sight of the beautiful girl, but Rob caught it and involuntarily took a step forward.

Gabriel quickly turned back to Rob, lifting the gun toward his head. "Don't." He looked at Rob for an extra minute, almost daring him to make a move. "Get back beside your partner in crime. As a matter of fact, both of you back up about five feet. You're making me nervous!"

They grudgingly did as they were told.

He yelled over his shoulder, "And you, slowly get out of the truck and come here."

Skye leapt out of the truck, landing on the dusty lot with a light thud.

"I said slowly!"

She just shrugged with defiance.

"Is this everyone?"

"Come on, man. Drop the act." Rob couldn't hide his disdain.

"Is this everyone?!" Gabriel shook the gun at him.

"It is only the three of us," Michael said calmly.

"And what did you do to Rebecca?!"

"Rebecca is fine." His voice remained steady.

59.

AT LEAST HALF OF THE COMPUTER monitors in the building were watching the spectacle. Sergeant Hutson wasn't one of them.

"The chief is gonna make sure I'm driving an Uber next week if we don't give her some answers!" He was storming past every desk with a new command, a new outrage. "This complete cluster is going to inspire fifty different conspiracy theories! And I hate conspiracy theories! Wanna know what I *like*? I like finding guilty people and convicting them and making my city safe! I also wanna know why our only witness is going all Charles Bronson! It looks like he's holding off three killers by himself! And let me tell you, if he gets himself killed, a lot of *your* heads will roll! So for the love of all things holy, is *anyone* able to locate this sideshow?"

Figuratively handcuffed to her desk for the duration of the investigation, Gradillas was hiding behind her monitor, where nothing seemed to be making much sense.

Something still wasn't right.

If she was just reading a manuscript of the feed, she would be convinced there was a group of disturbed people working together, but what she was watching over the feed seemed to hint at a different story. The story Rob had outlined so briefly. Even if it had epically backfired, maybe they *were* attempting to get her, to get anybody, evidence that Gabriel was the killer.

She stood up from her desk and made a beeline for Hutson.

"Oh, for God's sake! What, Gradillas?"

"Sir? I believe Gabriel Kane might be the killer."

"You know I appreciate your deductive skills, but our priority at the moment is to figure out where this is happening!"

"Why is the trace taking so long?"

Hutson shook his head, looking around. "Not that it's any of your business." He lowered his voice, confiding. "Based on a trace of Robert Safranski's phone, we already sent several units to the Corona del Sol neighborhood, but when they just arrived on the scene, it was some crusty old war veteran named John. He said he had no idea how he had a stranger's phone. We'll look into him later, but for now, we are working on putting a trace on his phone, in case they were swapped without the man's knowledge. So now we're in the process of explaining to the same carrier why we need a second trace."

Gradillas knew exactly what happened even if she didn't feel like sharing, seeing as it wouldn't do any good.

"So we should have authorities on the scene within five, ten minutes. Fifteen at most." He patted her on the shoulder condescendingly. He probably didn't mean it that way, but it sure felt like it to Gradillas.

"Sir? Please listen—"

"You listen to me." He cut her off. "This is how this arrangement works. I'm the sergeant. You are off this case. You have *been* off this case. This should not be breaking news."

"But—"

"End of discussion! Back to your desk or back home. I frankly don't care which!"

Gradillas decided home was preferable.

As she looked at the elevator doors, waiting for them to open,

Santorini approached her.

He cleared his throat, his beady blue eyes avoiding her from behind his glasses. "I know where they are."

She looked at him. "What?"

He nervously ran his hand through his red hair. "I know where—"

Gradillas forcefully shoved him away from the elevator down an empty hallway outside the restrooms. "Location!"

"After what Gabriel did to Alvarez,"—he glanced up at her—"I thought you should know first—"

"Don't care. Location!"

"I isolated a few frames of the feed and—"

"Santorini!"

"Pawnshop. Here's the address. I can only give you a head start." He handed her a slip of paper.

She grabbed it, then squinted. "You just said 'Gabriel' a second ago. You realize Michael is still the prime suspect?"

Santorini took off his glasses, looking down at them while he cleaned them meticulously with a cloth he pulled from his pocket. "Before the phone was tossed to the ground, this Gabriel was pretending to be nervous, but when he was forced to react quickly, he appeared to be supremely confident for a fraction of a second before regressing to his nervous state." He continued without looking up, determined to get every bit of each lens crystal clear. "Furthermore, the hints of genuine confusion in the suspect's voice seem to further confirm this is not the behavior he expected from the so-called witness. Finally, and this is really quite simple, why hasn't he just used his gun to force all three suspects to lay down in the dirt and driven directly to a police station? Holding them at gunpoint makes sense if he is confident in his ability to do so, and his primary goal is getting them arrested. But if he is in over his head and his primary goal is self-preservation, which is what his nervous performance would suggest, remaining with them would not be as typical. None of this stands

firmly as convincing in and of itself, but when put together—"
He looked up to see Gradillas running toward the open elevator
door.

As it shut, he heard her shout, "Tell Hutson what you just
told me about our witness, Santorini!"

60.

SKYE STOPPED A FEW FEET SHORT of Gabriel. "Now what?"

"Pick up your boyfriend's phone and film me."

"Pick it up yourself. Ya got two hands." Rob seethed.

"Rob. Stop," said Michael, trying to keep the situation from exploding.

"Tackle, dirt, door, sirens." Four words only Michael could hear. Barely audible. That was all.

"Robby? It's okay." Skye soothed Rob. She looked back at Gabriel with disdain.

"Pick it up and film me!" he yelled, gun still on Rob.

Skye slowly lowered herself before Gabriel, maintaining untrusting eye contact with him while she felt for and found the phone. She stood back up in front of him, took a step back, and finally aimed the camera at him.

"Are you getting this?" Gabriel asked.

"Yeah, scumbag. You're still on the air," Skye shot back.

Gabriel cleared his throat. "My name is Gabriel Kane. As far as I know, I'm the sole witness in an investigation into Michael Bale and his accomplices. I don't know if it is only these two or if there are more."

"This is ridiculous," Rob moaned.

"No! No! Your plan to frame me was ridiculous!" He shook the gun again. "I'm on Broadway and . . . and . . . 30th Avenue! Please just get here quickly! I need help!"

Just then, the phone Skye was holding flashed bright white.

"What . . . what was that?" Gabriel yelled.

"What was what?" Skye asked quickly.

"The phone . . . it just flashed."

Skye began doing something to the phone.

"Stop! Hand me the phone or your friend gets it!" Fright was still in his voice.

Skye's head dropped as she handed it over.

Gabriel backed up a step and raised the phone with his free hand. A text notification had popped up. He looked into the camera again. "Police? Please get here quickly. The phone is about to die!" Then, he turned off the camera, cutting the feed, before reading the message aloud. "Let me know when you are on your way. Meet you at TPD. Mill & 5th Street."

He shoved the phone in his pocket and looked up with an alligator grin, straightening his posture. "Glad that's over. It is absolutely exhausting being such a wuss. Michael! How the hell do you do it?" He jerked his head to the side, cracking his neck.

Skye took a step away from him toward her friends.

"Hang on, little missy! Get back here."

She took a step back next to him as he now openly leered at her for a moment. She began to tremble with disgust.

"Hey, Mike! Do me a solid! Take out your keys and toss them over that fence."

Michael didn't put up a fight. He didn't protest. He just did as he was told.

He heard the words again. "Tackle, dirt, door, sirens."

"Man alive, brother! Maybe callin' you a wuss was givin' you too much credit!"

Michael whispered, "Tackle, dirt, door, sirens."

"What was that?" Rob whispered back.

"No idea. Yet."

"Hey! Shut up over there!" Gabriel pointed the gun at them again. "I'm tryin' to concentrate." He looked at Skye and smiled, openly disrespecting her and taunting Rob.

"Bro!" Rob called to him. "Why don't you set down that gun and then we'll see what kinda man you are!"

Gabriel laughed with vigor. "I've always found it astonishing how some dudes think they can take me just because they get angry. You and I already had our dance. How are your ribs?"

"Can't even feel 'em." Rob's face was deadly serious, jaw clenched.

"Now, we both know that's a lie, Robert." He cocked his head. "I beat you senseless, but I left you alive. Didn't have to, but I did. And you aren't showing me an ounce of gratitude. And I gotta be honest with you, lack of gratitude is sort of a pet peeve of mine." Rob extended his hand and silently motioned Gabriel to come get some. "See? There ya go with that machismo idiotic behavior. Now, I completely understand trying to be brave in front of your girl, but you're disrespecting me again." The smile was still plastered across his face. "So I'll disrespect you." He grabbed the back of Skye's neck with his free hand and pulled her in for a hard kiss.

In the instant Rob charged toward them, Michael followed a few steps behind him.

Tackle.

Gabriel shoved Skye at Rob with one hand while aiming with the other.

At the moment he pulled the trigger, Michael blasted into both Rob and Skye, sending all three of them to the ground mere feet from Gabriel who quickly pointed the gun at Rob, the closest to his feet.

Dirt.

Michael grabbed a handful of the light dirt and flung it into

Gabriel's face before sprinting toward his truck. Gabriel tried to wipe his eyes clear.

Rob seized the opportunity to lunge at Gabriel who, despite being temporarily blinded, sidestepped him easily and unleashed an uppercut to his already broken ribs. Rob collapsed on impact.

Gabriel didn't have time to put a bullet in him because Skye had now scrambled to her feet, coming toward him. He used her own momentum against her, sending her flying off the rear quarter panel of his car with a thud, as she landed hard on the ground.

He pulled the trigger, but she had rolled quickly under the car, and the bullet smashed the dust where she had been an instant earlier like a miniature meteor.

He quickly turned and ran to the other side of the car just as Skye got back to her feet on the passenger side. Dirty and defeated, staring down the barrel of Gabriel's gun, and standing between the car and the truck, Skye raised her hands in the air.

"While it strikes me as a shame to shoot such a precious little thing, you've chosen the wrong side. But hey, thanks for that delicious kiss."

Door.

As Gabriel pulled his trigger a third time, the driver-side door of the old truck swung open, deflecting the bullet just enough.

Michael reached out from inside the truck, grabbed Skye, and yanked her into the truck across his lap, slamming the door shut.

Gabriel walked directly in front of the truck and took a moment to reassess the situation. "So let's talk this out. I'm standin' here with a gun. Still got enough bullets to do the job. Tough guy in the dirt over here can hardly breathe. Meanwhile, his girl is spending quality time with his best buddy hiding below the dashboard of a truck!" Gabriel looked over at Rob. "In all fairness, you can hardly blame them. If they got out of the truck, I'd just shoot 'em. The problem is, you guys don't give up. If I started toward either side, you'd just scurry out the other. So

I guess my only option . . ." He stepped onto the front bumper of the truck and climbed onto the hood. From there, he could see Skye and Michael through the windshield and Rob, still laying in the dirt lot curled in pain. "What's the matter, Rob? Wait! Don't tell me. Lemme guess! A couple of ribs are puncturing something important?"

"You . . ." The raspy voice came from Rob. "Really . . . never . . . shut . . . the hell . . . up."

Gabriel's temper almost got the best of him as he aimed the gun at Rob. There was no way he could possibly miss this time. His smile was gone. "You're ungrateful like the rest of them. Like Mikey here." He turned back to Michael, frozen low on the other side of the windshield. Gabriel lowered himself like a baseball catcher tapping the glass with the muzzle. "Change of plans because you've really pissed me off. I'm going to go get Rebecca. Then, I'm going to kill her. I'll do my best to make it look like it was you, Mikey. When the cops get here in a few minutes, it'll look like I lost control of the situation but managed to flee. When you eventually get out of prison, I'll hunt you down and kill you. But don't worry. I won't be bored. Rob? For your continuing disrespect, I'll kill your girl before I kill you."

Sirens.

Michael slowly and defiantly sat up behind the wheel of his truck. "Do you hear them, yet?"

"Well take a look, everybody! The lion appears to have finally found his courage!"

"The approaching sirens."

"What?"

"Do you hear the approaching sirens, Gabriel?"

"No. But I'll take your word on it." He turned to Skye and winked as he said, "And you, gorgeous. I'll be seein' you."

He jumped off the truck's hood to the ground, got in his car, and peeled out of the lot, kicking up a huge cloud of red dust.

Before the dust cleared, Michael was out of the truck and

sprinting toward the fence. He scrambled up and over it in a flash.

In the darkness beyond the fence, he ran directly to his keys, partially obscured by a pile of rusted car parts. He stuffed them in his pocket as he ran back and scaled the fence a second time with stunning agility.

His feet landed back on the right side. He saw Skye had gone to Rob and was cradling his head.

Skye yelled to him, "I'll take care of Rob! You take care of the psycho!"

Michael didn't respond. As sirens could now be heard in the distance, he jumped behind the wheel of his old truck and roared out of the lot.

61.

AS GABRIEL SPED NORTH, HE ROLLED down his window and finally began to hear the sirens in the distance as a light changed from green to yellow to red down the road.

He decided to stop, pulling the phone out to text Rebecca. *Done, but we have to talk before going to the police. Meet us in Tempe Beach Park in 15.*

The light turned green, and he accelerated onward. Now, entering an area with moderate traffic as he approached the freeway from the south, he slowed to only ten miles per hour over the speed limit. He didn't want to draw any attention to himself.

What was that back there? He thought as he continued toward the freeway. *I mean, I haven't lost a step, the way I dodged every attack. But freaking Michael. He was able to block every move. Hell, he even blocked two of the bullets. Why didn't I hear anything?* He shook off the thought and it was quickly replaced by another. *I can't believe I'm related to that guy. He was the only one too gutless to even try and come at me.*

Gabriel came to another red light just half a block from the freeway entrance.

As he waited for the light to change, Gabriel decided he'd exit on Priest and take Rio Salado to the park. The twin Mill Avenue bridges crossed Tempe Town Lake right next to Tempe Beach Park, but on the northern banks of the lake, Mill Avenue went under the freeway without access.

The light turned green and just as Gabriel pressed the gas, he thought he saw Detective Gradillas drive past him in the opposite direction. But it couldn't have been. She hadn't had enough time to get across town. He had only given away the location about ten minutes ago. She would've needed almost twice that. Those sirens he'd heard had to have been local Phoenix units.

He turned onto the freeway and hit the gas a bit harder than he'd planned just in case.

No. It couldn't have been Gradillas.

That was when Gabriel saw lights quickly approaching from behind.

62.

MICHAEL PRESSED THE GAS PEDAL TO the floorboard and paid no attention to red lights, knowing in order to have any chance of catching Gabriel, he had to max out the old truck's speedometer and hope to heaven he wouldn't hurt anyone.

Anyone but Gabriel. He deserved to die.

Michael shook his head.

No. He doesn't. He just needs to be stopped.

Gabriel was headed for Rebecca, and last he knew, she was on Mill Avenue. It would be a brazen place to kill someone, even for Gabriel, as it was one of the busiest places in the area late into the night, but it was Michael's only lead.

He blew through mile after mile and a few lights on his way toward the nearest freeway. As he approached the freeway, a light one hundred yards or so directly ahead turned from red to green. Then, Michael saw Gabriel's unmistakable Shelby accelerating up the ramp.

Michael pressed the gas pedal into the floorboard with even more force, almost clipping a turning car in the process.

He wrestled the metal beast onto the on-ramp and into

freeway traffic but not without incident. The driver-side of the truck slammed into a white sedan's passenger side, sending it into the next lane and causing several cars to narrowly miss one another. The Shelby was still in view but seemed to accelerate into traffic farther down the interstate.

Michael kept pushing his truck as hard as it would go, doing his best to navigate the slower cars, weaving left and right, testing his truck's ability to keep all four wheels on the pavement all the while.

63.

GRADILLAS REALIZED IT HAD TO BE Gabriel and decided to make a U-turn just beyond the light.

Slowly beginning her turn, she glanced back and saw Gabriel get on the freeway when a large battered pick-up truck almost clipped the front of her car as it flashed by. She immediately recognized it as Michael's. By the time she had completely turned around, the truck was disappearing up the on-ramp as well.

Unbelievable as it was, her mind had finally landed on the truth and what mattered.

Justice for Alvarez.

She turned onto the ramp and immediately had to hit her brakes to avoid several cars that were driving well below the speed limit. There was debris on the road from a sedan that was slowly making its way to the right shoulder.

Gradillas carefully made her way through the slowdown before finding some open space to speed into. Gabriel and Michael could only be so far ahead.

64.

AS GABRIEL TRANSITIONED FROM ONE INTERSTATE to another, he knew he only had about fifteen miles to lose Michael before his rendezvous with Rebecca, and although his car was the faster vehicle, traffic would hold him back.

He needed to do something to slow Michael even more.

He saw the Deck Park Tunnel approaching and had an idea.

Gabriel surveyed the traffic in every direction for a brief moment. Then, he pulled up to the rear bumper of the car to his left and swerved into it, using the pit maneuver to spin it out to the left just short of the tunnel entrance. With no time to spare, he accelerated again, catching a compact pickup truck to his right, and repeated the process. The truck overcorrected and veered back to the left behind Gabriel, smashing into an SUV just inside the tunnel. With the carnage piling up behind him, cars in all lanes were forced to a complete stop as he pulled away.

He glanced back and saw that every lane was blocked.

It'll take Michael at least forty-five minutes to get through. More than enough time.

65.

M ICHAEL WAS FINDING IT IMPOSSIBLE TO gain any ground on Gabriel. The muscle car was just faster and more nimble than Michael's truck. Then, things went from bad to worse. Every driver in front of him seemed to slam on their brakes at the same time.

As Michael slammed the brakes to avoid smashing into the congestion, he saw a car had crashed into the concrete center divider. Next, he saw a pileup that seemed to be blocking the tunnel altogether.

I've lost him . . . unless there is another way . . .

"There's still a way."

Michael took another look at the tunnel. Straight ahead, the blocked eastbound tunnel was five lanes across. To the left, cars were speeding out of the five-lane westbound opening, but between them was a much smaller opening to a two-lane tunnel he'd never noticed before, obstructed by chain-link fencing. Michael guessed it was reserved for emergency vehicles.

If this isn't an emergency, nothing is.

Michael spun the wheel to the left and punched the gas. A second later, the old truck smashed into the fencing, sending pieces flying and ricocheting off both sides, cracking the windshield before the truck suddenly shot into complete darkness. The faded headlights barely illuminated the soupy blackness of the unlit tunnel and did a wholly inadequate job considering the speed he was now achieving, but he instinctively seemed to know when to adjust to the left or right as the tunnel curved below the city.

Without warning, directly in his path, a second high wall of chain-link fencing glistened in the headlights. He was going to smash into it, and there was nothing he could do.

Another explosion of metal, sparks, and light engulfed Michael as the fencing on the far end of the tunnel was no match for the truck.

He swerved back to the right, barely missing the center divider.

But the freeway ahead was completely clear.

Michael stomped down on the gas pedal.

66.

GRADILLAS HAD HER SCANNER TURNED ON and heard there was an accident at the eastbound entrance to the Deck Park Tunnel.

It has to be my boys.

Minutes later, she rolled up on the mayhem.

For a second, she thought about reversing to the Seventh Avenue off-ramp, but then she saw the emergency tunnel off to the left. It was still partially blocked by a few lengths of twisted metal fence.

She drove over to it and jumped out of the car.

As she began dragging the metal aside, she grumbled, "Alvarez was right. I really need to get a freaking hobby."

She cleared the last of the wreckage, jumped back into her car, and drove cautiously through the darkness.

67.

AFTER LOSING MICHAEL, GABRIEL SLOWED HIS pace a bit. No need to be reckless or attract unwanted attention. He was approaching the Priest Drive exit and less than ten minutes from checking the first name off his list.

He began moving to the right lane when something slammed into his car, causing it to lurch forward, missing the exit.

He spun around to see Michael's truck coming at him again. He tried to hit the gas when the truck rammed the back of his car a second time.

He hit the gas to pull away, but the Shelby's backside was wobbling, and the car couldn't achieve any real acceleration. Looking in his rearview mirror, Gabriel saw the truck bearing down on him a third time, and all he could do was try to veer off to the right. The truck adjusted and clipped the rear driver-side corner, and Gabriel's world began to squeal and spin.

68.

MICHAEL SAW THE SHELBY DIRECTLY AHEAD and didn't hesitate for a moment. The truck was already at its maximum speed. All he had to do was aim.

He almost lost control with the first collision when one of his knees slammed into the metal dash, but he knew what to expect the second time around. The Mustang's back end was severely dented in and wasn't able to pull away. Despite the second impact slowing the truck's momentum, it gradually pulled back up to speed and was able to catch the car for a third time.

The final impact was the least violent, but the angle at which he ran his truck into the rear corner of the car sent it spinning into and through a temporary construction guardrail beyond the right shoulder. The car—and Gabriel along with it—seemed to drop off a cliff toward Tempe Town Lake and vanish.

Michael slammed on the brakes and was out of the truck almost before it had come to a complete stop. He scrambled to the hole in the temporary barrier and looked down. There, smoking and clicking, the mangled muscle car had landed directly in the center of Mill Avenue's two southbound lanes over twenty-five feet below.

Michael's mind flashed to another accident.

Is that what it looked like? Were my parents' bodies locked in a mangled cage like that one? They were so dignified, so gentle. They deserved to die peacefully, surrounded by love. Not in a temporary pile of twisted metal.

Michael looked up at the twin bridges stretching south across the lake toward the college district, illuminated by the strings of white lights arching from pole to pole on both sides of each bridge. Below, the lake reflected a deep blue hue emanating from all the glass office buildings on the southern shore. Everything seemed so quiet.

Some cars were pulling to a stop to check on Michael and see what happened when he heard metal slamming below.

He looked down to see a foot finally kick open the driver-side door of the mangled mass.

Ever so slowly, a bloodied Gabriel crawled out of the car and began limping south on Mill and toward the bridge. His left arm was dangling, lifeless.

Michael leaned over the edge and looked for a way down. To his left, next to where Gabriel's car had smashed through the construction, was scaffolding that rose from below. He ran over and began making a careful descent.

*

69.

GABRIEL COULDN'T FEEL ANY SHARP PAINS as he made his way across the bridge. Every injury had settled into a distant, throbbing ache.

Is this what shock feels like?

All his mind could focus on was getting to and hiding amongst the throngs of Arizona State students who routinely overcrowded Mill Avenue bars and clubs just blocks south of the lake. He could duck into a bathroom, clean himself up, and convince a coed to give him a ride out of the area.

He thought he heard someone shout his name, but that wasn't possible.

My mind is playing tricks on me. That ain't good.

He heard it again.

He wiped blood from a blurry eye and slowly turned just in time to catch a fist in the face. He landed hard with a thud on the cement sidewalk of the bridge.

I didn't see that coming. How is that possible?

Michael landed hard on top of him and unleashed another, but Michael's position left him exposed. Gabriel was about to thrust his knee hard into Michael's groin, when Michael rolled off him, sprang to his feet, and unleashed a kick to Gabriel's already-injured arm.

"If you've got a problem with me, you come after *me*!" Michael shouted at the wounded man at his feet.

"Dang it!" Gabriel grunted as the kick forced his pain to the surface and every wounded nerve in his arm came into sharp focus.

How is this happening?!

A siren could be heard from the other side of the lake.

From his back, Gabriel rolled quickly and reached in a futile attempt to grab one of Michael's ankles, but Michael easily took a step back.

Gabriel sat up slowly as if in surrender. His head felt foggy, and his arm was on fire. "I don't understand. I always see it coming."

Michael, seemingly content to stand out of reach until the police arrived on scene, shook his head. "What the hell are you talking about?"

In the distance, the solo siren was joined by several more.

Though his vision was becoming blurred by blood a second time, Gabriel could see several of their lights approaching the far end of the bridge along with several more passing them on the adjacent bridge.

"I think they are close enough, don't you?" Gabriel reached down and pulled a gun from his ankle holster. He managed to stand up and lifted the gun high in the air. Then, he aimed it at Michael. "Dang. I wonder why you didn't see that coming. It seems neither of us is on our A-game."

Word must've spread quickly because the cruisers on the far end of the bridge all slowed to a stop. A few more rolled up to the wreckage behind them while only a few dared to drive a bit closer. As they stopped, doors flew open, and police took up positions behind each of them.

Gabriel realized his exposure. As quickly as his broken body would allow, he circled Michael on his way to the edge of the bridge, still watching as another group of police set up on the eastern bridge directly across from him. He wiped more blood from his eye with the back of his right wrist and sat with his back against the low concrete sidewall, obscuring himself in its shadow.

"Get on your knees, Michael!" He shook the gun at him.

"What are you doing, man?" As Michael lowered himself slowly, he grimaced. One of his knees seemed to be messed up. "You aren't getting out of this! The cops are everywhere!"

Gabriel shook his head with a smile of disbelief. "You think that's what I want?"

"Then, what *do* you want?"

Gabriel's voice rose with uncontrolled vitriol. "I want you to pay, you ungrateful piece of crap!"

"For what, man?" Michael's voice sounded nonplussed. "For stealing a girl who was never into you?"

"You don't know?" Gabriel momentarily leaned forward from the shadow before realizing his error and leaning back. "How do you *not* know? For killing dad."

"For what?!" Michael blurted out.

"You killed dad. Indirectly, of course."

"And how exactly did I do that?"

Gabriel scoffed. "Oh, but wait! There's more!"

"You aren't making any sense, man."

"Before that, you killed mom."

70.

R EBECCA'S HEART WAS POUNDING.

We are so close to finishing this. Guessing the other three want to bring me up to speed before going to the police station together. Then, this will all be over, and I'll be able to get to know Michael without the tension of, you know, being hunted by the police and a serial killer.

She headed north on Mill Avenue past the old mill to her right. Up ahead were the beautiful Mill Avenue bridges, and off to the left was the beach park where Michael had tried to ditch her in the middle of a monsoon just days ago. It was lit fairly well along the paths but wrapped in shadows everywhere else.

Are they already waiting, hiding from the cops until I'm closer? Or have I just beaten them to the park?

Just as she finished circling the small park and decided she had arrived first, the relatively quiet Thursday night was shattered by a sudden crash echoing from the north side of the lake.

Whatever it was, she couldn't see it because of the trees and small scattered buildings. Her instinct was to run toward the crash, but she dismissed it as morbid curiosity. Besides, she had to sit tight until her friends found her.

Within moments, a siren fired up. A few moments later, the night air was filled with sirens. Mill Avenue was immediately overflowing with what seemed to be every police car in Tempe. For a moment, Rebecca thought this might be a good thing. The police would all be distracted, and the four of them would be able to safely meet before making their way through the front door of police headquarters and presenting their case on their terms.

But this isn't a good thing.

Deep down in Rebecca's gut, she knew it. Despite that, she couldn't bring herself to leave the park.

I'm probably just losing my mind a little bit. And after this week, who would blame me?

Three shadows were approaching through the park from the southwest. Rebecca decided it was a good thing she had waited. That was, until they walked into the light and she realized they were just three Arizona State students.

As they approached, a guy said to another, "No, dude. You should've seen it! They were trying to frame him, but he totally turned the tables on them."

The other guy, a bit of a meathead, said, "I still don't get it."

"They did it, but they were trying to make it look like the witness was the actual murderer!"

As they walked by, the girl chimed in, "Well, I think the witness was the real killer."

"What?" The first guy was shocked. "You seriously believed them?"

"Hey!" Rebecca called after them. "What are you talking about?"

The first guy turned around. "There was this crazy thing on the internet tonight. The guy they are saying is the Canal Killer and his two accomplices tried to frame the only witness in the case, but he had a gun and totally turned the tables on them."

Rebecca's heart stopped.

"I'm telling you, the witness is the killer, guys." The girl objected.

"Whatever. You're just saying that 'cuz you think that Michael guy is hot!" The guy dismissed her and looked back at Rebecca. "It was streaming live and totally went viral."

Rebecca's heart still wasn't beating. "What happened?"

"That's the crazy part." The girl took over. "The witness . . ."—she looked at her friend—". . . you know, the *guilty* one, was holding the camera when the battery must've died, and no one knew what happened. So Stevie here turned on his police scanner."

"Comes in handy for ragers." He winked at Rebecca.

The girl continued. "And the cops think the two guys are on the bridge right now."

"Yeah," Stevie said. "Right *now*. Let's go before we miss our chance at a viral video of our own!"

Before Stevie was done talking, Rebecca took off sprinting toward the bridge.

As she emerged from the park, she saw the police line at the entrance to the western bridge. They were keeping the first news outlets on the scene at bay. Other curious people were beginning to make their way to the spectacle. Rebecca slowed to a walk and blended in with the mass of curious bystanders. She watched carefully for her moment.

"What is going on?!" someone shouted at one of the officers.

He turned to give a typical say-nothing answer. "The bridge is temporarily closed due to a police matter. We'll let you know when it is open to traffic again, but it might be a while. For your own safety, please move along."

No one was going anywhere.

71.

T HE NIGHT SKY HAD TURNED TO day eight hours early. Blue and red flashes strobed in every direction as police headlights shone up both ends of the bridge. Helicopters quickly approached from the west with powerful spotlights aimed toward the scene, searching for the action. In the middle of it all, Michael found himself staring down the barrel of a desperate man's gun.

There is safety in witnesses. Right?

"Look around. There must be a lotta cameras on us by now."

"Then I certainly hope they have a three-second delay," Gabriel responded, still obscured in the shadow of the low concrete wall at the edge of the bridge. "You know, for the sake of the kiddies at home."

"Look, man." Michael pleaded from his knees. "You don't wanna do this."

"You don't think I wanna kill you? Seriously?" His face flinched without warning in obvious pain. "Be assured, brother. I do." The gun shook slightly in his hand. "Fortunately for you, I still have a to-do list I need to get started on." He tried to smile but could only manage another wince.

"I don't get it. You think you're gonna take out my friends one by one before eventually getting around to killing me?"

"Pretty much."

"But you are completely surrounded. There's no way out."

"This doesn't end tonight. I'm always one step ahead."

The Voice spoke up. "Ask the question."

But it doesn't make sense.

"Doesn't matter. Ask it."

Michael reluctantly asked, "Then how was I able to kill your parents?"

"*My* parents?" Gabriel lowered the gun, comfortable with the distance. "Michael, your ignorance used to be cute, but it's starting to wear on me."

"Ask again," the Voice insisted.

Michael took a deep breath and asked again, "How was I able to kill your parents?"

"You've taken everything. And this world is full of people like you," Gabriel responded, leaning back against the wall, gun now resting at his side. "The golden lives. Lives cushioned comfortably in affirmation and love. Center of the universe—"

"Again!" The Voice demanded.

Michael was losing his patience. "How was I able to kill your parents?!"

"—when a loved one dies, they ask themselves, 'How could they leave me?' As if it's about them! People who consider themselves undeserving of pain or long lines in the grocery store. People who get stuck in traffic behind a fatal accident and are angry at the inconvenience. People who just love to proclaim what they deserve and what they don't deserve—"

"Gabriel! How was I able to kill your parents?!"

Gabriel ignored Michael's question and continued his rant. "People who expect saving without a single solitary drop of gratitude for the savior! Well, brother, I got tired of it. I got tired of the people who never said, 'Thank you.' I got tired of the people who were upset because I didn't save them on *their* terms!"

"Gabriel!" Michael shouted, still kneeling, lights hitting him from both ends of the bridge.

"And yes! I got tired of my family! The memories of a father who was weak and took the easy way out. The mother who was taken from me before I ever knew her. And my brother who was behind it all. I'm done. I'm done. So if I can't have anyone, neither can you."

"Gabriel! You aren't making sense!"

"I'm not making sense? Nothing about this situation makes a dang bit of sense!" He managed to pull himself up to his feet, dug in his pocket, and left the gun at his feet. "You clueless piece of crap! This is gonna blow your mind." He pulled out a rolled-up sheet of paper and held it out.

"Get down!"

The words slammed into Michael with a sonic force so great, he almost felt it.

Michael dove onto the pavement.

72.

Detective Gradillas first saw Michael's truck haphazardly pulled off to the right shoulder of the freeway. As she drew nearer, she saw the hole that had been blasted through the construction by Gabriel's Mustang.

"Oh God," Gradillas whispered in disbelief as she peered through her windshield.

She rolled past the construction to where she could safely pull her car off the road and ran back to Michael's truck. Seeing it was empty, she backtracked to where Gabriel's car went through the barrier. On her way, she peered over the edge just in time to see Michael lay Gabriel out with a punch to the face. Then, she glanced straight down and saw the twisted metal that used to be Gabriel's car.

Gradillas fought to keep her adrenaline under control. She needed to remain calm on the slim chance she could diffuse the situation. And if she couldn't diffuse it, her aim might be called upon to end it.

She immediately saw the scaffolding and lowered her way down the entire drop to Mill Avenue below.

As her feet hit the pavement, two police cars came screaming up behind her. She spun to see Gabriel lift a gun above his head.

Crap.

She held up her badge as they pulled up next to her.

"Detective Gradillas!" She identified herself. "A gun has been pulled. Let everyone know!"

As the patrol cars rolled forward cautiously, Gradillas fell in next to them for cover.

Gabriel looked like he'd gone twelve rounds with a heavyweight champion and limped behind Michael, dropping against a low wall and into its shadow. Michael, still illuminated from all directions, was slowly getting on his knees.

Guess we've got a hostage situation. But to what end? He's got nowhere to go.

Little glints of light from the shadows were enough to know a gun was still in play but far from enough of a visual for a confident kill shot.

A sniper had just arrived at the third vantage point from the eastern bridge. Two helicopters were approaching from the west, but they were just media, not air support.

It was getting noisy and frantic. Radio chatter was picking up. A series of commands and responses, clarifications and confirmations. Air support was promised, but it would take a few minutes. The two media helicopters were circling overhead and another was coming in the distance. Their lights were flashing over a few small paddle boats and kayaks in the darkness below.

That's his only option.

Gradillas turned and yelled, "Where the hell is our boat?!"

An officer scooted up next to Gradillas. "We are working on getting it in the water, and our helicopter is just lifting off now."

"How the hell do the networks beat us every time?" Gradillas vented.

She looked back at the men on the bridge. Michael was still kneeling in the light while Gabriel was virtually impossible to see in the dark shadow.

The uniform's radio chatter continued until a clear message came across. "I've got the shot." Gradillas looked to the other bridge and saw the shooter who had just checked in.

The response from the commanding officer on the far end of the bridge came back immediately. "Does he still have the gun on the hostage?"

"No. I see both hands. No gun."

"Where the hell is it? He didn't throw it into the water."

"Northside. Do you have a visual on the gun?"

Gradillas grabbed the radio. "Completely obscured from here."

"Fine. East bridge. Keep on him. You see a gun aimed, put him down."

"Copy that."

Gabriel started yelling, but the helicopters were making it impossible to hear. "I'm not . . . nothing . . . this whole…makes a dang . . .!"

He's getting to his feet! Where's the gun? He's in the light! Where the hell is the gun? Going into his pocket!

Gradillas took up position, ready to shoot if necessary.

"He's partially blocked by the hostage." A calm voice came over the radio.

"You clueless piece of crap! This is gonna blow your mind." Gradillas heard Gabriel through the commotion.

Gabriel pulled out a rolled-up sheet of paper and thrust it at Michael.

Over the radio, another voice exclaimed, "He's got a gun!"

"Waiting for clear shot," the calm voice replied.

"No! No gun! No gun!" Gradillas shouted into her radio, but it was too late.

Michael dropped from his knees to a prone position as Gradillas heard a solitary pop from the other bridge.

The impact propelled Gabriel backward as blood flew from

his shoulder. He stumbled from the impact, legs undercut by the low wall and flipped over, falling into the darkness below with a faint splash. Michael leapt to his feet and ran to the edge of the bridge, looking down into the black waters.

The radio was suddenly filled with efforts to get a visual of Gabriel in the darkness. The paddle boats and kayaks were clearing out quickly as the fallen body was a bit too close for comfort.

A single figure broke through the police line on the far side of the bridge.

"Someone else is joining the party!" The radio chirped.

Another voice said, "Female. No visible gun."

"For God's sake. Stop her before she contaminates the crime scene!"

Gradillas got on the radio. "Closest to the scene. I've got it."

Rebecca beat her to the scene and didn't stop until she nearly knocked Michael over with a hug. This was because Gradillas was running along the edge of the bridge trying to get a visual on Gabriel, a virtual impossibility. The bridge was drenched in flashing lights from approaching squad cars and still-circling media choppers. As a result, the lake below was an inky darkness, broken only by a few tight beams from flashlights.

"We need that eye in the sky now!" Gradillas shouted into the radio.

"Almost there," a response came through the radio.

"Then I need the media to stop getting shots of my pretty face and refocus on the water! I know you can hear me! Which station wants credit for catching a murderer on live television?"

One at a time, the spotlights from above shifted away from the bridge and onto the water below.

Gradillas focused on surveying the scene instead of the hugging couple. She saw the gun laying on the sidewalk close to where Gabriel fell off the bridge. She knew that wasn't what he had in his hand when he was shot, but she didn't see anything else he could've been holding.

While a police line was being run all around them, several paramedics got to Michael, sat him down on the curb, and asked a flurry of questions. As the adrenaline finally began to subside, he realized his left leg was pretty bashed up and had been functioning well above its capability.

Then, in the midst of his pain, he remembered Rob and Skye.

He looked up at Rebecca, ignoring the continuing barrage, and said, "You've got to get to the pawnshop. Rob and Skye are still there."

"They're already in police custody," Gradillas interjected. "Don't worry about them."

"Detective." Michael looked up from the curb.

"Michael. I have a feeling I'll be apologizing for your eventful week very soon, but . . ." She looked over at Rebecca. "You need to come answer some questions."

"But—" Rebecca began to protest.

"And if you don't come of your own accord, I'm pretty sure I can charge you for breaking through a police line and interfering with a police action."

"You better go," Michael said. "This is not a detective to be trifled with."

"Okay. Fine." Rebecca turned to the paramedics. "Where are you taking him?"

"St. Joseph's," one responded.

"Okay. I'll look it up and get there as soon as I can."

"I know. You'll arrive at 4:32 in the morning."

Rebecca froze.

"Kidding. I'll see you when you get there. Now, get out of here before Detective Gradillas shoots you."

"I appreciate that, Michael." Gradillas grimaced. "If you come out of this clean, I'll use you as a reference." She headed off with Rebecca.

"Detective?"

Gradillas paused. "What?"

"I'm sorry for your loss."

"Yeah." Gradillas swallowed and quickly nodded in a rare show of subtle emotion. "Let's go, Rebecca."

"Detective?"

"What?!"

"One more thing."

73.

GABRIEL FELL THROUGH THE BLACK NIGHT with a burning ember searing his collarbone. A cold wall smashed into him, only to absorb him. He was somehow enveloped in the cold while burning up from the inside.

Then, Gabriel realized where he was and didn't know what to do.

He pulled himself to the surface for air and orientation, but he figured he would only have a second or two at most.

He broke the water to see he was directly beneath the bridge. *Lucky break.*

The night was loud with the sounds of competing helicopter rotors, shouting officers, and the water splashing against the support columns. He saw a few kayaks heading toward the dock on the south shore. The north shore was much closer. He also remembered it had significantly fewer police. Suddenly, the waters to both sides of the bridge's shadow lit up with more intensity than the midday sun. He took the deepest breath he could muster and dipped below into the quiet lake.

He used to be able to swim beneath the surface for seventy-five meters. A long time ago. That was high school, and he hadn't just been shot and survived the worst accident he could imagine.

On the other hand, his life hadn't depended on it like it did now.

With each pull, his shoulder felt like it might explode, but he didn't dare stop. He slowly, sparingly, let air escape his lips with the smallest spurt of bubbles. More pulls toward shore. His lungs began to ignite as the wildfire emanating from his collarbone spread. More pulls. He let go of the last of his air. A few more pulls. He had to breathe.

Gabriel exploded through the surface, shocked at how close he was to the shore. Lights were now swinging below the bridge behind him from the matching bridge to the east. He pushed forward. Time was running out. The shore ahead would be swarming with police within minutes. The southern shore might be already. It seemed the vicinity of his previous splashdown and the docks in the distance were garnering the most attention. That would only last for so long. He swam harder toward land under the noise cover of the commotion in the skies above the bridge.

On the shore, a single beam of light bobbed from around the right side of the bridge abutment. There were only ten feet of wet, sandy soil separating the wall of the abutment and the current waterline.

Gabriel stopped his advance and lowered 'til his eyes were hovering less than an inch above the water. Treading upright, he felt his feet tapping the slick bottom. As the light continued making its bouncing journey from right to left, Gabriel slowly advanced, staying low. When the light moved away from him, he could see it was held by a fresh-faced patrolman, probably in his first few years with a badge and looking to make a name for himself.

The light had almost made it to the far left end of the abutment where it would vanish around the corner. He looked along the shore to the right. There was nothing but the other bridge.

He looked to the left beyond the patrolman. There was an apartment complex about one hundred yards up a slight embankment that primarily served Arizona State students. That is where he'd need to go. He just needed to wait out the kid with the badge and cross the field.

Without warning, the beam of light swung around across the water and struck him flush in the eyes. He hadn't even had time to duck below the murk.

"Hey! Outta the water!" yelled the officer.

Gabriel couldn't be certain due to the glare of the flashlight, but he was pretty sure he was also staring at the business end of a pistol.

"Hey! Officer?" He seemed to question as he continued out of the lake. "Oh, thank God! That guy who fell off the bridge! He pulled me out of my kayak and paddled off!"

He continued to emerge until the water was at his knees.

"That's far enough!" the officer yelled a bit too nervously.

Gabriel shook his head as he continued cautiously. "Dude! The guy shot me in the shoulder and stole my kayak! Look!" The water was down to his ankles.

"Stop right there!" The officer took a step back as he latched the flashlight onto his belt and raised his radio. "Yeah. Twenty-four, ninety-three, thirty-eight here. I got a guy—What?" His face contorted ever so slightly. "I can't hear you!"

Gabriel took two more tentative steps. "I think it's the bridge!"

The officer glanced up. "What?!" His frustration kept him from registering the steps.

"The bridge, man! You're standing right below several tons of concrete!"

"Dang it! Hold on!" The officer turned halfway from Gabriel as he stepped further out from under the bridge. "I got a guy here who says he was pulled out of his kayak! What? Yeah! Badge number two, four, nine, three—"

The line went dead as Gabriel launched his good shoulder

into the officer's side, sending both men flying through the air before Gabriel landed hard on the young policeman. His bad shoulder felt like it exploded with both impacts. He scrambled after the loose gun, grabbing it just as the officer charged him. Then, he discharged three shots into the officer's vest, knocking him back to the ground. Gabriel knelt atop him and used the butt of the gun to knock him out.

Gabriel sized up the man below him.

Too small. Crap.

Blood from his shoulder began to fall onto the policeman's neck. He grabbed the officer's badge before getting to his feet and looked to the sky to make sure every helicopter's attention was still on the lake or the southern docks. Then, he sprinted up and across the field toward the apartment building's parking lot.

Headlights approached the lot from the far side. Gabriel dove into the grass. As he watched the car pull up in front of the main entrance, he saw a windshield sticker identifying a ride-share company. He jumped back to his feet and secured the gun into the back of his belt loop, brushing himself off, and running to the car.

He opened the rear passenger-side door and startled the driver who had been focused on the apartment entrance. He slid quickly into the seat and closed the door to extinguish the interior lights.

"Hey, friend." The fifty-something driver glanced in the mirror of his 2014 Acura TL. "I'm sorry. I'm picking up a Suzanne."

Without hesitation, Gabriel said, "Suzanne will just have to understand. See all those helicopters back there?"

"Can't miss 'em."

"I'm a cop, and I'm trying to find the guy they are looking for. I think he might be trying to get to the light rail. Can you get me there?"

"Can do." The driver shifted into drive before pausing and turning around. "Officer, your clothes are soaked."

"My apologies. No time to explain."

"Great. Getting my car soaked and I'm not even going to get paid for this."

"You will have to be content in the knowledge you helped apprehend a very bad man."

"Oh goody." He accelerated just as a woman in her young twenties bounded out while texting.

Within minutes, Gabriel noticed his ride was now driving next to the light rail tracks. He saw the glow of the light rail station ahead and immediately scoured the illuminated area for law enforcement. "No cops."

"What was that?" asked the driver from the front seat.

"Looks like I'm the first cop on the scene. Well done." He reached up and patted the man on the shoulder.

"Uh, yeah. Sure thing."

"Right here's good."

"But the station is still—"

"Here is good!" Gabriel insisted.

"You're the cop." The man stopped in the middle of the dark road about fifty yards short of the light.

"If you hurry back, you can probably still pick up that fare." Gabriel jumped out of the car and slammed the door without waiting for a response.

As the car pulled away, Gabriel began dragging himself the remainder of the distance to the station. He could hear the light rail approaching from Tempe Town Lake and pushed through the pain to get to the station in time. It was headed toward downtown Phoenix and away from his pursuers.

Survive today. Vengeance tomorrow.

74.

IF THIS DOESN'T WORK, I'LL BE FIRED. *Hell. If this* does *work, I'll be fired.*

As per Michael's instructions, she'd jumped in a patrol car, driven it across the bridge, and skidded to a stop just short of the police line, sprinting the remaining block to catch the westbound light rail.

Now she was sitting in the back of the empty third car waiting to approach the first stop after crossing the lake.

There is no way this is going to work.

As she thought the words, she crouched down below the seat in front of her.

The light rail slowed to a stop.

She heard the doors woosh open.

A man grunted his way on.

As the doors wooshed shut and the train car resumed its journey toward downtown, Detective Gradillas stood and saw Gabriel Kane sitting four rows in front of her.

She aimed the loaded gun at the back of his head.

Just shoot him. He deserves it. Alvarez deserves it.

75.

MICHAEL WOKE UP IN A HOSPITAL BED. His shirt had been removed, and his arm had an IV sticking out of it. A thin sheet was pulled up to his abdomen. He lifted it with the arm that wasn't plugged in and saw his jeans had been removed as well. His entire wardrobe consisted of boxer shorts and a huge knee brace. He had to find his jeans. He looked all around the room from his back when a nurse hurried in.

"Oh, there you are!" said the big nurse with impossibly red hair and a permanent smile.

She checked his chart and compared it to a monitor that was keeping track of several health factors. The only one he understood was the heart monitor. "How is Mr. Popular this morning?" She reached up, grabbed the curtain, and yanked it open to reveal the bright morning.

"How long have I been here?" asked Michael through squinting eyes.

"Oh, I wasn't on shift yet. I think about eight hours." She walked back over to the chart. "Let . . . me . . . see. B-I-N-G-O. Bingo! Just a hair over eight hours. So tell me. How do ya feel?"

Michael shifted uneasily in his bed. "Ever run a marathon?"

The nurse was not amused. "Look at me," she demanded, her fist on her hip. "So you're exhausted. That's what the fluids are for. What hurts, hon?"

"My left leg."

"Where specifically?"

"Everything around the knee."

"Is the pain sharp? Or is it more of a dull pain?" The nurse went back to the chart and picked it up.

"It feels like everything that is attached to the knee is hanging on by a thread."

"Okay. The doctor determined you needed your rest after we stabilized the knee, but we will be checking it out within the next few hours. X-ray. Possibly more."

"But I don't have insurance yet. I can't afford—"

"Your medical costs are being covered by a friend."

"What?"

"I heard about some of what you've been through. You need to rest up. We'll get to your leg soon enough." The nurse replaced the chart on the end of the bed and headed for the door.

"Nurse? One more thing. You called me Mr. Popular. Why?"

She approached the bedside. "Oh. Well . . ." She paused for a moment. "I was going to wait to tell you, but you've got a few people waiting just outside. I thought it'd be best to let you rest up first."

"No. Please. If it is all the same to you, I think it would help if I could see them. Just give me a minute before you send them in."

"Okay. You've got five minutes with the entourage. That's it. Then, rest."

She walked out of the room, and Michael heard her footsteps fade. He quickly sat up and swung his legs off the bed. His braced leg screamed.

How did I manage to run on this thing last night? How did I kneel on it without crumbling in pain?

He lowered his feet to the floor and slowly raised himself with almost all his weight resting on his right leg. He took a few hops away from the bed, surveying the room for those jeans until he saw them, along with his shirt, folded neatly on a small ledge next to the bathroom door. He took a few more hops, snatched the jeans from below the shirt, and quickly jammed his hand into their right pocket.

There it is!

His hand found the now crumpled-up sheet of paper Gabriel had tried to give him on the bridge. He had quickly stuffed it into his pocket moments after Gabriel took his dive.

Michael heard a small herd trampling up the hall. Standing on one foot, wearing only his boxers and knee brace, he didn't have many hiding places. He chose the better of the two when he stuffed the paper between the brace and his knee.

As the footsteps approached, the task proved more difficult than he anticipated. The brace was tight against his lower thigh, and the paper was refusing to be cooperative. The door swung open as he shoved the last bit in with his index finger.

Fr. Fitz filled the doorway, a look of amusement across his face as he saw his employee and young friend standing on a single leg in nothing but boxers, bent over with a finger shoved into his knee brace. "Got an itch, young man?"

Skye poked her head between the priest and the doorframe. "Hey bud—" Her eyes widened at the sight before her. "Oh. Uh. Sorry, Rebecca." She smiled and awkwardly backed out of the doorway.

Fr. Fitz looked back into the hall and said, "Give me a moment, ladies." He walked into the room and let the door shut behind him. "If you tell anyone about this, I'll come out of boxing retirement." He put Michael's arm over his shoulder and helped Michael back to his bedside, lowering him with paternal care.

Michael leaned back into the pillow. "Thanks, Father."

"Michael. Are you alright?"

"Yeah. Just a bad knee and still a bit tired."

"Good. Good." Fr. Fitz straightened up. "Now, cover up." He moved to the door. "And consider some weight training. Okay, ladies. The young man has recovered his dignity."

Skye appeared in the doorway a second time, hesitating at first. She looked up at Fr. Fitz, who was holding the door, and said, "Thank you, sir." Then, she scurried up to Michael's bedside and kissed him on the cheek. "How ya doin', Mike?"

Michael smiled. "Sore, but good. You?"

"I'm a warrior princess. That dude couldn't touch me." She gave him a quick wink.

Behind her, Fr. Fitz cleared his throat. "Oh! Sorry!" She stepped to the side and revealed Rebecca standing in the doorway.

She was slowly shaking her head with a small smile. "You dummy."

"Nice to see you too, beautiful," Michael said from his hospital bed.

Rebecca walked slowly to Michael and placed her hand on his chest. She leaned down and softly kissed him on his forehead. Then, she bent lower, her lips next to Michael's ear. "Skye told me everything. Thank you for saving my life." She straightened up and brushed Michael's hair with her hand.

Fr. Fitz made his way over to the lone chair in the room and eased into it. "Well, son, it appears you've come a long way. Less than a week ago, you didn't know how to get a girl's number. Today? You are getting lipstick all over your face."

"Until you sat down, I thought you might kiss me on the forehead too."

"Michael? I've quickly grown fond of you, but that is never gonna happen."

"Hey! Has this jerk even asked about me yet?" Everyone looked over to the doorway where Rob was sitting in a wheelchair.

Michael sat up quickly and painfully. "Whoa, buddy! What happened to your legs?"

"My legs are fine, bro. I just have a few ribs that have seen better days, so the medical pros think it's best that I stay off my feet for a bit. I'm not even supposed to wheel myself around, but since I'm such a rebel . . . " Rob slowly wheeled his way into the room.

Skye walked behind him and placed her hands softly on his shoulders. "He'll be just fine."

"Especially now that we've been cleared of all charges," Rob added.

"Wait. What?" Michael was surprised by this revelation.

"Yeah, dude." Rob nodded. "That badass detective dropped by and let me know that they were able to pin everything on Gabriel."

"So she . . ." Michael started before hesitating.

"Apprehended him on the light rail." Fr. Fitz finished for him.

"I wonder how that happened?" Rebecca said with a big smile, having personally witnessed Michael's instructions.

Behind her, the nurse reappeared. "Time's up! Everybody out!" She disappeared back into the hall.

"If you need, I'm three doors down, and Skye smuggled in a few gaming systems." Rob offered as Skye wheeled him out of the room.

"Love ya, big brother!" Skye called back into the room as she turned the wheelchair to roll Rob back down the hall.

Rebecca leaned back down and kissed Michael on the cheek. "Rest. I'll be back often until you get out." She stood up and slowly walked out of the room.

Michael took a deep breath, grateful for all these new blessings.

"Well, that was awkward," said Fr. Fitz from the chair. "I was going to leave before Rebecca so you two could have a moment, but I'm not as fast as I used to be." He slowly got out of the low chair.

"Father?"

"I'm not helping you go to the bathroom."

"If Gabriel is like me, how was I able to get the drop on him? And how did he get shot?"

"Well, son. If this is a God thing, and I suspect it might be . . ." He considered his next words. "How long will a gift intended for good continue to be given if it is being used for evil?"

"If memory serves, something like seven times seventy."

"That is in reference to God's forgiveness."

"Wouldn't that apply here?"

"If I'm being honest, I'm not sure."

"Thanks for coming, Father."

"I just wanted to know when my new maintenance guy would be back on the job." He smiled warmly and began walking for the door. On his way out, he said, "On your first day back, I want to see a doctor's note."

The nurse walked through the door, pulled the shades back down, and left the room.

Within a few minutes, Michael was out, completely forgetting about the note stuffed in his brace.

76.

MICHAEL OPENED HIS EYES TO SEE Gabriel standing at the foot of his hospital bed, the shoulder of his torn shirt covered in darkened blood. Every inch of him was soaked through.

"Well . . . hello, brother!" Gabriel said with a wink. Michael went to sit up, but Gabriel pulled out his gun and aimed it right at Michael's head. "Eh, eh, eh. Calm down. I don't want to kill you first. Don't make me."

"Then why are you here?"

"Read the letter."

"Psst." The noise came from somewhere above.

"What?" Michael asked, momentarily confused.

"Read the—"

"Psst." The sound thundered so loudly, it fractured Gabriel's face, silenced his voice, and smoked everything in Michael's view in swirling blackness.

He blinked his eyes open, and Gabriel was nowhere in sight. Instead, Detective Gradillas had found a small chair and had sidled it right up next to Michael's bed. The room was bright from the midday sun shining through the reopened blinds.

"Hey, detective."

"I swear. You don't sleep. You hibernate."

"Really? I usually have trouble sleeping."

"Well, maybe you've kicked it. Anyway, I've gotta be quick. Nurse Wilkes is taking her protection of you and your sleep pretty seriously. We need to talk about Gabriel Kane."

"Still in custody, right?" Michael slowly sat up.

"He's not going anywhere." She hesitated. "Michael? I need to explain why we were so sure."

"You've got my attention."

"You had just been interviewed for stalking a young woman. Then, you found the body of another. A body that no one saw over twenty hours or so even though they walked right by it. Evidence was missing from the scene. Then, a witness came forward and said he saw you dropping things into a church dumpster. You ran from the police. When my partner pursued you, he turned up dead with a taunting message. And, to top all of it off, we had DNA evidence connecting the canal murder and Alvarez's murder. And Michael? Testing proved conclusively that it was either you or an immediate family member."

"So he set me up." Michael reasoned.

"He did. But do you want to know *how*, Michael?" Gradillas' face showed nothing.

"How? I mean . . . I've never even set foot inside Dead Horse Ranch State Park. When did he get my DNA?"

"He didn't have to." She shook her head.

"Then how did—"

"He used his own, Michael."

"But that doesn't make sense. You said—"

"He used his own."

"But you said it proved it was either me or . . ."

Gradillas waited a moment for the reality to sink in before she explained. "There was plenty of blood left in his car and on the bridge. I had a rush put on it."

Michael swung his legs off the side of the bed and looked at his knee brace. He quietly said, "Cousin?"

"Michael? You have a brother, a fraternal twin."

"Alright!" He laughed nervously. "Very funny!"

"After the results came back, I had a guy at the station do a little research. He put together a file for you. When you have the time, read through it, okay? But Michael? Don't read it alone. Trust me. Bottom line? You were given up for adoption, and your brother wasn't."

There was silence as Michael just stared into the empty air. He was remembering how many times Gabriel had called him "brother" over the past few days.

Even in his dream.

Then, he looked toward Gradillas, but his eyes couldn't meet hers. "I think I need to be alone for a minute."

"Are you okay?" Her genuine concern was kind, but he really needed to be alone.

Now.

"No, but I will be."

"Alright. I'll go. If you need anything, call me." She placed a large manila envelope on the bedside table before pulling the blinds shut.

The envelope contained details of Ruthie Kane's death during childbirth. There was information on Dr. Wood's negligence. Next, were the particulars of Billy Kane's resulting payout. The final contents were some press clippings from the accident where Michael's birth father accidentally killed his adoptive parents.

Gradillas placed her business card atop the envelope. She had written her personal number on it. Then, she left.

Michael immediately set about the task of digging the note out of his knee brace.

77.

Dear Billy,

You don't know me, but I need to say I'm sorry. I'm sorry for the loss of your beloved wife. I'm sorry for the pain of having given up one of your sons for no fault of his own.

And this is why I'm writing to you today.

My husband Ezekiel and I have adopted him. We love him as our own. He is our only child, and he is our entire world. Please know he is happy, safe, well cared for, and loved beyond comprehension.

We do not want any financial support. As a sign of this, I will not include a return address or our last name. Although it will never make you whole after what you've endured, the entire settlement should be yours and for the son you are raising.

Please do not try to figure out how I was able to get your address.

Suffice it to say, I have a friend who was able to bend a few rules. I pray you will forgive her.

Be assured of my condolences, prayers, and of my love for the son we have the honor of raising.

Phyllis

78.

MICHAEL WAS SITTING AT HIS NEW dining room table as the fall morning sun broke through his open window. Before him, the table was set for two with his new dining ware.

He had struggled on and off with the events, along with the fallout, of that week three short months ago, but blessings had been born of the chaos. The greatest blessing of all was sitting across from him, waiting.

"I'm not sure I understand what this is about," Michael said, puzzled.

"Don't worry." Rebecca reassured him. "I already told you I talked to Father. You've been approved for a half day, and after I explained, he said you'll still get paid for the morning. Just don't get used to it."

"What did you *explain?*"

"That today is a special day, so I'm making you a special breakfast."

"With your mind?"

"We all have superpowers." She tilted her head and smiled. *Ding!*

Rebecca hopped up and ran into the living room. A muffled conversation followed. She burst back into the kitchen with a bulging plastic bag and a large container of coffee that she set on the counter.

She grabbed the plates off the table with a flirty smile.

"So your superpower involves a credit card?"

"Used well," she said over her shoulder. She spun around to reveal two stacked plates replete with eggs, French toast, and piles of bacon.

"I thought I smelled bacon."

As she set a plate down in front of Michael, she said, "Over the last three months, if there is one thing I've learned about you, it is that bacon is your love language." She set her own plate down and headed back to the counter to pour the coffee. She set a huge mug in front of Michael. It was closer to white than black. "And here is your creamer with a splash of coffee." Then, she sat down with her own mug of jet-black rocket fuel and picked up a huge piece of bacon before Michael stopped her.

"Rebecca? I hope I don't get in trouble for asking this, but what makes today so special?"

She smiled and set the bacon back down. "Well, Michael. Today is my twenty-fourth birthday, and I wanted to start it with you."

"Rebecca . . ." Michael looked a bit sad. "Why didn't you tell me?"

"Because this is precisely what I wanted. A few minutes with you."

"Well, the pleasure is mine."

"The pleasure is shared."

"Mind if I say a quick prayer before we eat?"

"It's a big part of who you are . . . so . . . you do you."

"In the name of the Father, and the Son, and the Holy Spirit, I thank you for this amazing woman. Her heart. Her intellect. Her warmth. Her beauty. Thank you for the gift she has been to all who know her. Bless this coming year and help me become more of the man she deserves each day. Amen."

He opened his eyes to see her grinning across the table at him. "How could I take issue with that? Now, can I eat some of this bacon before it gets cold?"

Michael responded by grabbing two strips off his own plate and stuffing them into his mouth whole.

Rebecca shook her head. "Overwhelming maturity. That must be why I kinda like you."

Michael swallowed down the bacon and with a serious look, said, "I kinda like you too, Rebecca."

"More than bacon?" She went to take a sip of coffee.

"Bacon never stood a chance." Rebecca's lips curled into a smile above the brim of her mug. Michael went on. "By the way, I want you to know that is possibly the most romantic thing I have ever said to anyone in my entire life."

"Now, that's just sad."

"You obviously underestimate my love of bacon."

Ding!

"They're early." Rebecca set down her coffee.

"Who?"

"Just some crazy people I know."

She walked into the living room and Michael heard Rob's booming voice. "Birthday girl!"

Then, he heard a cheerful voice. "Gimme a hug, sis! Happy birthday!"

Michael snuck a few more bites of bacon before standing up just as Rob sauntered around the corner.

"Bro! What up, dude?" Michael reached out and gripped Rob's hand as they pulled close for a single-slap-on-the-back bro hug.

Rob saw the spread over Michael's shoulder. "Woah! Bacon!" He released Michael and moved past him to the table.

Rebecca and Skye walked in, and Rebecca quickly laid down the law. "Touch *my* bacon, lose your hand."

"Which is yours?"

Michael quickly pointed to his plate.

"Lies!" Rebecca countered.

Rob sat in Michael's chair and began munching.

"Come on!" Michael protested.

Through a mouthful of bacon, Rob replied, "Really, bro? After Brindy completely furnished your apartment? You're gonna quibble over a plate of carnitas?"

"She was thanking me for saving your life!"

"Uh, I'm pretty sure I saved *your* life." Rob countered.

"When?"

"Well, I provided safe refuge, so I'm pretty sure I saved both your lives," Skye quickly interjected.

"I think Skye has a point," Rebecca responded.

"As you should," Rob said, suddenly beaming. "She is completely amazing, tough as nails, hot as hell, and entirely engaging."

"Well, that was certainly descriptive." Michael smiled.

The room fell silent.

"Wait!" Rebecca narrowed her eyes and looked at Skye who couldn't contain an ear-to-ear smile. "Let me see that hand!"

"Ahhh!" Skye exclaimed as she held out her left hand, which was sporting Brindy's ring.

"Oh my gosh! Skye!" Rebecca exclaimed while almost tackling her.

"Wait." Michael grinned and looked at Rob still sitting at the table, eyes just sparkling.

"Yup," was all Rob needed to say.

"Dude!" Michael pulled him up into a huge hug. "I am so happy for you!"

Michael and Rebecca switched as Rebecca gave Rob such a strong hug, his ribs hurt for the first time in over a month. "You are one lucky guy."

Rob was glowing. "I know. I know. She's the best."

Michael grabbed Skye by the shoulders and looked down at

her. "Are you really sure about this?"

From behind him, Rebecca said, "Shut up, Michael! Ignore him."

Skye looked up at Michael, tears suddenly welling up. "Absolutely, big bro."

"Of course. He is incredible," Michael said as Skye wrapped her arms around him and squeezed. When she finally let him go, Michael continued. "I just don't know if it is a smart move to work with your fiancé."

Rob punched him in the shoulder.

Rob had begun working at Humboldt Camping Supply again. Skye was able to get a job there as well. For Skye, it was the best of both worlds. She was an expert in the outdoors, and she was able to spend more time with her boyfriend. The minor celebrity status resulting from the incident months earlier brought in more than enough new business to justify the hire.

"It's okay. I'll only have to work with my fiancé for a year." Skye smiled.

"Sounds about right," Rob said as he sat back down at the table. "Then you'll have to deal with your husband." He winked at her before taking another big bite of French toast.

Michael suddenly stopped smiling and went to the window. All conversation stopped as he looked outside. Every smile disappeared.

Then, noticing everyone was watching him, Michael said, "We should head to the park. It's beautiful out."

Air seemed to rush back into the room and smiles reappeared.

"Well, you know I prefer to be outside." Skye offered.

"Sounds like a plan!" Rob chimed in.

"I'll box up the food," Rebecca said.

"To bring along, right?" Rob asked, concerned.

"You act like we never eat." Skye laughed.

"We never eat enough," Rob shot back.

All three were in good spirits while they cleaned up.

"Guys?" Michael said, looking out the window again.

They didn't even hear him.

"Hey, guys?" he said, a bit more urgently this time.

"Even on my birthday?" Rebecca looked a bit sad.

Rob and Skye turned, recognizing what was happening.

Michael was exclusively focusing on Rebecca. "I'm so sorry. I didn't—"

She took a step toward him and touched his cheek. "Go." Then, she gave him a gentle kiss. "Just be safe out there."

79.

———————————

"HELLO, GABRIEL."

This voice sounded different than the one he'd heard in the past.

"Hey. Uh, do I know you?" he whispered in his cell.

"I think you might. You've been listening to *me* for years."

If you enjoyed reading
A LIFE OF NO COINCIDENCE,
leave an online review, let your friends know
you enjoyed it, and spread the word.
It truly makes a difference.

Please also look for the David Martin Lins debut novel,
SKULL VALLEY.

DavidMartinLins.com

where you can also sign up to be the
first to know about upcoming projects,
find exclusive content, and get insider info.

Connect with the author at
facebook.com/davidmartinlinsauthor
instagram.com/davidmartinlins
twitter.com/davidmartinlins

ACKNOWLEDGEMENTS

ALTHOUGH *A LIFE OF NO COINCIDENCE* is my second published novel, it is actually the first I ever wrote. Thus, it will always hold a special place in my heart. Here are some of the special people who have helped me bring it to life:

Maryrose, your love and support makes my writing possible. I love you.

Stephen Prat, you helped with early edits, alternative ideas, and moral support from very early in this process. Your fingerprints are all over this work.

Adrian Bumgarner, your friendship has been a blessing, your gift of editing has been a godsend, and your generosity has been inspiring.

Mike Snozek, your expertise in certain "arenas" both inspired and informed much of my previous novel. Your incredible support encourages my present and future efforts.

Lorin Petrazilka, your help, patience, and friendship is more than I deserve. You are a creative force in a million ways and—once again—I love what you did with the cover.

Inner Keep, your support of (and reaction to) *SKULL VALLEY* is the reason *A LIFE OF NO COINCIDENCE* exists. I hope you enjoy it as much as I've enjoyed its creation.